"Did your captors say anything?"

"Anything to give you an idea of what they wanted?" Gabe asked.

She shook her head. "They never spoke to me."

"How did they know you'd be there at the orphanage at that precise time and day?"

"I have no idea." Cassidy watched him. His features still showed the strain of their ordeal. Fatigue roughened his voice. A shave and a haircut should be at the top of his priorities.

"No one knew my exact plans. Who would send someone to kidnap me?" Cassidy asked.

"I don't know, but our rebel didn't want to report his failure. Which means someone hired him. Which also means that person is still out there and probably knows by now that you've escaped."

Cassidy shivered. "Which means someone may still want me dead."

D1570636

LYNETTE EASON

grew up in Greenville, South Carolina. Her home church, Northgate Baptist, had a tremendous influence on her during her early years. She credits Christian parents and dedicated Sunday School teachers for her acceptance of Christ at the tender age of eight. Even as a young girl, she knew she wanted her life to reflect the love of Jesus.

Lynette attended the University of South Carolina in Columbia, then moved to Spartanburg, South Carolina, to attend Converse College where she obtained her master's degree in education. During this time, she met the boy next door, Jack Eason—and married him. Jack is the executive director of the Sound of Light Ministries. Lynette and Jack have two precious children, Lauryn, eight years, and Will, who is six. She and Jack are members of New Life Baptist Fellowship Church in Boiling Springs, South Carolina, where Jack serves as the worship leader and Lynette teaches Sunday School to the four- and five-year-olds.

Lethal
Deception

Lynette
Eason

Steeple
Hill®

Published by Steeple Hill Books™

STEEPLE HILL BOOKS

Steeple
Hill®

ISBN-13: 978-0-373-44280-5
ISBN-10:   0-373-44280-7

LETHAL DECEPTION

www.SteepleHill.com

Printed in U.S.A.

May the God of hope fill you with all joy and peace as you trust in Him, so that you may overflow with hope by the power of the Holy Spirit.

—*Romans* 15:13

Dedicated to Jesus Christ.

Thanks to:

My husband, Jack. I love you, appreciate you, respect you
and thank God for you.

My children, Lauryn and Will, who understand when Mom
orders takeout for supper—six times a week.

My parents, Lewis and Lou Jean Barker, brother Lane, and
in-laws, Bill and Diane Eason. Jason and Jennifer Dorris.
You guys are so great!

My grandma, Freda Trowbridge, in Amarillo, Texas.

My fellow teachers and coworkers at the
South Carolina School for the Deaf and Blind.
You guys are awesome!

Shirlee McCoy, Ginny Aiken and Dee Henderson.
Thank you!

Brandilyn Collins for posting me on her blog!
Check out February 28, 2007 at
www.brandilyncollins.com!

ACFW. You're fabulous.

To the girls: Margaret Hall, Dawn Barnes, Joni Quinn,
Becky Smith, Tracy Krout & Sarah Couch.

Eastside Spartanburg Martial Arts. You're a blessing!
And you don't look at me weird when I come to watch
my kids' karate classes with a laptop in hand.

To my home church, Northgate Baptist, and
my new church, New Life Baptist Fellowship.

Jesse and Carolyn Hartley.
Jesse, keep writing, you're next!

ONE

Danger hung heavy in the air around her. It was time to go. Instinct, a nudging from God or just plain common sense told her the time was now. She'd been here a month getting to know the child in her arms, but even this three-hour wait for the taxi she'd called was too much time. Cassidy McKnight loved Tefé, a poor city located in the state of Amazonas, situated in the northern part of Brazil. But now, uneasiness rolled through her as she shifted two-and-a-half-year-old Alexis higher on her hip and scanned the dirt path that was supposed to pass for a road.

Tropical green trees swayed in the slight breeze, and the humidity pulled Cassidy's natural flame-colored curls even tighter against her head, causing the mass to lay heavy against the back of her neck.

"Come on, come on," she muttered, alternating amongst pacing, standing and tapping her foot. Patience had never been her strongest virtue. Where was the cab?

"My Cass-ty," Alexis said, and lay her curly, blond head on Cassidy's shoulder.

"My Lexi," she answered, and planted a smacking kiss on the child's rosy cheek.

Alexis grinned, then sobered. "Want Mama."

Cassidy's heart lurched. "I know, sweetie. I wish your mama was here, too."

"Daddy?"

Cassidy nodded. "Yes, Daddy, too."

Alexis looked up at the sky. "In heaven with Jesus?"

Cassidy blinked back tears and whispered, "Yeah, in heaven with Jesus."

Anna, one of the relief workers from the orphanage and also a woman Cassidy called friend, walked up. "Taxis take forever around here. You might be better off hiking it."

Before Cassidy could respond, Alexis pointed to the sky and said, "Mama, Daddy with Jesus."

Anna blew out a sad sigh, looked at Cassidy and said, "You'd think God would have a special protection plan for people who build orphanages, wouldn't you?"

Cassidy gave a humorless smile, a mere twitch of her lips, although she nodded her agreement. She was ready to leave for more than one reason. Being here, the same country, the same jungle, where her brother had disappeared two years ago was taking its toll. They'd never found his body and Cassidy still had trouble accepting his death.

The taxi finally squealed around the corner and pulled up in front of the Amazon Orphanage. Dust swirled as it stopped.

"About time," Cassidy muttered, and moved through the gate. The sun beat hot as she nodded to the bearded driver and pulled open the back door. Anna followed and handed over a booster seat. Cassidy placed it in the backseat and tossed the diaper bag on the floorboard.

Alexis in her arms, she turned back to the relief worker who had short dark curls and compassionate dark blue eyes.

Anna said, "Here are the papers. I sent another copy to your fax machine. It should be waiting for you when you get home. God be with you."

Cassidy stuck the rubber-banded bundle in the back pocket of her jeans and leaned over to give the sweet woman a one-armed hug. "Thank you so much for all you've done."

Anna squeezed back and said, "Take care of the *bebê pequeno*—and yourself. You need to go. You really shouldn't have taken the risk to come here—not with the enemies your father has made with our local rebels."

Cassidy stepped out of the embrace. "I know. You're right, but I just couldn't stand the thought of some stranger picking up Alexis. She's had enough turmoil in her little life, and that would have added to her confusion."

Anna's expression said she agreed. Cassidy assured her, "I managed to e-mail Amy and let her know we were leaving and would be home by tomorrow late. Everything will be fine." Amy was a childhood friend taking care of things in the States, like decorating the room for Alexis, while Cassidy took care of things in Brazil.

Anna allowed a small smile, and Cassidy knew the woman would have done the same thing had she been in Cassidy's shoes. Anna motioned back toward the taxi. "I understand, but now it's time for you to leave. After that villager saw you, too many people know you are here."

No sooner had the words left her mouth than Cassidy's taxi churned its wheels and, with the passenger door still open, disappeared around the curve beyond the orphanage.

"Hey! What?" Choking on the swirling dust, she waved a hand in front of her face and stared after the vehicle.

She turned at the sound of another engine and understood.

A jeep full of four men all holding rifles was headed directly toward them.

Anna grabbed her arm. "Run back through the gate!"

As Cassidy turned to obey, bullets kicked up the dirt around her and she froze in shock, terror causing her to shake. Eyes closed, shoulders hunched, she clutched Alexis close. The child howled her protests and fear. Cassidy flinched with each report, but she knew that if these men wanted to kill her or the baby, they'd both be dead.

God, what is going on? Protect Alexis, please!

The shooting stopped; the silence screamed in her ringing ears. Before she could raise her head, rough hands pulled at her.

"Put down the baby!" ordered a hard-eyed man dressed in jungle fatigues, his rifle held negligently in his hand, pointing to the ground.

Automatically, Cassidy pulled Alexis closer.

The gun barrel rose and pointed at the child. In precise English, he stated, "Put her down or I will shoot her."

And he would. Like he would shoot an annoying dog. Terrified for the little girl, Cassidy kissed the top of her head and bent to put her on the ground. "Go to Anna," she whispered in Alexis's ear.

When she tried to straighten, Alexis clung to her, her chubby arms like steel bands around Cassidy's neck. "No! No! Want up!"

All too aware of the gun still pointed at the child, Cassidy kept her eyes trained on the rebel, reached back and wrenched the clinging arms away from her, feeling like her heart was being torn from her chest in much the same way.

Alexis fought and grabbed at her. "No! Stay with my Cass-ty!"

Cassidy's stomach cramped at the little girl's fear and confusion, but she took a step away, holding the child's hands so she couldn't latch on again. "Shh, sweetheart. It'll be okay."

She shot a pleading look at Anna who stood off to the side with the other two relief workers, eyes narrowed, lips tight. Anna stepped forward to grab up the screeching child and hand her off to one of the other women. She turned back.

The hard hand clamped around Cassidy's upper arm hauled her toward the waiting jeep. Alexis still cried for her. And these brutes had threatened her.

Cassidy exploded. She struggled and resisted the hands that gripped her. But she was no match for their sheer strength.

Out of the corner of her eye, she saw Anna turn back to the jeep and race toward her. Horror chilled her as she realized what her friend meant to do. "No, Anna, get back!"

Anna ignored her.

Cassidy renewed her fight and landed a solid kick on a hard shin. Her captor grunted and twisted her arm. Pain shot through her shoulder, and Cassidy shrieked.

Anna delivered a solid right hook to the man who held her. He grabbed his bloody nose and hollered, but didn't lose his grip on Cassidy. One of his companions in the jeep yelled a curse, gripped his rifle and dropped to the ground to help. As Anna turned to face him, he swiped the barrel across the side of her head. Blood squirted; she went down and didn't move.

Cassidy fought harder until the man grabbed a fistful of hair and brought her face up to his. His black eyes glittered in his filthy, unshaven face. She tried to turn her face from his rancid breath, but he held her head fast as he told her in slow, measured English, "Continue to struggle and I will snap your neck."

Cassidy froze and whimpered at the pain in her scalp. *God, please!*

"That's better." With no more effort than it takes a cook to toss a pizza, he hurled her into the back of the jeep. Cassidy hit the floor with a grunt. Pain shot through her left shoulder and her hip throbbed.

A third man grabbed her arms and yanked them behind her back. Rough rope chewed her tender wrists. Cassidy stopped fighting. Her muscles quivered from the exertion. She had no more strength left. Struggling now would only earn her more bruises.

The jeep screeched off, churning up dust as it bumped down the pitted dirt road. Alexis's screams echoed in her ears and fury mingled with the terror choking her.

Cassidy rolled over to see the man who had knocked Anna out. He sat slightly ahead of her, perched on the edge of the jeep instead of in one of the seats. She drew knees up to her chin then kicked out as hard as she could. The bottom of her feet landed on his backside and toppled him over the edge. His harsh yell and shouted curse gave her a brief moment of satisfaction.

His comrades howled with laughter; the driver slammed on the brakes and backed up. They taunted him as he came up over the side of the jeep, dusty, the gash on his forehead matching the one he'd put on Anna's. However, the rage in his eyes turned Cassidy's satisfaction back to terror.

She was dead.

His fist shot out and connected with her left eye and cheekbone. Pain exploded, bright lights flashed, then darkness blanketed her.

Cassidy awoke and choked back an agonized moan as the ropes bit into the tender skin of her wrists. She lay on her right side, her cheek pressed into the dirt while her heart beat in time with her pounding head. She couldn't decide what hurt more—cheek, eye, hip or wrists.

With the return of consciousness came memory. Unfortunately, memory brought forth such a surge of terror she gasped.

She'd been kidnapped.

Oh, Lord, help me. Give me the strength to endure. Be with Alexis. Cassidy whispered the prayer then inched her way to sit up as straight as her bonds would allow. She tried to shift into a more comfortable position.

Impossible.

With her hands bound behind her, fire shot along every muscle in her shoulders, arms and back, her body protesting the strain of being in one position for too long. A bead of sweat dripped off her chin; her head throbbed harder and nausea churned.

Gritting her teeth, she gathered every ounce of strength and managed to shift into a sitting position. Panting from her efforts, she dropped her head to bent knees and told herself to keep breathing.

Finally, the nausea eased and she dragged her head up to look around. Misshapen boards were stacked on top of each other and nailed haphazardly to keep them from falling in. Through the slits in the walls, she could see movement. Shifting closer to lean against the wall, she looked out. A dark-headed, dark-eyed preteen was cooking over a campfire, occasionally turning the meat on the skewer. Cassidy sucked in a sharp breath. Next to the young girl stood the man Cassidy had kicked out of the jeep. Rafael, they'd called him.

She watched, unable to pull her gaze from the sight before her. This man, this rebel, leaned over and gently kissed the top of the girl's head. The girl looked up, smiled and said something. Cassidy couldn't understand all of it, but caught the word, *Papai*. That awful man was a father? Ugh. *Oh, what are these people doing to their children, Lord?*

Cassidy shook her head and pain splintered through it. She gasped out a groan and waited. When the throbbing faded, she looked out once again. Garlic, peppers and other spices tantalized her. Dogs barked and children played soldier, shooting each other with toy guns fashioned from sticks.

Several older preteens carried the real thing.

Cassidy shuddered; fear clawed up her spine.

Did anyone other than her kidnappers know she was here? She bent her shoulders forward. No relief. Cassidy looked through the widest crack again. Rustic huts, no electricity, no phone lines. She felt caught in a time warp… surrounded only by towering trees, a rushing river and the occasional monkey calling to its mate.

Oh, God, please get me out of this! And get us out before Mom hears I've disappeared. Please, God, first Micah and now me. She'll die. Literally.

Micah, a Navy SEAL on a mission, had disappeared two years ago, and the navy had declared him dead, based on the report of one of Micah's fellow SEALs.. Her father continued to search and her mother swore Micah was just on an extended mission. And now this.

The door opened and a short, round, dark-skinned woman with gray-streaked black hair stepped inside. Silent, flat, black eyes stared and Cassidy swallowed hard. The bruise above her left eye continued to throb and the nausea returned with a vengeance.

She muffled a groan, regretting her brief fit of temper in the jeep. Shaking uncontrollably, she focused on the figure in front of her. As though by magic, a knife appeared in her visitor's hand. Cassidy inhaled sharply and shrank back. Unable to tear her eyes from the fearsome weapon, she waited for the worst.

The old woman stepped toward her and shifted the knife higher.

"No, please." Cassidy meant it to be a scream, but only managed a weak whimper.

The woman moved behind her and Cassidy held her breath, expecting to feel the knife plunge between her shoulder blades. Instead, there was a slight tug and her hands popped free.

Agonizing pain sucked the air from her lungs as her muscles screamed their protest at the sudden movement. Tears filled her eyes again, but this time she refused to make a sound.

A short grunt brought her attention up to the face in front of her. The woman motioned for her to follow. Cassidy stood, swaying slightly. Her stomach protested, her eye throbbed, her legs shook, but she obeyed. I can do all things…

"Tell me why I'm here, please," she asked in English with a surprisingly steady voice.

Another grunt answered her.

Cassidy sighed and looked around. No way to escape; no weapon to be found. She had already examined every inch of the small hut and other than a lumpy-looking cot with a blanket, the place was empty.

Once outside the dark hut, the bright sunlight intensified the throbbing in her aching head. She bit her lip. What she wouldn't give for a sip of water and a painkiller. Rubbing her rope-burned wrists, she stumbled after the woman to a small hill that held—of all things—an outhouse.

Although grateful for the moment of privacy, she wrinkled her nose and held her breath as she finished her business as quickly as possible. She opened the door to find the woman waiting with a small canteen.

"Água." The word came out as a grunt, but Cassidy understood. She eagerly grabbed the container, put it to her mouth and drank slowly; small sips to quench her thirst, but not enough to make her sick. The nausea subsided.

"Obrigada," she said. Thank you. With a shaky hand, she wiped her mouth and asked in Portuguese, the official language of Brazil, "Who are you?"

"Maria." Just one word, but at least it wasn't a grunt.

The woman's dark eyes never changed from their dull flat expression, but her face softened by a fraction. Again, Maria motioned for Cassidy to follow. Again, Cassidy obeyed. The woman's girth should have made her clumsy; instead, she moved quietly and gracefully, skirting over the rough ground.

As she followed, Cassidy tried to formulate an escape plan. She had to get out of here. She had to get back to Alexis. The poor baby must be scared to death. All the adults in her life kept deserting her.

But the question was—*where was here?*

Cassidy cherished the few precious moments of exercise on the way back to her "prison." Never in her wildest dreams would she have imagined that her mission of mercy would land her in the middle of a rebel camp deep in the Brazilian Amazon jungle. Confusion reigned. *Why me, Lord?* It wasn't a complaint, but a sincere question. What did they want with her?

"Eat. *Entende?*"

Cassidy blinked. Yes, she understood.

She entered the hut and noticed a plate full of food on the old cot. Her stomach rumbled, but no way was she sitting on those bug-infested blankets. Cassidy grabbed the plate, made sure no little critters had crawled into the food and moved to the wall beside the door. Eyes on Maria, she slid down to sit on the floor, resting the plate in her lap.

She scooped up a tortilla and took a bite. Warm and surprisingly tasty, the food energized her and she settled back to eat. A canteen of tepid water finished off the meal.

The door to the hut banged open and the vigilant Maria narrowed her eyes as she saw who entered. Cassidy yelped, scrambled to her feet and bolted for the back of the hut, trapped. Terror thudded through her, beating in time with her pulse. He came closer.

Before Rafael could reach her, Maria planted herself in front of Cassidy, silent, yet ready, if necessary. Rafael stopped and glared at the two of them as though judging whether offending the old woman was worth it.

To Cassidy's relief, he backed toward the door and left without a word. She looked at Maria, "Why?"

"You're more valuable unharmed right now."

Cassidy swallowed hard. "Oh."

March 16
Thursday morning

Gabriel Sinclair patted the pocket of his plaid shirt. The papers crinkled reassuringly. He just hoped he didn't get killed before he got to show them to *o patrão*—the boss located in the rebel camp just ahead. Gabe's sleekly muscled arm gave the machete another vicious swing, his anger fueling his strength. How had he managed to get himself talked into this?

One week ago, he'd been minding his own business when the ambassador to Brazil, Jonathan McKnight, had come to him at the hospital, tracking him down in the busy South Carolina emergency room and pulling him away from a patient.

"I need you."

Curious, wary, Gabe motioned for the nurse to take over, and led the man down the hall to an empty office. He waved a hand toward one of the metal chairs, then Gabe took the chair behind the desk. Once Jonathan was seated, Gabe asked, "What do you need with me?"

He watched the ambassador's jaw work, the muscles flexing as the man clenched and unclenched his teeth. Something was obviously terribly wrong, but what?

"Cassidy. She's done a really stupid thing."

Now, *there* was a surprise, Gabe thought grimly. Cassidy and stupidity just naturally went together, didn't they?

"She hopped a plane to Brazil and got herself kidnapped."

"What?" Gabe clenched his fists, his attention fully focused on the man in front of him. That was a little more serious than stupid.

"I need you to get her back." Ambassador McKnight sat

ramrod straight in the chair, his jaw tight, hands resting on his thighs. But his emotionless facade couldn't cover the turmoil rolling in the man's green eyes.

"Kidnapped?" Gabe sputtered.

"She was taken from a Brazilian orphanage and is being held somewhere in the jungle. Here." He pulled a note out of his shirt pocket and shoved it into Gabe's hand.

Brazilian jungle? Orphanage? Gabe read the note. It was written in Portuguese.

He read aloud as he translated it, "'We have your daughter. Our boss wishes for you to meet with him. He wishes to learn the secrets of your government. Should you wish to have your *filha bela* returned to you, you will contact us to set up a meeting. You will also refrain from bringing in any police or authorities of any kind. If we even suspect that you have done so, we will send your daughter back to you…in pieces…or sell her to make the profit you denied me.'"

Gabe tried not to picture a terrified Cassidy as he looked up in the ambassador's eyes. Cassidy's eyes. "Isn't there someone else who could help her?"

Jonathan shook his head. "I promise, if there were anyone else, I wouldn't ask. But you owe me after that last mission…" He trailed off. Micah had been declared dead after the navy heard Gabe's story. But his testimony had been sealed. He couldn't tell the family exactly what happened.

Gabe thought to himself, *You have no idea about that last mission.*

"Also for Cassidy, I'm asking," the ambassador finished. The man swallowed hard and stood to pace to the door and back. "I don't know what will happen to my wife if she finds out about this, not with what happened with Micah. It would probably kill her. Right now, I'm able to stall her.

Cassidy's always running off somewhere. But she's been gone way longer than usual with no contact for the last two weeks, so pretty soon I'm going to have to tell her mother something. I've responded to the kidnappers and managed to set up the meeting. It's two weeks from today, but I want Cassidy out of there now."

"What was she doing at a Brazilian orphanage?"

Jonathan shifted his eyes, paced toward the door then back. "I don't know. She was supposed to be on vacation in Paris."

Gabe lifted an eyebrow; he had a funny feeling the ambassador knew exactly why Cassidy went to Brazil. Instead he said, "Paris, huh? Tough life."

Jonathan ignored the sarcasm and narrowed his eyes. "All I know is that I need you to get in there, get her, and get out. I'm home in Spartanburg on leave right now dealing with another situation. Any other time, I would have been in Brazil, but I came home to…" He sighed and trailed off.

Gabe raised an eyebrow in silent inquiry. "Another situation?"

Jonathan swallowed hard and said, "I don't want to go into detail, but before I became a Christian, I had an affair. Almost thirty years ago. Christina found out recently about it and she's not dealing with it very well. We're trying to keep our marriage together. Losing Cassidy would destroy us."

Gabe blinked and tried to absorb all that the man was saying. He decided to ignore the part about the affair and said, "Why do you think she was taken?"

"It wasn't mentioned in the letter, but I somehow wonder if this has to do with what I'm working on with the president," Jonathan said.

"You mean, your stand against human trafficking?"

Jonathan nodded and said, "Cassidy's been a tremendous help with the entire project." He shrugged. "Human trafficking is a nine-point-five-billion-dollar-a-year income that goes right into the pockets of criminals and organized-crime groups. Men, women and children sold like cattle to work in sweatshop factories and that's the best that happens. I can't imagine the horrors these people live with every day."

Gabe knew the horrors the man talked about: sexual exploitation, modern-day slavery. It was a profitable enterprise in many parts of the world. Ambassador McKnight had been a huge mover and shaker in putting a lot of these people out of business—or at least putting a dent in their income. And if Cassidy had fallen into their vengeful hands…

He shuddered and stood, unable to complete the thought or sit still any longer. Agitation echoed in each step as he paced around the office. He really couldn't imagine Cassidy taking the time to be involved in something like politics. It seemed completely out of character for the girl he'd once known. Didn't match up with the stories Micah had shaken his head over.

Take care of Cassidy.

Gabe shook the words from his head, finally stopped pacing and stared out of the third-floor window. Not bothering to turn, he said, "Sir, no doubt, I owe you." *More than you realize.* "I would be dead if Senator Graham hadn't tipped you off to what was going on with that last mission. I still don't know how you managed to send in that helicopter, I'm just grateful you did. But that part of my life is over now." And there was nothing on the face of this earth that would make him accept that kind of responsibility again. Except…

Take care of Cassidy. With what was probably one of his last breaths, Micah had asked him to watch over his sister.

Gabe's mind flashed. Men scrambling for safety and screaming at him to help. Machine guns popping, the explosion and raging fire.

Death.

And that gun in his ear. *Three, two, one.* Then the ominous *click.*

He sucked in a deep breath and forced his thoughts away from those memories. He had yet to face them and get over the guilt of being the only one to survive. Memories had remained buried and questions had gone unanswered for two years. Gabe figured he could go at least another two.

Now this man was asking him to come face-to-face with the demons of his past. For Cassidy. A spoiled little rich girl. He turned from the window to stare at Jonathan. "I know you have enemies, people who would lose big if you and the president succeed in passing certain human-trafficking laws, and it's possible that's why they took Cassidy. I know I owe you, but I can't just leave…" He trailed off weakly, knowing he might as well give up. He was going.

Take care of Cassidy.

"You are the only one who can do this. You know this jungle and you know it well. I don't have the time to set anything else up. And you can leave. I've already checked. You have six weeks of vacation built up. I've had all your patients reassigned. So, in fact, you can leave today."

The ambassador handed him a piece of paper with a name on it. "This guy is your ride in. He'll have your parachute and rebel identification and the name of your contact. After that, he's gone and you're on your own. There's no team, no backup. Only a supply plane that will land once a week, every Monday, at five in the afternoon, Brazil time, on the little airstrip in the village of La Joya. The pilot is a friend of mine. He'll wait for two hours each time he lands for the next six weeks. Here's a map, the name of my contact in Brazil and the approximate location of this rebel camp. Figure out how to infiltrate it and get the job done."

If it had been anyone else, Gabe might have simply walked away. But this was his father's best friend, a man who had the president's ear, a man who was welcome in elite political circles—and the man whose son had died on Gabe's watch.

He owed it to Micah.

And to Cassidy. She might be a spoiled rich girl, but he'd never been able to forget her.

With a sigh and a disgusted mutter, he took the papers. Responsibility for another human being's life in the jungle was the last thing he wanted. Emergency-room responsibility didn't bother him. The E.R. was stable and sane compared to the jungle. The jungle would kill him, if not physically, then emotionally.

Now, a week later, the deadline looming, Gabe's muscles flexed each time he hacked at the dense growth as he headed for the rebel camp, wondering if he could fully trust the guide ahead of him. With each swing of the machete, he pushed the nightmarish memories down deep inside.

Gabe's cover fully established him as Miguel Sanchez, rebel for hire. With his raven-colored wavy hair, black eyes and dark skin, he looked the part. The scar slicing through his right eyebrow added to his menacing appearance. No one had to know he'd gotten the scar when he'd been showing off at his parents' house and cracked his head on the diving board.

He ignored the sweat dripping off his face and sliced another thick vine. He'd stopped praying two years ago after
the mission with Micah went terribly wrong, but as the
camp finally came into sight, he decided today might be a
good day to start up again.

TWO

Cassidy used the rock to scratch another tally mark into the wall of her hut. At the end of each day, she added another mark.

Seventeen miserable days.

What was her father doing? Her mother was probably in need of a straitjacket by now. Cassidy paced and kicked the dirt floor. What was taking so long? Why hadn't she been rescued, ransomed or killed? Or, she shuddered, sold?

That last thought scared her more than the idea of being killed. In fact, she was sure she would much prefer a bullet to the brain. Working with her father in the political arena had exposed her to a twisted evil she'd never suspected existed. Since she'd started the Stop the Traffic Foundation, human trafficking in Brazil had taken a beating. Unfortunately, a fatal blow never seemed to land.

The men who'd snatched her had told her only that her father had been contacted, but said nothing about what they wanted. The constant tension had her ready to scream. She'd lost weight and had to tighten the knot in the rope that she now used as a belt. Her jeans sagged, and her T-shirt had definitely seen better days. Washing in the creek every other day just didn't quite measure up to her normal hygiene habits.

Cassidy groaned and knelt on the dirt floor. What were they waiting for? And now, she had another worry plaguing her. Sometimes she had to go to extreme measures to avoid Rafael. Almost every time she stepped out of the hut, she felt his leering gaze follow her, making her skin crawl.

The days blended together in an endless fashion. Recently, Cassidy had caught a glimpse of the newest rebel to join the camp. Three days ago he had marched into the camp and his eyes had caught hers for a brief moment before he turned away without expression. She knew this man. She didn't know where or how, but she knew him. It would come to her later.

Right now, exhaustion threatened to snap her sanity… and it was getting dark. Fear snaked up her spine to twine itself around the base of her neck. She hated the nights and the suffocating terror.

She would lay rigidly still deep into the night listening to the old woman snore, reassuring herself that as long as she was there, nothing would happen to her. It was probably a lie, but she drew comfort from it anyway. And she prayed, over and over the scripture from Psalm 91, *Do not be afraid of the terrors of the night.*

Cassidy sighed and rubbed her burning eyes with shaky hands. Eventually, exhaustion overtook her and she drifted off.

Hard fingers dug grooves into her cheeks and she opened her eyes to see the newcomer she'd just been thinking about staring down at her, his black eyes even darker in the shadows of the cabin. Terror exploded her into consciousness and she froze.

He brought a finger to his lips and whispered, "Shh."

Cassidy managed a slight nod against the hand still clamped over her mouth. *What was he doing?*

And then she was free. She scrambled away from him and bumped into a warm body. She cut off a scream.

Maria! Had he killed her? Cassidy struggled to her feet, and backed up, her eyes never leaving the man's face. He said, "I'm here to get you out of here, you understand? Maria is busy with the outhouse, but that won't last long. Rafael there was about to pay you a rather unpleasant visit. He should be out for a while, but we need to get moving, now, okay?" His low voice eased her fear somewhat. He was here to rescue her? But…her brain felt too fuzzy to take it all in. Who was he? Who'd sent him? Why was this rebel risking his life to save hers?

Gabe reached down and pulled Cassidy to her feet. Dazed green eyes stared up at him. If she shook any harder, she'd come apart at the seams. When he'd first seen her, he had been appalled at how thin she was. He worried if she would have the stamina to make the trek through the jungle.

"Who are you?" she asked. "I know you."

"Your knight in shining armor, m'lady," he quipped without humor. "Now, please, let's go." He gave a firm yank on the hand he still held and pulled her out the door. He wasn't sure how much time they had to put as much distance between them and the camp as possible, but he didn't want to waste any of it. Unfortunately, he'd caught

Rafael sneaking into Cassidy's hut and had to act. Rafael had seen his face; Gabe's cover was blown. If they were going to escape, it had to be now.

Cassidy stumbled along behind him. Within seconds, they reached the hut that Gabe had been assigned and he reached in, grabbed the pack that he always kept ready and slung it over his shoulder. "Come on, let's get out of here." He took her hand again.

"Why are you helping me, anyway?" she asked.

"I'll explain on the way out of here." He looked up. The sun, just peeking over the horizon, made him groan silently. Great, running from rebels in broad daylight ranked pretty much last on his list of fun things to do. He pulled her along behind him. "We don't have a lot of time, moving fast is top priority, got it?"

Thankfully, Cassidy held her questions, nodded and fell in behind him as he headed for the dense forest trees directly ahead. They were just about to the edge of the camp and ready to disappear into the jungle, when he heard, "*Ei!* You there! Stop!"

Gabe gave Cassidy a shove and whispered, "Run!"

Cassidy obeyed, and Gabe followed close behind. A well-worn path led to the river. Soon the men would form search teams. They would spread out to make a big circle and gradually narrow the diameter to capture their prey in the middle. Somehow, they had to slip through that circle.

Gabe stayed beside Cassidy, helping her when she stumbled. Branches and bushes slapped at them, as though trying to hold them back. "Wait." He stopped and bent double, winded. Cassidy flopped beside him, gasping and holding her side. Blood dripped from a gash on her cheek.

Gabe sat down beside her and said, "They'll be coming. I don't think we can outrun them, so we're going to have to outsmart them."

Cassidy finally had enough breath to say, "Sounds good to me. But first I want to know who you are and why you're helping me."

Gabe gave her a sad smile. "Look a little harder, Cass."

Her eyes narrowed as she gave him the once-over, and he knew the moment she recognized him. She gasped then her green eyes narrowed and she pursed her lips. "Gabriel Sinclair. Daddy sent you, didn't he? The man who knows how my brother died, but isn't talking. That's just great."

Gabe tried to form an answer while he waited for the sting of her words to lessen. He knew she'd been upset, but that zinger told him a lot. She still blamed him for Micah's death.

"Which way's the orphanage?" she asked.

His mind still reeling from her hostile shot, Gabe fumbled with one hand and managed to get his compass out of his front pocket. "Uh, that way. Why?" He pointed to the north.

"Okay," she said. "Let's go."

Anger started to push its way past the hurt. No way, uh-uh. Gabe protested, "Now, see here, Princess, your daddy managed to talk me into playing hero to get you out of here. This is my job, my mission. Now, *we*—as in you and me—are going that way. No orphanage, got it?"

Cassidy frowned, pursed her lips and said, "I'm on my own mission, Gabe. I'm heading that way." She pointed north.

Gabe grabbed her extended arm and pulled her right up into his face. "This isn't some game. You're going with me. Now."

She tried to jerk out of his hard grip, but failed. Anger lit a fire in her eyes. "Now, listen here—" She stopped. Demanding was getting her nowhere, so she changed tactics. She reasoned, "Look, Alexis is waiting for me. I have to go back."

Gabe shook his head and pulled a fairly clean bandanna from his backpack to swipe at the blood dripping from the cut on her cheek. "You could probably use a stitch in that. Who is worth risking your life—excuse me, *our* lives— for? And who is Alexis?"

Cassidy took a deep breath and pushed his hand away, "My daughter."

She turned on her heel and headed north.

The shot from the rifle cracked the branch above her head. Gabe tackled her from behind and brought her down on the jungle floor.

THREE

Gabe whipped up his weapon, caught a blur of movement through the trees and fired off a round. The scream of pain told him he'd found his target. He turned back to Cassidy. "Run," he ordered through clenched teeth.

She ran. Another bullet pierced the tree beside him and Gabe swerved and shot back. Finally, they made their way through the undergrowth to a group of trees that offered some shelter. He stopped, listened.

Nothing. Yet. Hopefully, the kidnappers had stopped to help the wounded man. Gabe decided they'd lost them for the moment; however, he didn't count on that to last long. He leaned against one of the trees and checked his gun. Cassidy sank to the ground.

"Your *what?*" He picked up where they'd left off. *Please, anything, but a child. Not a child. The ambassador knew. Gabe had had a feeling he'd been hiding something.*

Gabe steamed as frustration boiled through him. This was not in the game plan. Get in, get the girl, get out. That was the plan. Nothing about a child. Especially *her* child. The twinge of jealousy took him by surprise, but he quickly forgot about it as he watched her disappear through the mess of twisting vines and leaves.

He quickly caught up and caught her arm. "Slow down," he hissed. Then he focused on the fact that his fingers wrapped around her upper arm almost effortlessly. Gabe frowned, appalled at her fragile state. Once the adrenaline wore off, she wouldn't last long without some rest and nutrition.

She yanked away from him; blinked back tears. "You don't understand. I made a promise and I'm going to keep it. I have to." Desperation flashed.

Gabe groaned, "Cassidy, those men aren't going to give up. They're closing in on us even as we stand here arguing."

"Then I suggest we argue while we move. And if you're supposed to keep me alive, could you do a better job of it with me than you did with Micah?" With that flat question, she headed north when Gabe desperately wanted to head west. These last few days had been his nightmare come true. And it wasn't over yet.

And Cassidy scored a bull's-eye every time she opened her mouth.

He squeezed his eyes tight to tamp down the memories of the explosion, the gun in his ear. *The click.* He swallowed hard, blew out a frustrated sigh and stomped after her, catching up quickly. Just in time to reach out and pull her weaving, swaying form into his arms.

"Gabe? I don't feel so good." She slurred her words and moaned. He could tell she was on the verge of passing out.

"Sit down for a minute." Holding her close scrambled his thought processes, but somehow he managed to ease her onto the jungle floor. She rested against a fallen log, leaned her head back and shut her eyes.

Gabe asked, "When was the last time you ate?"

Her brow crinkled as she thought. "Um…I'm not sure. Yesterday, lunch, I think."

Gabe growled, "Not smart. Here. Your blood sugar's probably getting ready to bottom out." He swung the backpack down beside her and rummaged through it until he found what he was looking for. "It's not exactly the seven-course meal that you're used to, but it's all I've got and it'll get some nourishment in you."

With what little strength she had, she yanked the jerky out of his hand and muttered, "You have absolutely no idea what I'm used to."

After two pieces of jerky and half a canteen of water, Cassidy looked slightly better. Gabe pulled a cell phone out of the backpack and turned it on. The battery was good, but no signal. He dropped it back in his pocket. His satellite phone had disappeared within an hour after his arrival in the camp.

"What daughter?" he probed.

Cassidy stared at him for a moment then sighed. Her eyes misted, closed again, but she spoke. "Her name's Alexis."

Gabe thought about all the pictures of Cassidy he used to see in the society pages of the newspaper. She was with a different man every week. "So who's her father?"

"Jacob Foster." Her eyes shot open and he found himself ensnared in her wild green gaze. Tears slid a silent pattern down cheeks flushed from the run. "He loved God with a passion I envied, he was one of the most wonderful men I've ever known."

Jealousy snagged him again. "Was?" He didn't want to know, but had to.

She nodded. "He was killed almost two months ago in a raid on his village. He was a missionary."

Gabe flinched. "Ah, Cass, I'm sorry."

She shuddered. "No, I'm sorry. I don't mean to be hateful.

I'm still working on the forgiveness issue when it comes to you and your silence about what happened to Micah."

A twig snapped.

Gabe bolted. He grabbed his machete and cut a shallow path through the dense underbrush, pulling Cassidy behind him. Sweat beaded and slipped down his face. There was no time to try to cover the path completely.

Hide us, Lord. The prayer slipped through his mind unintentionally. He reminded himself he wasn't speaking to God because God didn't listen. Why talk to someone who didn't care about listening to you? Gabe was working this mission alone. He trusted and depended on no one but himself. Somehow that thought didn't offer the comfort he'd hoped it would.

A hollow tree trunk lay horizontal just off the path. About six feet in diameter and rotted on the inside, Gabe was willing to bet all kinds of creatures probably called it home. Right now, he would call it an answer to his prayer—if he thought God heard his prayers anymore.

He ignored the smell of must and decay and pulled Cassidy into the trunk, her small hand clutched in his. As he made his way in, he moved aside debris, hoping he didn't dislodge anything poisonous. Scorpions, spiders and various other insects scuttled from under the rotted bark, but when nothing jumped out at him, he leaned against the tree-trunk wall and drew Cassidy in behind him.

A shaft of light through a small crack in the top subtly illuminated the inside. A finger to his lips communicated the need for silence and her nod let him know she understood.

They were going to have to stay hidden and hope the men weren't looking very carefully, because if they were, their snug little hiding place would most likely become their grave.

* * *

Cassidy shivered and moved deeper into the trunk. She squeezed her eyes shut as she tried to control her panicked breathing. *Thank You, God, for sending Gabe—I'm grateful for his help even if he won't tell me how Micah died.* Her brother had been reported dead on a secret mission that Gabe led. His body was never recovered. Cassidy had written Gabe begging him to tell her what happened so that she could have closure, but he'd refused. She was grateful for his help, but she still resented his silence.

He put a hand on her shoulder and gave her a slight squeeze before moving toward the opening to keep watch. Her heart still raced from their dash through the jungle and she shifted, trying to put a little more distance between them.

"Be still," Gabe turned his head and whispered into her ear.

She froze. He still had that effect on her stomach. She'd worked hard to get over her teenage crush on him, but apparently she hadn't worked hard enough.

"Don't even breathe," he whispered.

Prayers trembled silently on her lips. Footsteps crunched closer. She bit her lip and his right hand brought up the gun to point it toward the sound.

Someone grunted a question in Portuguese, but Cassidy, who spoke the language fluently, couldn't quite make out the words. However, the answer left her shaking even harder than before. "Kill them immediately. The ransom is not important. I do not want to have to report this failure."

The footsteps faded. They hadn't noticed the trampled underbrush and the cut vines. Yet.

Oh, thank You, Lord. Thank You for the protection. Sweet relief flowed through her, leaving her feeling weak and a little nauseated. *When I am afraid, I will trust in You.*

Gabe's arms slowly relaxed; the rest of his body soon followed. He stuck the gun into the back of his jeans and leaned his head against the wooden trunk.

Cassidy didn't bother to move. "Are they gone?" She whispered the words as quietly as possible.

He whispered back, "I think so. Hopefully they're closing their circle. But soon they'll realize we managed to slip through and will start looking outside that circle. We have to be gone and on a plane by the time they widen their search."

"Gabe, I've already told you I'm not leaving without Alexis." Cassidy stared into his flashing dark eyes and whispered, "I made a promise, and I'm going to keep it. God's brought me this far, He's not about to desert me now."

"Whatever. Right now, we're going to sit tight. Now, be quiet so I can listen."

Cassidy rolled her eyes and started praying again.

A slight snore brought Gabe's gaze down. Cassidy had moved in and rested her head against his arm and fallen asleep. Standing up. It finally registered how absolutely exhausted she must be. Lack of sleep and terror had all taken its toll.

He knew they needed to move on, but she had to rest before she went unconscious and he had to carry her out. Holding her steady, he slid down the wall to sit in the mildew-infested debris that littered the base of their hideaway.

Cassidy never stirred, her form remaining limp in his arms while her chest rose and fell with each deep breath. She must have finally felt safe enough to relax—or maybe she'd simply just passed out.

He needed to rest, himself. Feeling as if he'd been back in the midst of fighting for much longer than a week and a half, Gabe decided to stay put for the moment. He dug through his pack and pulled out a dirty T-shirt. It would have to do. Wadding it up, he placed it behind her neck to give her some support. The now sweaty and dusty riot of curls she'd never been able to tame spread over the T-shirt and across his hands. Gabe pulled away, fighting the memories even as they surged through his mind.

In his third year of medical school, compliments of Uncle Sam, Gabe had been a very self-confident twenty-four-year-old. He'd stopped by the McKnight house to talk to Micah about something. And then *she'd* appeared at the top of the stairs; a vision of loveliness in a gown of white. Green eyes drew him; her smile tangled his thoughts. This girl he'd always considered a bratty little sister. But this night…

She floated down the staircase to stand next to her date, the top of her head barely reaching the middle of his chest. When she'd said goodbye to her adoring onlookers, she'd laughed and flung that riotous cascade of flaming curls. They'd brushed his nose and mouth—and singed his heart. Micah had noticed—and stared daggers through Gabe.

Micah. Just the thought of that name was enough to bring Gabe back to reality. Cassidy's brother. Dead. Because Gabe had failed him. Had requested—no, ordered—him for the mission then allowed him to die. Cassidy was mad at him for not talking about that day, but if she knew the whole truth, she'd hate him forever. He put the mental brakes on the memories, refusing to go there now. Cassidy stirred and frowned; whimpered, in her sleep. Gabe wanted fiercely to wipe the bad memories away and replace them with good. But that wasn't his right.

That had been someone else's privilege.

She'd been in love with another man. Had his baby.

Why hadn't Cassidy's father mentioned a child? Hadn't he known? Gabe laughed sardonically at his mental question and answered it. Oh, yeah, the man had known. And he'd not mentioned it because he'd known Gabe would flat out refuse to take the mission.

He let his eyes drift shut, but made sure the gun was tucked close and his ears were tuned to the jungle noises. He wasn't afraid he'd fall asleep only to wake up dead. Too many years of training, too much intensive conditioning— too many nightmares to keep at bay—would keep that from happening.

"Cassidy." She ignored the faraway voice. The sleep her body had craved for so long had her in its grip and wasn't about to let her shake it. "Cassidy." This time a rough shake accompanied her whispered name. Sleep disappeared fast.

"Gabe?" She blinked to bring his face into focus. Brown-black eyes bored into hers. "What? What is it?"

He brushed the hair out of her eyes for her, his fingertips gentle, lingering. "We need to get going. Since you're bound and determined to head to the orphanage, we've got to beat these guys at their own game."

Cassidy moved and couldn't stop the groan that slipped out.

"Sore?"

"To say the least. I thought I was in shape up until a few weeks ago."

His short bark of soft laughter made her jump. She frowned. "What's that supposed to mean?"

"Trust me. There's not a thing wrong with your shape."

Cassidy flushed. She gave him a punch in the gut that made him grunt. "That's not what I meant and you know it, Rambo."

"I know, Cassidy. I know." Cassidy could have sworn his expression went tender for a brief moment before returning to its usual unreadable gaze. He turned and edged cautiously toward the end of the trunk and Cassidy followed him. She cleared her throat and asked quietly, "So, you're going to help me?"

Gabe cut his eyes to her. "What do you think?"

She allowed a small smile to cross her lips. "I think you hate it when I get my way."

Gabe's lips curved into a rueful smile, but he didn't respond. Cassidy brushed leaves and debris from the seat of her pants then pulled her hair up into a ponytail with the rubber band she'd had in her pocket since opening the papers about Alexis.

"Let's go," he said.

"You think it's safe?"

"You mean, you care what I think?" he taunted.

Now, *that* hurt, but she covered it with, "Of course I care. I've always cared about you, Gabriel. In spite of whatever happened with Micah and my anger at your silence, you were my brother's best friend. Now, can we get going before those creeps come back?"

When she looked up, surprise at her confession was reflected on his face. He opened his mouth to confront her and when he did, Cassidy pretended not to see it. She wasn't in the mood to discuss matters of the heart—her heart—when she was finally doing something totally unselfish for someone else. Something that not even Gabriel Sinclair and his stubborn personality would be able to deter her from.

FOUR

I've always cared about you, Gabriel. The statement taunted him.

He hiked slowly, keeping his ears tuned to the sound of anything that didn't have to do with nature. Nothing set off his worry alarm, so he decided to give Cassidy a little space while he mulled over her words.

They'd seen each other off and on over the next couple of years when they attended certain social functions at the request of their respective parents, and Gabe had visited often because of Micah, but Cassidy lived in a different world; one Gabe hadn't wanted to be a part of. Yet, he'd been fascinated by her. And saddened by her wild lifestyle, thinking she was on the road to destruction. And then all of a sudden, her face and exploits were no longer mentioned in the paper. He'd wondered what happened. He realized now that this was when she'd become a Christian and changed her lifestyle.

And then came the mission.

And Micah had died.

And Gabe couldn't forget how.

And he couldn't forget Cassidy.

It galled him that he could be so attracted to a flighty

debutante, but there just seemed to be something about her…something deeper, like her shallowness was some kind of cover-up and there were many layers to her personality that the public never saw.

So, he'd gone to attend her college graduation. To see if he could find the deeper layers. Only, before he could see her, he'd read about her engagement in the paper. He'd been disappointed, but not surprised.

Without contacting Cassidy, he'd said goodbye to his parents and joined the SEALs. He'd thought he could make a difference with his medical skills—and he had. He'd saved the lives of good soldiers. And still, his dreams were haunted by the green-eyed princess. He knew her engagement had fallen through, but Micah was always tight-lipped about why.

What was it about her that wouldn't shake loose from his mind? His heart? He'd thought about looking her up again a few years ago, but Micah's death changed everything. And now he'd learned she'd had a child.

"Are you coming or not?" Cassidy asked.

Gabe jerked like he'd been shot. Horror swept over him. He'd totally lost his concentration for a brief moment. His carelessness could have gotten them killed. Fury with himself for his lapse made his low voice harsh. "Keep your voice down."

Cassidy's eyes widened then narrowed to slits, her displeasure with his curt tone evident. Her lips thinned and she planted her hands on her hips. Gabe caught up with her, and Cassidy kept her glare at full power. He knew he should apologize, but frankly he just didn't feel like it. Besides, when they argued, he didn't think about his nightmares.

"How much farther do you think it is?" Her words came out stiff, as though she begrudged having to ask the question.

"We can probably be there in a couple of hours."

"That soon?" Surprise chased away her anger.

"Yeah, the camp where you were held wasn't that far. By jeep, only a couple of hours or so. Seeing how we have to keep off the beaten path, it may take a lot longer."

"Okay, once we get there, how long do you think it would take us to get to La Joya?"

Gabe shrugged. "If we could borrow a jeep, and don't get lost or killed, probably not that long."

"And if we don't have a jeep?"

"A lot longer. Today's the twentieth. The plane will be there tonight for its weekly supply drop. If we miss it, it'll be another week before it comes back."

A raindrop chose that moment to roll down one of the large canopy leaves through the drip tip and splatter on Gabe's nose. He groaned. "We'd better get moving so we can find a dry place to hole up for a while."

"Where do you find shelter from the rain in a rain forest?" she asked.

Gabe felt a few more drops and said, "I have no idea. Let's see if we can find something before we get saturated."

The sky opened up. Gabe groaned again. Barely able to see in front of him, he pulled the machete from the sling across his back and swung with a vengeance, not caring about the trail he was leaving. If they were getting wet and looking desperately to get out of the downpour, chances were so were the guys behind them.

After an hour of backbreaking work, struggling to walk and see through the pouring rain, Gabe was so tired he was ready to drop. Cassidy wasn't faring much better. She lagged, and he pulled. However, she never voiced a complaint.

Gabe shook his head and brought his arm up one more time to swing, refusing to give in to the exhaustion plaguing him. His SEAL training had been a long time ago, but right now, it was like it was yesterday. When the machete cut through the vine in front of him, then came to a bone-rattling halt, Gabe's shoulder felt as if it was going to bounce out of its socket.

His abrupt halt brought Cassidy slamming into him. He grabbed her to steady her and her soggy ponytail slapped the side of his face.

Gabe parted the vines and leaves and realized that his hand rested on knotted wood. They'd found a cabin. He wiped the rain from his eyes to no avail. It still came down in sheets, blinding him. Cassidy forged on ahead.

He followed in Cassidy's rapidly disappearing footsteps and found them standing on a small porch, finally out of the never-ending rain. Cassidy curled her fingers around the knob.

"Wait!" he hissed in her ear.

She jerked back and stared at him.

"I need to check it out. Stand here and be quiet, okay?"

He scrubbed the water from his eyes and moved to the edge of the door. He pulled the gun from his waistband and motioned for Cassidy to get behind him. Using the butt of the gun, he gave the door a hard rap.

No response. Gabe repeated the procedure and still, there was nothing to indicate that anyone was inside.

Holding the gun steady with his right hand, he twisted the knob with his left. It turned smoothly and Gabe pushed the door open. When the object hurled itself from inside, screeching at the top of its lungs, Cassidy's scream echoed in its wake as Gabe tackled her to the floor of the porch.

FIVE

Heart thudding, adrenaline pumping, Cassidy watched the colorful macaw land on the railing then jump to the wooden floor of the porch.

"It's only a bird." Cassidy shook with relief.

"He almost scared me to death," Gabe grunted in disgust, got up and brushed himself off. He hauled Cassidy up next to him.

"But at least we now know no one's home." She eyed the entrance. "Nothing human anyway."

Gabe stepped into the cabin and Cassidy followed, stopping just inside the door to stand beside him. The place stunk. Cassidy wrinkled her nose and pulled the neckline of her soggy shirt up over it. Water pooled around their feet.

Cassidy saw that the cabin consisted of one large room with a kitchen off to the side. The large room boasted a sofa that mold, mildew and animals had attacked with a vengeance, and two chairs that matched the ones in the kitchen. The kitchen held a rickety wooden table and two chairs that sat rotting in one corner.

Obviously no one had been there in a long time. The broken window in the kitchen revealed how the birds entered and left. Cassidy didn't bother to close the door as she made her way farther inside.

Gabe said, "I'll check that back room."

Cassidy nodded and moved to stand in front of the fireplace. Leftover wood lay on an iron grate, like someone had readied the kindling for burning later, but then never returned. She wondered if she could light a fire without a match.

Gabe came out of the back room and said, "It's a bedroom. Nothing there. I doubt the guys on our tail can follow a trail through this mess, but we'll still have to be careful. If they know about this place, they may head straight here. As soon as it quits raining, we need to be out of here."

"Okay." She nodded. "But first things first." She walked back onto the porch, "I'm starving and since I'm already soaking wet, I'll see if I can gather some fruit from these trees."

Gabe agreed and joined her, squinting through the downpour to keep an eye out for their pursuers while Cassidy picked the fruit. His hand never moved very far from the gun at his waist. She appreciated his vigilance.

Working quickly, she gathered their next meal then re-entered the cabin. Gabe brought up the rear. She walked into the kitchen, set the fruit on the dusty counter and asked, "You think you can get a fire going?" She tossed him a papaya.

He caught it easily, took a bite and said, "Better not risk it."

Cassidy nodded, seeing the wisdom in his caution. She wrung the water out of her hair and picked up a piece of the fruit she'd gathered. Stepping next to the dark fireplace, she sat down near it, imagining she was back at home, safely ensconced in her home. It didn't work.

"What happened to those quick little showers that quit after five minutes?" she grumbled under her breath and took a bite. Sweet juice slathered her tongue then coated her throat. Wonderful. She asked, "Are we going to end up spending the night here?"

"I hope not. If the rain keeps up, I guess we'll have to. I don't like the idea of staying in one place too long, but if we can't travel in that mess, neither can the guys chasing us. If it comes down to it, you can have the bed. I'll sleep on the floor."

Cassidy frowned.

He taunted, "Don't worry. Your questionable virtue is safe with me."

"Questionable virtue?" She planted her hands on her hips, resisting the urge to stamp her foot. "How in the world after a few hours of running through a jungle did you come to the conclusion that I have 'questionable virtue'?"

"Are you married?"

"What? No, I'm not married. What's that got to do with anything?"

"Are we not going to the orphanage to pick up your daughter? Although, now that I think about it, why is your child at the orphanage?"

Cassidy's anger disappeared as she realized that he thought Alexis was her biological child. She silently ran through each conversation she'd had with Gabe over the last several hours.

"I never explained, did I?"

"Explained what?"

"The baby's not mine by birth, she belonged to Kara and Jacob Foster, my best friends, missionaries to Brazil, who were killed in that village raid two months ago. I'm now her official guardian. They asked me to take her if anything ever happened to them. I said I would."

SIX

Relief edged out his embarrassment at jumping to conclusions. Gabe shifted his gun and checked the door one more time. Then he walked over to sit on the floor next to Cassidy. He was exhausted—and fighting feelings he thought he'd buried a long time ago.

Ten years ago, he'd been attracted to her outward beauty. And while she had physically matured from a beautiful teenager into a lovely woman, his attraction now went beyond that. He admired her spunk, her spirit. Her determination to keep her promise to her friends.

"I think I could sleep for a week." Cassidy yawned and her eyelids fell to half-mast.

Gabe nodded. "Why don't you rest for a little bit. Hopefully, the rain will let up and we can move on."

"Sounds good to me." She tapped her fingers against her leg, nervous, tense and still running on adrenaline. She kept tapping. Gabe reached over and grabbed her hand. She froze. "Cass, relax," he soothed.

"I am relaxed." She held herself stiff. Gabe thought if he moved, she might snap in two. This was ridiculous.

"Hold on a minute." Gabe got up and walked into the bedroom. When he came back, he held a dusty blanket and a ratty pillow. With swift, efficient movements, he made her a pallet on the floor, then pulled mosquito netting from his waterproof pack to drape over her. "I'll keep watch. You rest, all right?"

She huffed a sigh and tentatively lay her head down on the pillow and mumbled, "I'm probably going to get lice, you know."

Gabe watched her fall asleep almost instantly. His eyes felt gritty and he used the palm of his hand to rub them. He could use a few hours of sleep himself, but that wasn't an option. Careful not to wake her, he walked over to the door and peered out. Then he looked back at Cassidy and silently wondered if she'd ever be able to forgive him. If he'd ever find a way to forgive himself for practically forcing Micah into a mission he'd wanted no part of.

Regrets and guilt covered him as he remembered....

Gabe dialed the number to Micah's private encrypted cell phone. "Micah, I need you on this mission. You know the language, you can get past the security and get the kid. I need you to pull one of your famous quarterback sneaks. Cancel whatever you're doing and get your tail on board."

Micah refused. "Gabe, people in that compound know me. I've managed to gain the confidence of one of the ringleaders in a human-trafficking deal. He's cutting me in. I'm just about ready to bust this guy and his slimy business, and I can't get my cover blown. Get someone else."

Gabe snapped back, "There is no one else. At least not someone available now. And I need you ASAP. If you don't help out, a little kid could die. Don't make me pull rank."

Micah went silent. He knew the same thing Gabe knew. Micah was the best. And Gabe needed the best on this mission.

Gabe could practically hear Micah's back molar grinding before he said, "Fine. But if anything goes wrong, it's on your head."

Cassidy woke with a start. She couldn't believe she'd actually fallen asleep. The rain had stopped and now she heard only the occasional drip of a raindrop against the porch. Gabe stood by the door, his gaze unfocused and staring. She wondered what he was thinking about.

She'd always had a little crush on him, but he only thought of her as Micah's little sister. So she'd dated guys at college— even agreed to marry one. But that love hadn't lasted.

Gabe had remained friends with Micah, but always seemed to avoid being around her. And so she'd moved on, and given her life to the Lord. And now He'd brought Gabe back into it. Gabriel Sinclair. The man who'd been there when her brother had been killed, but wouldn't talk about it. Not with her, not with her family. It hurt.

Lord, get us there safely. Keep Alexis in Your care. Bring Gabe to You. Let him know You're more than just God… You're a Heavenly Father to lean on and trust. And help me deal with my anger. Let him know he can trust me to tell me what happened with Micah.

She shifted slightly and looked up into his face. The beam from the sun shed enough light in the room so that she could clearly see his face fuzzy with the beard, head resting against the doorjamb. Even though he was motionless, he still seemed restless. The frown lines between his brows stayed pronounced and she wondered if he ever truly smiled.

Oh, yeah. He smiled when he pushed her buttons and riled her temper. Silence echoed and she sat up with a start. "Gabe?" she whispered. "It's stopped raining. We can leave."

He blinked and she gulped at the longing that speared through her. She did her best to ignore it. Now wasn't the time. And she still wasn't sure how she felt about him and his role in her brother's death.

He asked, "Are you sure you're up to it? You've only slept about two hours."

"I'm fine." She stood to stretch the kinks out. She ached all over, but ignored it. Alexis was waiting.

"All right," Gabe agreed, "we've probably stayed here too long anyway."

Cassidy joined him. Her hair brushed against his chin and he sucked in a breath. She smelled like rain mixed with sweat. When she turned to look up at him, Gabe wondered what the flickering behind her eyes meant, wondered what she'd do if he leaned down the fraction of an inch separating them and kissed her. No time to find out as Cassidy blinked, pulled away and moved out the door. The moment fizzled. She said, "Come on, Gabriel, we've got a baby to rescue."

Gabe walked back into the bedroom and gathered up his pack. He came back and handed her the Ruger. He said, "Do you know how to use this?"

"I can hit what I aim at."

He hesitated as though trying to decide if he should leave the gun with her. "I'm going to backtrack a bit and see if they're on our tail or not. Keep your eyes and ears open. And shoot anything that moves. Except me. I'll whistle as I get close."

Cassidy hefted the gun and its weight felt comfortable and familiar against her palm. She knew a thing or two about guns and shooting.

"I'll be all right. I don't like you leaving me, though.

And won't you need it if you run into them?" She chewed her bottom lip.

"Don't worry, I don't plan on letting them see me. These guys might not let a little downpour slow them down. If not, we're in trouble." He gave her a pointed look, a quirky grin and said, "And I don't need any more trouble."

Cassidy rolled her eyes, but couldn't hold back her answering smile.

"Go," he said. "I'll catch up in a minute."

Cassidy sighed and did as ordered. Gabe took off in the opposite direction. She thought about how close Gabe had come to kissing her—and how close she'd been to letting him. But this was not the time to explore old feelings…or discover new ones. She walked and prayed.

Fifteen minutes later she heard a soft whistle and set the safety back on the gun. He appeared from behind a tree and water dripped from the dark hair that curled around his ears and down his neck. The bristly beard he'd grown—one of the reasons she hadn't recognized him right off—glistened with moisture. He looked good. And a lot different from ten years ago. Harder, leaner…and meaner. But definitely good.

"Well?" she asked, trying to distract her wayward thoughts.

"Nothing. But they're still looking for us and no doubt following our trail. We need to keep moving to put as much distance between us as possible."

Gabe took the lead and she followed. Cassidy still had to pinch herself to make sure she wasn't dreaming. Never, in all of her rescue fantasies over the past two weeks, had Gabriel Sinclair played the starring role.

She took a deep breath and shoved a branch of leaves

out of her face. Gabe swung the machete into a mess of tangled vines and cleared the way. She could tell he didn't like using it, but knew he had no choice. The undergrowth grabbed at their ankles making it impossible to traverse without help. They were leaving a path a blind man could follow as he whacked and sliced, leading the way and grunting with the effort.

Admiration for him swelled within her. Fatigue gripped him, but he kept going. She felt ready to drop in her tracks, too, but exhaustion ignored, they pressed on. Gabe grunted and hacked some more. After another hour, she asked, "Where do you think they are?"

Gabe hesitated for a long moment then finally said, "I don't know and I don't like it."

"What do you mean?"

Gabe shook the water from his head then answered, "They should have caught up with us." He stopped and took a deep breath. Cassidy stopped beside him. Gabe pulled his backpack around and extracted two bottles of water. He passed one to Cassidy.

She uncapped it, took a long swig and stated, "I'll never take the sweet taste of water for granted again." Then she asked him, "When you backtracked, you didn't see anything?"

"Nope, not a thing. That means they're not chasing us blind. I didn't have a lot of time to work out the chain of command in the camp, but my guess is Rafael is the one on our tail. And while he may be paid muscle, unlike most of these guys, he also comes with a brain. And that makes him more dangerous than ever." Gabe tossed his empty bottle into the pack and said, "I don't know where those guys are and I don't like it."

Cassidy frowned at him. "Maybe they gave up because of the rain."

"Guys like that don't give up. No, they've got a plan. You realize they may be waiting for us when we get to the orphanage."

Cassidy shuddered at the thought. "So if they've got a plan, what's *our* plan?"

Gabe sighed. "I have no idea."

Cassidy stared at him for a moment then flopped to the ground and shut her eyes. She said, "Well, you'll think of something."

SEVEN

You'll think of something. Gabe shuddered and sat down beside Cassidy, ignoring the moisture soaking through the seat of his pants. He had no desire to have that responsibility heaped back on his shoulders. Once he'd been the best; the most trusted leader. And he'd led those men who trusted him right into a death trap. Including his best friend…

"Let's go, guys. Follow the plan. We've got a drug-cartel-slash-kidnapper to bring down and a little boy to rescue."

Normally a SEAL team consisted of six men, himself included. He'd asked for another full team and gotten the all clear. Now he had five on land with him and six in the water—plus one extra, his secret weapon, Micah McKnight. Six men, two from the north, two from the west and two from the south, in camouflage dress, slipped silently up to the hedge that hid the iron fence surrounding the property of Diego Manuel Cruz. The guys on the water had the eastern part of the estate covered. The man had kidnapped his own son to spite the boy's mother who'd left to raise the child in a different environment, one free of crime and hate. She'd gone to the authorities with enough evidence to lock up Cruz for a long time. Only Cruz had slipped away and grabbed the boy.

Gabe lifted his hand to signal his men to stop and follow procedure. The South American beach-front home exuded a peace and serenity that Gabe knew covered criminal activity including drugs, human trafficking, arms smuggling and who knew what else.

He motioned one more time and four of his men broke off to scale the fence surrounding the property line. Two headed to go over the wall perpendicular to the one their comrades were already over. Two others would wait on the Advanced SEAL Delivery Vehicle for the rest to come back. The other four would approach from the water, rising from its depths like a silent sea monster.

Hopefully they would be Cruz's worst nightmare.

Gabe shoved his earpiece farther in his ear and forced himself to breathe normally. Adrenaline raced, and as always, a healthy respect for the unknown edged his consciousness.

He double-checked the security system. Unarmed. Micah McKnight had done his job. He'd been right to request that Micah join his team this time. No dogs barked. Gavin had accomplished his part of the mission. All that remained was to slip in to the bedroom of the drug lord and—drug him.

Gabe allowed himself a quick smile at the irony. Only chloroform, not cocaine, was the SEAL choice of drug in this operation. Once drugged, Cruz would be cuffed and brought to the States to stand trial. Of course, the official story would be he was captured on U.S. soil.

Normally, SEAL teams operated in a more amphibious environment, but their training allowed them to succeed on land, too. In the ASDV, two more SEALs waited in the rocking waters to transport their "guest" back to the States.

Gabe checked his watch. A voice whispered in his earpiece, "Something not right here, Gabe."

Nerves tight, Gabe gripped his Ruger and scanned the perimeter. Nothing moved. Infrared goggles hung around his neck. He picked them up and did another scan. It was quiet. Too quiet. Where were the guards?

Gabe spoke into the microphone that would transmit his voice to all twelve men, "Get out. If it doesn't feel right, it's not. Get out now. Micah, you got the kid?"

"Affirmative." Micah's husky voice reached his ear two seconds before the explosions that rocked the ASDV, then seconds later the house, rocked Gabe's world. One minute, he had twelve experienced men on his team, the next minute, he had twelve dead friends—and a dead child. Gabe had been SEAL number thirteen....

"So, have you come up with anything yet?"

Gabe crashed back to his current surroundings. He shuddered, focused on the quiet voice and opened his eyes.

Cassidy.

He looked at his watch. "We've been here for about ten minutes. Long enough."

Thankfully, she didn't ask him what he'd been thinking about and they were able to move out with Gabe acting like a rogue scout, backtracking, then catching up, moving ahead, then making his way back. Finally, they broke through the jungle, and the Amazon Orphanage sat in front of them. High, thick adobe walls surrounded the perimeter. Closed and locked, the iron gates looked like the prison bars of a jail.

Cassidy's hushed voice broke the silence. "I don't see anyone, but I don't think we should go in the front. I bet the reason you didn't see them behind us is because they know I'll come back here for Alexis. It might be a bit of a stretch, but I think I know another way in."

Gabe agreed and Cassidy took the lead. She made her way around to the side wall of the orphanage then stepped up to one of the trees that grew alongside the west wall. She gestured. "Climb up and over into the playground, then we can go in the side door. At least there are no nails spiked up on the wall at this orphanage." Some orphanages used them for added security. She rubbed her hands together and smiled grimly. "Piece of cake."

He said, "I'll go first. I can pull you on up if you need it."

"I'll be fine," Cassidy assured him.

Gabe grabbed the lowest limb and started up. Cassidy followed close behind and muttered, "All those times climbing out of my window *were* for a reason after all."

He gave a soft chuckle and stepped off the limb onto the top of the wall. He straddled it and looked down. Cassidy stopped on the limb next to him and asked, "Is it too far down?"

"No, not too bad. Probably about a twelve-foot drop. Grab my hand and I'll let you down a bit." She scrambled over, grasped his hand and was on the ground within the blink of an eye. Gabe swung over, gripped the top of the wall, paused, then landed like a cat beside her.

She headed for the nearest door and slipped inside.

Cassidy breathed in the clean scent of the orphanage. She'd desperately needed to see that Alexis was all right.

"Oh! Miss Cassidy? *O senhor?*" The squeal of a relief worker in her late seventies brought them up short.

Cassidy spoke, "*Sim,* Francesca. We escaped." She reached out to hug the shaking woman. "*Estou tão pesaroso.* I'm so sorry. We frightened you. Have you seen any of the rebels?"

"No, no one. Since they took you, we have had no trouble and seen no one. Of course, we are in the process of fixing what they destroyed, but mostly everything has been quiet."

Cassidy gently gripped the hands of the woman. "Please, tell me where Alexis is. Is she all right?"

Francesca smiled warmly at Cassidy, "Oh, *sim.* Fine. Waiting for her new *mamãe* to come get her. We were very worried about you. And here comes Anna."

Cassidy turned quickly and gasped, "Anna! You're all right. I'm so sorry you got hurt because of me." She hurried to Anna to wrap her in a relieved hug. The cut on the woman's forehead had almost healed.

Anna squeezed back and asked, "Are you okay?"

"We escaped thanks to my father sending in Gabe here. But I'm afraid we need to hurry. The longer we stay, the more danger we put all of you in."

"*Sim, sim,* follow me." Francesca hurried off and the trio followed her through a maze of hallways until she reached a set of double doors.

As they walked, Anna continued, "I've been thinking about one of the men who kidnapped you. There is one named Rafael? I think I know who he is."

"What? But how?" Cassidy asked.

"He's on the Most Wanted list here in Brazil. Rafael Morales," Anna explained, "Not only is the orphanage a place of refuge for children caught in the drug or political wars, we're also connected with the Brazil version of the Department of Social Services system. If we get an abused child, we go through proper channels and report it, or if it's already been reported, we try to keep up with the status of the case and the child. Not that it always does any good,

but we do it. Which means I'm often in the police station—
waiting. I've studied the posters on the walls. It finally
came to me that that's where I know that guy from. He's a
well-known human trafficker."

Cassidy gasped, shuddered. "So, you think my kidnapping had something to do with my father's political stance?"

Anna shrugged and turned a corner. "Could be. Then
again, they could have heard about you being at the orphanage and decided to add a pretty redhead to the auction
block. Then later, somehow they learned who your father
was and decided they could get more money out of him
than a slave trader."

Gabe looked a little sick and Cassidy knew her expression said she felt the same. If Gabe hadn't come along
when he had… "Thank You, Lord, for sending Gabe," Cassidy whispered the prayer out loud.

Anna nodded. "Yes. God is definitely watching over
you. Rafael's sister, Juanita Morales, is also on the police
station wall. As a missing person. She disappeared over
thirty years ago. They keep her picture there next to
Rafael's in hopes that if someone sees her, it will lead
them to Rafael. Although, many people say that she was
Rafael's first victim. That he kidnapped her and sold her
and has been in business ever since."

Cassidy groaned and dropped her head in her hands.
*God, let what we're doing be making a difference. Please
get us home safe.*

Francesca threw open the door to the cafeteria, and the
sound of laughter and children's voices greeted them. Approximately seventy children sat around wooden picnic
tables finishing up their midday meal. Cassidy ignored the
rumble of her stomach as she made her way over to the

only towheaded child in the room. Alexis was adorable, dressed in a little red-and-white sleeveless jumper with red tights and white tennis shoes. Cheese, rice and beans covered her rosy-red cheeks.

Cassidy approached slowly and bent down next to her, hoping that all of her hard work in getting to know Alexis the previous month hadn't been wasted.

"Hello, Alexis."

The child stopped eating and blue eyes looked up to frown into Cassidy's. Alexis tilted her head as she studied Cassidy, then she grinned wide and laughed, "My *Cass-ty.*"

Cassidy let out a sigh of relief and leaned over to place a kiss on the head covered with wispy blond curls. "My Lexi."

"We've got to go. They're here."

Gabe's tight whisper in her ear brought her joy crashing down. She quickly stood and picked up the child, whispering reassurances in her ear. Alexis didn't protest.

Anna appeared next to Gabe. "Come on, you three, no time for goodbyes. There's a jeep around back in the garage. I don't know how great it runs, but it should help you put some distance between you and them."

Cassidy looked up at Gabe. "Now we can head west."

Gabe cranked the vehicle and felt responsibility sit heavily on his shoulders. How was he going to get them out of here and safely home? He punched the gas and the jeep lunged from its hiding place in the ramshackle garage. Gabe's knuckles turned white from his grip on the wheel and Cassidy struggled to hold on to the squirming child and keep the seat belt around both of them.

"Hang on!" Gabe shouted.

"Behind us!" she yelled.

Gabe spared a quick glance in the rearview mirror. Rafael sat on a seat with his head sticking out above the roll bar, balancing a rifle against his shoulder. Gabe spun the wheel to the right and swerved around a fallen tree. The jeep followed.

Gunshots sounded and Gabe ducked and hollered, "Put Alexis on the floor and cover her with your body. Keep your head down and hold on tight!"

Cassidy fumbled to obey. Gently but firmly she put the child on the floorboard, then bent over her to keep her own head down and Alexis covered. Cassidy winced as Alexis screamed her fury. Gabe continued to do his best to keep them on the makeshift road, one of the government's many unfinished projects, and out of range of the bullets. His only hope was to outdistance them. There was no way he could get his gun out, drive and shoot all at the same time.

"Go faster!" Wind whipped Cassidy's hair around her pallid face. A bullet cracked the window and Gabe jerked the wheel to the left, then back to the right. Another shot sounded and whizzed past his ear. "I'm going as fast as I can without blowing a tire on this road. Now, pray!"

"I am. Give me the gun," she hollered back.

"No way." Gabe whipped the wheel to the left and missed a hole the size of a crater, but hit a large tree stump. The jeep went airborne for a few brief seconds, then smashed back to the ground with a bone-jarring thud. Cassidy let out a squeal and Alexis yelled even louder. But at least the jeep kept going.

"Gabriel Sinclair, give me the gun!" Cassidy demanded over the whipping wind and screaming bullets. Keeping the baby between her legs, trapping her from moving, she leaned toward Gabe and grabbed the gun from the back waistband of his pants.

"This situation is a lot different from just holding the gun in the jungle. Are you insane?" If his fury had been fire, she'd have been toast.

"Probably. Now keep us upright and moving while I try to make these guys back off."

Gabe was scared to death. Not just scared of the guys behind him, but that he'd failed once again to keep safe those entrusted to his care.

Gabe decided to concentrate on driving—and praying. *Oh, God, why a child?*

Cassidy checked Alexis one more time, not bothering to try to take the time to reassure the terrified tot. Hopefully, there would be time for that later once they were all somewhere safe. With the gun in her left hand, she released the safety and leaned out the open window only to pull back in and yell, "When I say 'now' you turn the wheel to the right so they'll come toward this side of the jeep."

"You'll be exposed!"

"I'll take that chance, okay?"

She didn't wait for his response, just turned to position herself so she could keep Alexis safely pinned to the floor yet have a clear shot as soon as Gabe turned the jeep. Dust and dirt swirled in the air about them, but she thought she could see well enough at the right time…

"Now!" she yelled.

Gabe spun the wheel. Cassidy waited for what seemed like an hour but in reality was only a few gut-churning seconds then fired the weapon three times with deadly accuracy.

Several shots from the jeep behind zinged wildly by.

Cassidy pulled in from the window and leaned back with a grunt. Gabe waited for more bullets to come their way, but the only sound now was the rushing wind, Alexis screaming and the jeep's whine.

"Did you get them?"

"I don't know about them, but their two front tires are out."

Sure enough, the men behind them had stopped and Gabe quickly pulled away to leave the other jeep behind. He looked over at Cassidy, who lifted Alexis from the floor, wiping her tears, cuddling her and offering much-needed reassurances.

Cassidy prayed and Gabe put as much distance between them and the rebels as he possibly could, considering the fact that he couldn't go much over forty miles an hour due to the road conditions.

But after a few miles, the jeep sputtered, choked and died. Gabe whacked the wheel with the palm of his hand and muttered, "Not now."

"What's wrong?" Cassidy said.

Gabe didn't answer, just pushed the jeep as far as it would go, then finally let it roll to a stop between two trees on the side of the makeshift road. Cassidy absently shifted Alexis to her other knee. The child's cries had finally slowed to a whimper every now and then, but her big blue eyes followed the adults' every move.

Gabe leaned his head back against the seat and closed his eyes. "The jeep's done, but I've got to ask. Where'd you learn to shoot like that?"

EIGHT

Gabe hopped out of the jeep, wondering how much time they had. He rounded the front of the vehicle and popped the hood.

Steam hissed.

"Guess that's not a good sign, huh?" Cassidy said as she came into view. She had Alexis on her hip. Tear tracks streaked the little one's cheeks, and she scrubbed a grimy fist against one eye.

Gabe grunted, "Nope, not a good sign and I don't have the tools to fix it. Wonder how far we are to the next village."

"Here, hold her and I'll raid the glove box for a map. And to answer your question, Micah taught me. Said it might come in handy one day." A sad smile flickered across her face. "Guess he was right. Here."

Before Gabe could respond or protest, he found himself clutching the toddler. Alexis reared back against his hold to stare him in the eye. She poked her bottom lip out and frowned. Gabe frowned back, unsure what to do with her. Finally, she whimpered and turned to watch Cassidy, but at least she didn't cry. Probably too tired out from her last meltdown. Not that he blamed her. He patted her small back reassuringly.

"You find one?" Gabe walked over to the side of the jeep.

"Yep, look." She shook out the map so he could see it and pointed to a village by the name of St. Lucia. "I know this village. It's not too far from where Kara and Jacob were killed. They have friends here, Jorge and Selena Manuez. Their names are on the will as witnesses."

"Will they help us if we can get there?"

"Probably. They're missionaries, too."

"Then, that's where we'll head. Here, take her back." Alexis went willingly and put her head on Cassidy's shoulder. Gabe's heart softened at the sight. He could see why Cassidy had fought so hard to get back to the orphanage.

"I'm going to have to push this jeep off the road and cover our tracks as best I can."

"All right." She set Alexis in the passenger seat and settled herself behind the wheel. Gabe focused on the task at hand; getting the jeep off the path and hidden in the woods.

After twenty minutes of pushing, grumbling, resting and watching their backs, Gabe managed to hide the jeep then use the machete to strategically cut branches and vines to cover it.

Hopefully, the men would be so intent on the path and catching up to their prey that they wouldn't notice this spot. Sweat trickled down his face to drip off his chin. Gabe used the hem of his shirt to wipe his forehead then walked over to the tree root Cassidy was using as a seat. Alexis gnawed on a banana and sipped water from one of their sparse bottles. Cassidy offered him one and he took it.

"We've got to get going." He swigged the last of the water and put the empty container in his pack. He reached out to pick up the little girl, who frowned but thankfully didn't cry, just rubbed her eyes, gave a huge jaw-popping yawn and lay her head on his shoulder to snuggle down for a nap. Gabe's heart clenched. He had to get her and Cassidy to safety.

They continued the trek in silence, slowly eating up the distance. No jeep passed them on the road and no one jumped from the undergrowth to open fire. Two hours passed without incident. Gabe was worried about the lack of activity. Where were they?

Gradually, the dense trees began to spread out little by little and then a clearing opened up to reveal a village, populated with huts similar to the ones in the rebel camp.

Gabe felt eyes watching him and steeled himself for an ambush. "Here, hold Alexis."

Cassidy took the still-sleeping child and Gabe shifted the machete for easier access and then felt for his gun in the belt at his back. "They know we're here. I just hope they ask questions before they start shooting or tossing spears." Rushing water gurgled from the river to his left; a dog barked and the squeal of a pig came from one of the huts. "All right. Follow my lead."

Hands in plain sight to present a nonthreatening appearance, Gabe stepped into the clearing. Their arrival stirred the interest of several children who eyed them curiously then scattered in various directions.

A dark-skinned man, lean and strong-looking, emerged from the hut at the far end of the village. Gabe felt Cassidy start at the sight of the spear in the native's left hand. He placed a firm hand on the small of her back to propel her forward.

Silent dark eyes watched their approach. The native eyed the child in Cassidy's arms then held up his spear. Gabe immediately stopped. Cassidy followed suit.

"Why do you enter our village?"

Gabe blinked at the perfect English and responded in kind. "We need to find the missionaries Jorge and Selena Manuez."

The dark eyes never changed, but the spear shifted higher. "And your purpose with them is?"

Before Gabe could answer, Cassidy offered, "This is Gabriel, I'm Cassidy and this is Alexis. The Manuezes were friends of Alexis's parents."

"Alexis?"

The woman's breathy question turned all four heads in her direction.

Cassidy stared at the pretty, heavyset woman bearing down on them. She huddled Alexis closer and readied herself to run.

"Is that Alexis?" Panting gasps escaped as she held out dark brown arms in the child's direction. Full brown lips pulled into a beaming smile.

Alexis, awake and frowning at the woman, wrapped her arms around Cassidy's neck, shook her head and said, "No, stay, my Cass-ty."

Immediately the arms dropped, but the smile remained and the woman's dark eyes locked with Cassidy's. "Cassidy? Kara and Jacob's friend."

Cassidy knew immediately who this was. "Selena."

The chubby sun-browned round face creased into a smile, showing every wrinkle this kind woman had earned over her lifetime, which Cassidy judged to be around sixty years.

Selena turned toward the native who had originally greeted them when they entered the village and shooed him gently away. Cassidy thought she saw humor in the old eyes before he turned to leave, but couldn't be sure. She turned back to the smiling woman.

"Selena, I'm so glad to meet you. This is Gabe and yes, this is Alexis."

The smile disappeared and tears pooled for a moment before Selena blinked them away. "Kara, oh, I do miss her. Well," she sniffed, "come, come. Our hut is this way. I saw the little blond girl and knew who this must be."

Cassidy hefted Alexis higher and wearily offered Gabe a smile. "Well, we made it."

He brushed the hair from her eyes. "Yeah, now we've got to make that plane."

Cassidy nodded and started after the bustling woman, whose bright red, brown and yellow muumuu swayed with her every step. "I can't wait to get home and get everything finalized. And I'm dying to brush my teeth."

She stepped into the darkness of the hut and noticed it was much nicer than the one she'd been held captive in. This one actually had a small bathroom attached. A curtain down the middle separated the sleeping quarters from the living.

Selena waved them in. "Jorge, we have company."

Jorge emerged from behind the curtain, a short stocky man whose smile matched his wife's. Dark brown eyes twinkled with curiosity. Selena said, "Jorge, meet Kara and Jacob's friend, Cassidy. You remember we witnessed the new will they made out naming Cassidy as guardian if something happened to them? And this is Gabe."

The men shook hands and Jorge offered Alexis a smile.

"Good to meet you," Gabe offered. "Unfortunately, we probably bring trouble with us. We just need a jeep or some kind of transportation then we'll be out of here. Or your lives may be in danger for helping us."

Jorge frowned. "Oh? Well, danger's never stopped us before."

Selena stepped forward and told Cassidy, "Feel free to use the bathroom. There are washcloths and extra toothbrushes on the shelf behind the sink. There is plenty of soap and water, so you can wash your hair if you like."

Cassidy smiled at Selena and said, "Thank you." She looked at Gabe. "What do you think? Do we have time?"

He shook his head. "Just for the basics. No time to linger."

Jorge spoke up. "Selena, pack some food for our friends and I will see if I can find a jeep. They must get going."

Selena headed for the kitchen. While she loaded down a small sack, Cassidy asked, "Do you know where I can find some diapers?"

Selena laughed. "We have many children in the village, I will find some for you." She handed Cassidy the packed food and hurried out the door, promising to be right back.

Jorge came back as Selena left. "No jeep. We have one in the village and it's not working." He stepped into the kitchen and said, "Sit for a moment. Eat something while you can. Let's think." He placed fruit and bread on the small table and after everyone was seated said a short blessing.

"Our Father in heaven, we ask Your blessing on this food and these young ones on the run for their lives. Place Your protection around them. Confuse their enemies. Give our new friends safe passage home. In Your precious son's name, Amen."

"Amen," Cassidy whispered.

Gabe shifted on his seat, the beautiful simplicity of the prayer grabbing his heart. Was God listening? He shrugged off the thought, promising himself that he would deal with it later. Gabe held on to the soggy child while Cassidy finished her food, every once in a while feeding a bite to Alexis, who gobbled it down with delight.

He couldn't help stealing a glance at Cassidy every now and then. He realized he admired her. Her maternal feelings for the child were clearly displayed on her face, in her actions, and his chest ached at the thought of someone doing her harm. "You may have your hands full trying to feed this one. She's got a healthy appetite," Gabe teased.

Cassidy's green gaze rose to lock with his and he had to work to ignore the false feeling of family. The door to the hut banged open and Gabe jumped, his hand reaching automatically for the weapon at his back, his other arm curved around the child. Selena hurried in and shut the door. She held pins and burp cloths that would function as diapers for Alexis. Cassidy took the items, but Gabe saw the worry stamped on the missionary's leathery features. He asked, "What's wrong?"

"There are men on the way. They are powerful men with many guns. Our village does not have a way to defend itself against such machines. You must hide. Jorge, show them where they must go—and tell them about the motorcycle."

Jorge jumped up and ordered, "Selena, get rid of the dishes." Then to the others, "You three follow me."

Selena hurried to comply while the others followed Jorge behind the room's dividing curtain. The old man's knees popped as he knelt and reached under the bed and pulled out a box, then two more. Finally, he pulled out a piece of wood that was square and about three feet by three feet. It matched the floor's grooves and lines perfectly.

Jorge grunted and hurried to explain. "Due to all the

violence in this area, Selena and I knew we may need a way out. It's a tunnel about fifteen feet deep, but once you get down there, it is only about four feet tall. You will have to crouch. It is approximately one mile long. It will lead you to the river. Once there, you will have to climb up some log steps and push hard on the piece of wood covering the exit. It will be difficult because of the growth, but if you push hard enough, it will move. Look for a motorcycle. It's hidden near the exit."

Gabe sucked in a breath. Fifteen feet deep. Great. He kept his thoughts to himself and said, "Don't fight them. Tell them what they want to know. They'll kill you if you don't."

"The Lord will be with us."

Gabe narrowed his eyes and secretly thought that Kara and Jacob probably thought the same thing. Then he turned his gaze on Cassidy. She stood trembling but holding it together.

A gunshot echoed from somewhere outside the small hut. Jorge paled and Cassidy jumped. Jorge pushed them toward the floor. "Hurry, go, go. I must cover the hole back up."

Gabe took Alexis from Cassidy's arms and motioned for her to crawl under the bed and down into the hole. She hesitated, terror written all over her.

Men yelling. Gunshots. The explosion. Then the gun in his ear. Gabe blinked against the harsh flashes and shoved the memories aside. He couldn't fail again.

Cassidy finally scrambled under the bed and then Gabe heard her call in a shaky voice, "Okay, send Alexis down."

Gabe quickly passed the child down to Cassidy.

Cassidy held her breath and caught Alexis as Gabe eased her down into the darkness. Gabe's pack and the bag containing the food landed on the mud floor near her feet. She stepped back, hugging the little girl close as she waited for Gabe to follow.

Coarse shouts and loud banging sounded from somewhere above. *"Abra a porta!"*

The rapid-fire Portuguese sizzled Cassidy's nerves. Open the door, he'd shouted. Rafael. She'd know that guttural, harsh voice anywhere. She swallowed back the nausea. Now wasn't the time for panic.

Gabe dropped beside her and grabbed up his pack to slide it over his shoulder. Wood scraped against wood as Jorge slid the door back into place, darkness enveloping Cassidy so quickly she gasped.

Thuds and stomps above told Cassidy that the men were searching. Had Jorge been able to move fast enough to slide the boxes back under the bed?

"No one is here!"

The scream punctured the floor, the sound so heartrending, Cassidy took an unconscious step back toward the opening. Gabe dragged her back, pulling her close, his warm breath whispering against her ear, "We can't go back."

"But we can't just leave them, they'll kill them." The desire to get Alexis to safety warred with the desperate need to help the two people who had risked so much for her.

"Jorge will handle it. Go before they find us."

Cassidy shivered in the dankness, the reality of their situation lodging in her throat and stealing her breath. Fifteen feet underground. Mud, dirt, decay. All they lacked was the coffin. She gave a violent shudder.

Alexis whimpered and Cassidy patted her back, knowing she'd risk anything for this little girl. "Okay. Let's go."

She put one foot in front of the other, following the

sound of Gabe moving ahead until she heard a thud, then a grunt. "Gabe, you okay?"

She ran into his back, smashing her nose against hard muscles. "Ouch."

"Hold on, this is where the tunnel narrows. I just found out the hard way. I have a lighter here somewhere."

Alexis gave another mewling whimper, "Mama? Want Mama."

Cassidy fought tears and struggled to breathe in the suffocating darkness. "I know, baby, I know."

A light flickered on and Cassidy gave a strangled shriek. Damp mud walls were alive with roaches as big as her thumb. "I think I was better off not knowing what was down here. Turn the light off, Gabe. Please!" She felt the hysteria building and swallowed to contain it.

"Here, give me Alexis." Gabe let the light flicker out and took the child. Cassidy grabbed his belt in a death grip. She crouched to follow as best she could, and while Gabe whispered assurances to Alexis, Cassidy took them to heart.

"Please, Jesus, get us out of here." Cassidy didn't even realize she'd started praying aloud until she heard her voice echo off the walls.

"That's it, just keep praying. Do what you have to do to keep calm. We're going to be fine. I have to turn the light back on, so get ready."

Cassidy tensed, but kept walking. She heard the scrape of the lighter that once again lit up the underground. Cassidy struggled to focus on his voice and not her current location. Gabe spoke. "Okay, there's a turn up ahead, just a slight curve to the right."

Cassidy felt light-headed, short of breath. And her back was killing her from walking in the stooped position.

Alexis began to wail. Cassidy panted, trying desperately to take even breaths even while feeling the panic rise to overwhelm her. Her heartbeat threatened to explode from her chest. Dizziness made her stumble and she felt the moisture of a cold sweat break across her neck. Harsh voices echoed down the tunnel to send more shivers of fear dancing across her nerves.

"I hear them. How much farther, Gabe?" she whispered.

"Not much, I don't think."

The light flickered and died. Gabe rasped it again as they made their way around the curve. Cassidy kept a tight rein on her nerves, but was starting to lose the battle. Alexis started crying and Cassidy ached to hold her and reassure her. She whispered, "It's all right, baby."

"That's it, Cass. You can do this," he encouraged.

She didn't agree, but decided to keep up the prayers and do her best to ignore her surroundings.

NINE

"Gabe, stop. I can't breathe. I'm sorry. Just stop for a minute." Cassidy's hitched whisper brought him back around to face her. Gabe shifted Alexis. Her cries had faded to whimpers. He had to let the lighter flicker out.

Panicked gasps whistled from Cassidy's lips and Gabe ground his back teeth. He vowed to make those responsible pay for doing this to her. He grabbed her hand and pulled. He said, "Keep it together for Alexis, Cass. They're coming. We need to hurry."

"Alexis, right. Okay. I can do this, I can."

"Go. Too dark. Mama? Don't like," Alexis whined.

Gabe flicked on his lighter again and listened to her harsh breathing. He was relieved she seemed able to keep her terror under control. Panic attacks were no fun at all. He could relate. Gabe let the light go out and they marched together in the dark, in the awkwardly stooped position for the next fifteen or so minutes, keeping just ahead of the noises behind them. He stopped and reached for the lighter again. "We should be almost at the end. Let me take a look."

The small flame revealed the end of the tunnel. The log steps were directly in front of him. Steep, but manageable.

"Thank God," he whispered under his breath.

Alexis squirmed in his arms, anxious to get down. He passed her to Cassidy and said, "I think we're only about five minutes ahead of them. I don't hear anything. Let me go up and get the top open, then I'll come back and help you two up. Can you handle it for about a minute?"

"Of course." She was being a good sport.

Gabe paused and listened again. Still nothing. *They* were probably listening for *them*. He had to hurry. Without any further hesitation, he scaled the steps and reached up to feel the hard piece of wood covering their exit. With a grunt, he shoved, but nothing happened.

Straining, he shoved again. Nothing.

"Gabe?"

"Yeah?"

"I hear them again. They're getting really close!"

Adrenaline surged and he realized that saving Cassidy and Alexis was out of his hands. He begged, "God, if You're listening, I could really use some help here. Please."

"Gabe!" Panic surged in her voice. "They're getting closer. I can see a flashlight. I'm coming up."

Gabe took a deep breath and shoved with everything in him, praying at the same time. The wood moved, popped up and shifted to the right. Dirt and debris rained down on him and fresh air surged over him. Sweat ran off him in rivulets.

"Thank You, God." Maybe God did listen after all.

By this time, Cassidy was right behind him, the strain of climbing with Alexis in one arm and pulling herself up with the other evident on her already drawn features. The steps were spaced diagonally enough that it was possible to climb this way, just difficult.

Gabe grabbed Alexis and pushed her through the opening off to the side. She whined and started crying. Gabe hauled himself out and set her on the ground beside him. He quickly turned back to the hole to help Cassidy.

"Gabe! They're right behind me!"

Gabe could hear the clatter and pounding feet below him. Cassidy's hands stretched through the opening, and Gabe grabbed both wrists and pulled to haul her up. She jerked against his hands.

"He's got my foot!" she screamed. "Pull!"

He felt her kick; her wrists slipped. *No! Please, don't let me lose her, God.* Gabe looked down through the opening to see a bearded, leering face contorted into an evil grin. A rough hand held Cassidy's booted foot; the other hand swung a snub-nosed pistol up to center on Gabe's heart. Cassidy twisted, one wrist slipped from his grip. Terrified, he grabbed for it, but she flailed her arm wildly, and the rebel below her clamped hard on the foot he still held. At least Cassidy's flailing threw the man's aim off. The bullet went over his head.

Gabe was determined not to let go of Cassidy's wrist—even if it meant dislocating her shoulder. Then, as though in slow motion, Gabe watched Cassidy bring her other booted foot around and smash it into the man's chin. A harsh scream echoed up from the tunnel as the rebel dropped down the steps to land on the hard-packed earth below. Gabe gave one last desperate pull and Cassidy popped through the opening, panting; mud and sweat covered her face. She scrambled away from the hole and Gabe moved fast.

He shoved the wood back into place and looked for something heavy to place on top of it. He urged Cassidy, "Shove all the dirt you can on top."

She quickly complied and Gabe noticed a fallen tree to his right. The trunk was thick, about six feet in diameter, and it definitely looked heavy. He just hoped he could move it. Straddling the log, he reached down and wrapped his arms around the base.

Already tired muscles strained to the limit, he heaved the trunk inch by inch across the uneven jungle floor.

"Gabe!"

At Cassidy's panicked cry, he looked to see the wooden covering moving. He heard the shouted orders. One last groaning effort dropped the tree on top of the wood covering the hole. Satisfaction soared when he heard a muffled yell. He hoped the fall had knocked the man out.

"What about Selena and Jorge?" Cassidy worried. Absently, she rubbed her throbbing arm and said, "The men will go back through the tunnel."

"Hopefully Jorge had the foresight to nail that opening shut and run."

Cassidy whispered, "It won't matter, they'll just shoot their way out."

Gabe agreed but didn't say so. He was worried about the missionary couple, too, but there was nothing that could be done at the moment. His primary concern was getting Cassidy and the child to safety.

Never had hot, humid, soggy air felt so good to Cassidy's already overheated, dirt-plastered skin. The Amazon River roared close by. The damp earth smelled of decay and life and all things that made Cassidy feel grateful to be alive—even though her arm and shoulder throbbed with torn ligaments and pulled muscles.

Eyes clamped shut against the light of day, she clutched

Alexis to her. Fortunately, the wide canopy of leaves blocked most of the bright sun, so it didn't take long for her eyes to adjust.

She looked around and wondered how in the world they would make it to the airport. Right now, walking was not an option. She didn't even think she could crawl.

Alexis howled, tears streaming down her flushed cheeks. The banging from below stopped. Muffled shots sounded and Cassidy flinched. They were trying to shoot their way out. *God, I'm so tired. I can't take much more.*

"Shush, baby, it's okay," Cassidy crooned to the child, stroking her cheek.

Gabe had his hands on his knees bent double, catching his breath. Finally he looked up, "Ready?"

He looked at his watch and grimaced. "We've got to hurry. The plane leaves in two hours. These guys will go back through the tunnel and try to figure out where it comes out, then pick up our tracks."

"How far away are we from the plane?"

"You still got that map?"

She set Alexis down and with her good arm, Cassidy dug in the back pocket of her filthy jeans pulling out the map. "Um, yeah. Here."

Gabe snapped it open and studied it for a minute. "We're about two hours away by jeep. It's three o'clock. The plane leaves at five. There's no way we can make it on foot."

"Gabe, where's the motorcycle? The one Jorge said to look for."

"He said it was near the exit."

"There. I saw a flash of something." Cassidy ignored the pain in her arm and trudged over to one of the heavily vined trees for a closer look.

Gabe picked up Alexis and followed behind Cassidy. "Do you see anything?"

"No… Wait a minute, yeah."

Using one hand, Gabe started pulling the vines off and Cassidy gasped. "Thank you, Jorge."

"With a side seat," Gabe exclaimed.

"Wonderful. How old is this thing? You think it works?"

Gabe grinned and said, "One way to find out. The key's in the ignition. Hop in."

Cassidy climbed into the passenger car hooked to the side of the motorcycle. Gabe set Alexis in front of Cassidy then climbed on and twisted the key. The machine roared to life and Alexis started. Cassidy thought she was going to cry again, but then she grinned, laughed and clapped. "Ride. Go, go. Go zoom."

Cassidy laughed the laugh of pent-up tension and stress. "Please, Gabe. Go zoom."

Knuckles white with the strain of holding on and keeping Alexis steady while Gabe maneuvered the bike down an overgrown path had Cassidy clenching her jaw.

Finally, the path smoothed out a bit and they were on their way to the little airstrip in La Joya where the medical mission collected its supplies each week.

Two hours and ten minutes later, they reached the airstrip. Gabe let out a relieved breath and gunned the motorcycle toward the plane sitting on the runway. "Come on, let's go home."

TEN

Ten minutes later, the plane taxied without incident down the small runway and lifted into the air. Cassidy leaned back against her seat and let out a breath she felt she'd been holding for the last month.

Using the plane's radio, she'd managed to contact Anna at the orphanage and let them know they were in the air. Alexis, stretched out on the double seat behind her, slept fitfully.

"What are you thinking?" Gabe's voice sounded over the drone of the plane's engine.

"Well, now that terror isn't clouding my thought processes, I'm finally able to analyze the last couple of weeks. There's something else going on besides my kidnapping."

Gabe's raised eyebrow encouraged her to express her thoughts out loud. "In the jungle when we were hiding, I overheard one of them say, 'Don't worry about the ransom, kill them immediately. I don't want to have to report this failure.' Or something along those lines."

"Yeah, I heard it, too."

"So, it sounds to me like someone wanted me…us…dead, and these guys may have gone out on their own and tried to milk my kidnapping for more than they were supposed to or…of course, they weren't counting on you to show up and—" She broke off with a shrug. "I don't know. Something's not adding up, I just can't put my finger on it."

"You know your father's going to want some answers. Fortunately, no law-enforcement agency knows about your disappearance, so there won't be any attention on that front. No media waiting for you at the landing on your parents' estate."

Cassidy watched him as he spoke. His features still showed the strain of their ordeal; fatigue roughened his voice. A shave and a haircut should be at the top of his priority list.

She realized she really did care about him. He'd always been Micah's best friend, in and out of her home on a daily basis. She was six years younger and had had a fierce crush on him as a teen. And now, she realized that in spite of his involvement in Micah's death, she wanted to get to know him. Get to know what made him happy, sad and what lay behind the shutters he tried so hard to keep over his eyes. And she felt guilty for wanting that. After all, he knew what happened to Micah and refused to tell her.

He was saying something.

She blinked. "What?"

He frowned. "You okay?"

"I will be." Cassidy sighed. At least she hoped so.

"Did your captors say anything else around you to give you an idea what they wanted?"

She shook her head. "No. They never really spoke to me—or around me."

"How did they know you'd be there at the orphanage at that precise time and day?"

Cassidy stopped and thought. She spoke slowly. "I have absolutely no idea."

"Who knew you were going to get Alexis?"

"No one, really. At least I don't think so. I mean, I didn't make it a huge secret that I was leaving, but I didn't advertise my destination, either, because I knew Dad would try to stop me. He thought I was going to Paris. Mom and Dad knew Kara and Jacob had been killed, but they didn't know about the custody arrangements. At least not until Amy told Daddy about it later. I'm sure they probably traced my plane ticket, but I went via Paris, hoping Dad wouldn't think much of it other than I was resorting to my childhood pranks. I should have known his connections would be better than that. He managed to trace me to Brazil, I'm sure." Cassidy chewed her bottom lip as she thought. "Oh, and Amy and her parents knew because I was eating supper with them when Anna called. Amy agreed to take care of my house and get the room ready for Alexis while I was gone. Really, anyone could have figured it out if they tried hard enough."

"So, that's how you knew where to find Alexis? Anna called you?"

"Yes, she was the third witness to the hand-written codicil." Cassidy reached back and felt for the papers in the pocket of her jeans. They were gone of course. Thankfully, Anna had faxed a copy to Cassidy's home. Still, from memory she was able to tell him the gist of what it said.

"What does the original will read?" Gabe asked.

"I have no idea. I took off to get Alexis before the reading of it."

"Does the lawyer have a copy of the codicil?"

"I'm sure he does. His name is Oliver Morgan. But he wouldn't have any idea that I'd hop a plane and go to Brazil."

"So, Anna called you to tell you what happened to Kara

and Jacob. Is it possible that she would have called the lawyer also?"

Cassidy stilled. Kara and Jacob had made it clear that if anything happened to them, Anna was to take temporary custody of Alexis until Cassidy could get to her.

"Yes," she said thoughtfully. "She probably would have."

"So, the lawyer knew you would have to go get the child. He also would know the location of the orphanage."

"But why on earth would he send someone to kidnap me?"

Gabe shrugged. "I don't know that he did. All I'm saying is that he knew you'd be traveling to get Alexis. Like you said, it wouldn't be hard to track your itinerary if he wanted. You flew a commercial airline, right?"

Cassidy felt dazed. "Yes."

"So, we need to start with Mr. Oliver Morgan, the lawyer."

"Start what?"

"Tracking down whoever was behind your kidnapping. Because our rebel didn't want to report his failure. Which means someone hired him. Which also means that person is still out there and probably knows by now that you've escaped."

Cassidy shivered. "Which means someone may still want me dead."

The plane landed and Gabe had never been so glad to be back on American soil. He hung back and held Alexis while Cassidy ran to greet her parents at the end of the runway. The three-story mansion set in the middle of twenty-seven luxuriously manicured acres, boasted its own hangar and landing strip, two pools—one indoor and one outdoor—a movie theater, a state-of-the-art security system, a helipad and, if Gabe's memory served him right, twelve staff members. These were just a few of the niceties Cassidy had grown up with.

Gabe shook his head. Born to comfortable, but definitely not wealthy, parents, this lifestyle remained beyond his comprehension. Gabe also noticed that Cassidy's parents had aged well. Cassidy's mother, Christina McKnight, in her late fifties, looked as though she could pass as an older sister.

The woman had her hair dyed an expensive auburn red with blond highlights, and had it piled artfully on her head. She still had a trim figure and a classy style of dressing in designer jeans and a flowing flower child-type blouse.

Mrs. McKnight grabbed her daughter and covered her in kisses and tight hugs. Finally, Cassidy sputtered, "Okay, Mom, I'm glad to see you, too. I have someone you need to meet, though. Gabe?"

Gabe walked toward the three McKnights. The ambassador looked at him, and for a moment, Gabe swore he saw the sheen of tears in the man's eyes. Then he pulled Gabe into an unexpected embrace.

"I don't know how I can ever repay you, son." His rough voice was low, but Gabe caught the words…and the thanks. Gabe still resented the way the man had taken control and forced his hand on the issue of rescuing Cassidy, but he decided against holding a grudge.

"Consider us even," he said. He couldn't help asking, "Did you know about the child?"

Jonathan McKnight pulled back and met Gabe's eyes. Guilt flashed and he nodded. "I managed to track Cassidy to Brazil, so I figured that's what she was doing. When I questioned Amy about it, she concurred. I planned to let

Cassidy have it when she got home about doing something so dangerous. Then the note came…" He shrugged. "I knew if I told you about Alexis, you'd never go for it after… I don't know all the details of the mission you were on with my son, but I knew there was a child involved that didn't make it. I guess I owe you another apology."

Gabe took a deep breath. "Forget it. It's over." He shifted Alexis on his hip and looked over at Cassidy. "You want to introduce the munchkin?"

Pleasure and sadness mingled as she introduced Alexis to her parents and explained to her mother how she came to be named guardian. Cassidy's mother responded as expected…with worry and doubt about Cassidy's sanity, but her father supported her wholeheartedly—now that he was over his anger about her taking off by herself.

Christina finally smiled then hardened her gaze toward her husband. "Now that the niceties are taken care of, why don't we discuss this more while Marguerite fixes us something to snack on?"

Gabe almost laughed. The words may have been phrased as a question, but they were not a request.

Jonathan cleared his throat again. "Yes, let's all go inside and get reacquainted."

Gabe followed behind, his hand on Cassidy's back for support. He had a feeling she might need it.

Cassidy clutched Alexis close and followed her mother through the French doors that led to the sunporch and then on into the informal den. She frowned at the undercurrents she sensed arcing between her parents. What was going on?

Knowing she'd have time to ask about that later, she plopped down onto the blue-and-green patterned love seat and placed Alexis beside her. The little girl promptly slid to the floor and began exploring her surroundings.

Christina sat on the matching couch opposite Cassidy, and Gabe stood in front of the fireplace, hands in the front pockets of his jeans. Marguerite Sayers, the family cook for over twenty years, bustled into the room carrying a tray laden with snacks and hot tea. Jonathan took the tray from her and passed out the treat. She rushed to Cassidy and hugged her tight. "I'm so glad you're home."

Cassidy returned the hug, smiled and said, "Me, too, Marguerite. Could I get a cup of milk for Alexis, if you don't mind?"

"Sure, Miss Cass. I'll get it right away. I'll also see if I can round up a few toys. Will she come with me?"

"I'm sure she would, especially with the promise of milk and toys." Marguerite may have been the hired help, but she was also family. Alexis looked up and grinned at Cassidy, "Toys, my Cass-ty. Play."

"Yes, you go play with Miss Marguerite, okay?"

"Marty?"

Everyone laughed at the child's mispronunciation, but Marguerite just said, "Marty it is, sweet one. Come on."

To Cassidy's surprise, the little girl went.

Her mother asked, "Why didn't Kara's sister and brother-in-law get custody?"

Cassidy shrugged. "Kara's never really liked Brian. She said he was sneaky and that he only married Susan for her money. And Jacob's parents were killed in a car wreck when he was fourteen. Kara's grandmother was initially listed in the will as guardian but has since been admitted to a nursing home. So—" she held up her hands "—I'm it."

"Oh, my." Her mother rubbed her forehead.

"I know, Mom. I think after I became a Christian and Kara and Jacob saw how my life changed, they realized they could trust me with Alexis."

Cassidy couldn't fight the fact that her eyes kept straying over to Gabe during her tale. He was staring at her with a look that she couldn't identify.

Her mother said, "So you just decided to hop a plane and go get the child? The least you could have done was let us know and take some bodyguards!"

"Mom, I don't know how to explain it. I just know I was supposed to do it."

Jonathan jumped in. "All right, Christina, let Cassidy finish."

Cassidy watched her mother frown at her dad, but at least she let the topic drop for now. Her mother still didn't understand about her becoming a Christian. Her father did. He'd given his life over to God about six months before she'd left for Brazil.

"So, we did all the paperwork naming me as guardian and sent it to the lawyer. Everything was fine for about nine months, then one night I was eating supper with Amy and her family and I got a phone call from Anna telling me that—" Cassidy swallowed hard and finished her sentence "—that there had been a raid on the village and Alexis was at the orphanage."

"Why didn't you let me help you?" her father demanded, intruding on her memories.

Cassidy smiled fondly and said, "Because you would have stopped me, and I had a promise to keep."

He harrumphed and said, "Well, you're home safe and sound now. That's all that matters. Christina, why don't you and I go get to know our newest addition to the family."

Cassidy breathed a sigh of relief that her mother said no more but frowned as the woman stood and brushed past Cassidy's father without a backward look. What in the world? Her mother had never treated her father with such disrespect. At least not that Cassidy remembered.

Cassidy wilted into the cushion. Gabe came over to sit beside her, which instantly set all of Cassidy's nerves on high alert. She picked imaginary lint from the hem of her shirt.

Gabe took her hands and she froze. Her fingers tingled as she laced them with his. The attraction she'd felt in the jungle still simmered. And yet, her brother still lay between them like a concrete block, seemingly unmovable. But, maybe in time, they could chip that block away, piece by piece, until there was nothing left to keep them apart. She sighed and squeezed his fingers. Maybe she was dreaming.

Gabe couldn't help the feeling of relief that shook him hard. He'd done it. He'd gotten her and Alexis home safe. He'd done his job, and he really should move on. No matter how much he wanted to explore a relationship with her, he knew he couldn't. He could never accept her love, not while knowing he was responsible for Micah's death. His secret stood between them. So he summoned up all the anger he had inside him. He needed to break this bond.

"Cassidy," he began, and looked down at their clasped hands then up into her eyes, "that was a really dumb stunt you pulled going off to Brazil on your own. You know, growing up, I always thought you were a brat. You had everything you ever wanted materially, a big brother who doted on you, and yet you still found ways to cause your parents and Micah worry and frustration. Partying, out with a different guy each week and other things that the tabloids took great pleasure in reporting. I think you still have some growing up to do and you need to get busy doing it if you're going to take care of a child."

He watched her flinch as though he'd slapped her. Her face went white and she snatched her hands from his and stood. Anger and hurt simmered in her eyes as she pointed a finger at his nose and stated softly, "You don't know anything about me, Gabriel Sinclair. Maybe taking off for Brazil was a dumb thing to do, and maybe I didn't think through all the ramifications. Yes, I knew there'd be danger because of who my father is, but I wasn't thinking about the danger. I was thinking about a child who'd just lost her parents. I was thinking about the promise I made to one of my best friends and I was thinking that finally, finally, I could do something for the person who helped me find myself—and God. So, no, Gabe, I don't think I have any more growing up to do, but maybe you need to come down from that pedestal you've placed yourself on and rethink why you believe you can judge my actions. I also think it's time you left."

ELEVEN

Cassidy decided to forget Gabe and her anger from the night before and take Alexis for a visit with the child's new grandmother. She'd also decided to stay at the main house rather than at her own house across town. She needed the security of the home she'd grown up in. And besides, it was time to find out what was going on with her parents. The tension between them was suffocating—and it would distract her from her thoughts of Gabe.

Cassidy got up and dressed before Alexis woke. The child finally sat up and popped her thumb in her mouth. Sleepy eyes surveyed Cassidy, and Alexis smiled around her thumb.

"Good morning, munchkin."

"Mornin', my Cass-ty." The words were slurred because of the thumb, but Cassidy understood her. Someone had found some clothes in Alexis's size and laid them out in the bathroom that connected to the bedroom.

Fifteen minutes later, hand in hand, Cassidy and Alexis walked up to her parents' fifteen-hundred-square-foot suite. Alexis giggled and chattered the whole way and Cassidy took delight in answering the many questions the child had for her. When they arrived at the door of her parents' suite, she knocked and cracked it open. "Mom? We're here," she called.

Cassidy shifted Alexis higher in her arms and went on into the sitting area to her left. A full bath joined by the bedroom spread out off to the right. Tray ceilings above her; floor-to-ceiling windows with heavy purple-and-gold window treatments surrounded her. French doors to her left led to a glassed-in sunroom with a five-person hot tub.

Cassidy thought about the missionaries in the jungle and their simple, uncomplicated lives. Uncomplicated in material things anyway. After her experience in Brazil, the sheer magnitude of the luxury around her now took her breath away. She thought about what the money used to live like this could do for those living in poverty and shook her head. What she'd once taken for granted…well, no longer.

"Cassidy?" Marguerite came out of the bathroom and smiled. "I thought I heard you. And hello, to you, my new little friend." She tapped Alexis on the nose and the little girl grinned at her. "Do you remember me?"

"Uh-huh. Milk and toys. Play." She looked up at Cassidy and said, "Me down. Play with Marty."

Cassidy and Marguerite laughed and Cassidy handed over the child. She said, "I'm going to find Mom and see what she's doing."

Marguerite frowned and chewed her lip.

Cassidy asked, "What is it, Marguerite? Tell me what's going on with my parents, please."

The woman shook her head. "It's not my place, Cassidy. I've been praying a lot for this family, my dear. For God's timing in all things. It's now time for you to talk to your mother."

Fear took a firm hold in her gut, replacing the mere concern she'd been feeling. "Okay," she agreed. "Will you keep an eye on Alexis?"

"Now, that's a silly question if I ever heard one. Your mother's upset, but I think she's ready to talk to you."

Worried, Cassidy went. Sobs greeted her as she pushed open the door. "Mom!" She rushed to sit beside the woman on the bed. "What's wrong?"

Red-rimmed eyes looked up from her mother's sad, blotched face. Mascara ran down pale cheeks. She begged, "Tell me, please. Is this about whatever has come between you and Dad?"

Christina gasped and stared at Cassidy.

Cassidy shrugged. "I could sense it right off when I first got home, but to be honest, I was so tired and weary with all we'd been through that I didn't have the energy to focus on anything else. I'm sorry if that sounds selfish, but…I just…I wish…" This time it was Cassidy who couldn't finish her sentence.

Her mother sighed and patted Cassidy's hand. "It's all right, honey. I guess I just need to say it." A deep breath. "Your father's had an affair. More than twenty-five years ago. I recently found out about it. And when I start thinking about it, I can't seem to stop crying."

Cassidy felt the room spin. Once again, she couldn't breathe, just like when she'd been in that tunnel in Brazil. She gasped, "Wha—huh? How? When? No, I don't believe it."

Fresh tears sparked in her mother's eyes, but Cassidy ignored them and backed away, shock ripping through her insides as if she'd been skewered with a metal rod. Her mother said in a choking voice, "And that's not the worst of it. I found out because the woman he had the affair with died, and she left your father a letter. Oh, Cassidy, they had a daughter together. You have a half sister out there somewhere."

* * *

"Micah! Abort, abort. Everyone out, now!"

Bullets popping sounded through his headset; an agonized scream followed and Gabe yelled, "Evan, what's going on?"

"Ambush, Gabe, they knew we were coming!"

"Where's the boy?" Gabe ignored the hurt pulsing through him. His men. He had to save his men.

"The boy's gone, disappeared somewhere. Micah's chasing him. They're—"

The next explosion ripped the air and Gabe tore the headset off, left ear ringing. It would take time to get his hearing back in that ear, but that fact hardly registered as he stared in horror at the fireball the massive estate had become. Everything in him wanted to rush into the flames and pull them out one at a time. But he knew it would be foolish. His men were gone. And so was the four-year-old little boy they'd come to rescue. The drug lord, the boy's father, had killed him rather than give him up to his mother, who'd tried to escape the life of drugs and crime. Gabe felt his heart break. *Micah! I'm sorry, Micah.*

When the muzzle of the gun pressed against his right ear, he froze.

Heavily accented English ordered, *"Don't even think about moving."*

Adrenaline pumped. *"I'm not moving. What do you want?"*

"I want to know how you knew where to find me. Who was your source?"

Gabe bluffed. *"Man, I just take orders."*

The gun pressed harder and Gabe winced.

"You have five seconds to answer the question then I pull the trigger."

"How did you know we were coming?" Gabe countered with a question.

The figure behind him laughed. "You Americans think everyone is on your side." The man hissed, "Now, your source. Five...four...three."

Gabe didn't move.

"Two."

Gabe clamped his mouth shut and closed his eyes. He wondered where he would open them. Heaven, or hell?

"One."

God, I want to come to heaven. I'm sorry...

"Bye-bye."

Gabe's own scream yanked him from the world of his nightmare. When would he stop reliving it? He threw back the covers and went into the adjoining bathroom to splash water on his sweaty face. Adrenaline caused his nerves to jump along his skin. He felt restless; needed to move. Get away from the dream. Get away from Micah haunting his thoughts. The man's body had never been recovered and Gabe was under strict orders to keep the details of that failed assignment to himself. The military didn't want it getting out that they'd left a man behind.

He wasn't even allowed to discuss it with Jonathan, even though the ambassador had been responsible for rescuing him. Protocol. Gabe sometimes hated the whole concept. Today was one of those times. The family knew Micah was presumed dead and that was all he could say about the mission. Period. And yet, his body had never been recovered. That just didn't add up in Gabe's opinion.

Less than ten minutes later, he jogged along the path that circled Lake Bowen and turned his thoughts to last night.

He'd been a jerk.

The look on Cassidy's face would stay with him the rest of his life. After putting him in his place and telling him to leave, she'd risen from the love seat and left the room.

He'd called after her. She'd ignored him. Gabe had let himself out of the mansion reassuring himself that he'd been right in what he'd said. By the time he arrived home, he realized he owed her an apology. But she'd scared him.

He'd seen her interest in him as a man. As a result, he'd lashed out in self-defense because he found the attraction mutual and didn't want it to be; didn't deserve her affection. In the jungle, he'd seen a different side of her. A side he'd liked…a lot. She'd been scared, but she'd displayed a courage few people in her situation would have shown.

She'd kept her promise to her friends despite every conceivable effort to stop her. Her determination to get to Alexis had endangered her life and yet she'd persevered. He'd accused her of needing to grow up and she'd said he didn't know anything about her. But he did, and he wanted to know more. He also wanted to hear about how God had changed her life.

Cassidy planned to stay with her parents until the reading of the original will on Monday morning. Gabe and the ambassador had discussed, via telephone, safety precautions for Cassidy and Alexis. If the people that kidnapped her went to that much trouble to track her down, it seemed reasonable to suspect that they would try again.

Gabe's stride faltered at the thought, but he reassured himself that she was safe as long she was behind the walls of her parents' security-protected home. Ambassador McKnight and his wife planned to leave after the reading of the will to head back to Brazil. His short-term leave was up, Cassidy was home safe, and the man had work to do. Gabe just hoped all would go as planned.

April 3

Monday dawned bright, warm and windy. The third day of April promised to be a hot one. Cassidy stepped into the offices of Morgan, Cline and Edwards and breathed a sigh of relief. Finally, it was all going to be over with. She'd left Alexis with her friend Amy.

Cassidy desperately tried to keep her thoughts from lingering on Gabe and the anger she'd felt when he'd accused her of being thoughtless. And her mother's confession about her father's affair. She'd have to sort through her emotions later. She loved her father and understood that the circumstances of her parents' life had been vastly different all those years ago, but still...

Another thought struck her. Her father hadn't been a Christian then so he'd not had the spiritual protection that would have allowed him to resist temptation. Sure, he'd known right from wrong, but what was to keep him from giving in? Where could his strength have come from if he didn't have the Lord?

Cassidy shook her head. The affair was wrong, but she could see why it happened. After all, what was going on in his life at the time? A lousy home atmosphere, loneliness, pressure from his job, feeling like he wasn't loved or understood—and no peace that comes from being able to lean on the One that would have been there through it all with him—Christ.

She took a deep breath. Yes, she could understand that. But she didn't want to think about it anymore. Instead, she thought about Amy and how blessed she was to have her as a friend. Amy had come along after Kara and Cassidy had already formed their friendship, but Amy had been such a fun, cheery girl that she'd been welcomed with open arms and the twosome had quickly become a threesome.

Thank You, God, for Amy. Keep them safe today.

Cassidy walked up to the receptionist. A name plate on the desk read, Sheila Simons. In her midforties, Sheila wore an understated blue business suit and her creamy complexion was free of makeup. She had her reddish blond hair pulled back into a thick bun at the base of her neck. Large, thick glasses sat perched on her finely crafted nose shielding piercing hazel eyes. She oozed professionalism.

As Cassidy approached, the woman peered over the top of her frames and asked in a low, cool voice, "Hello. May I help you?"

Cassidy smiled. She said, "Hello, I'm here for the nine o'clock appointment with Mr. Morgan."

"Certainly." A heartbeat later, she spoke into the phone. "Mr. Morgan, Ms. McKnight is here for the reading of the will."

The Coopers, Kara's sister and brother-in-law, arrived. After stilted hellos, Sheila paged the lawyer and all four walked down to the conference room.

Susan seated herself then spoke through clenched teeth. "Kara would have wanted me to raise Alexis. We plan to sue for custody, you know. There's no way she would have agreed to allow you to raise that child if she really thought something would happen to her and Jacob. I want her, Cassidy."

Cassidy bit back a response and turned her attention to the lawyer. Thirty minutes later it was all over. There were a few touchy moments when Mr. Morgan claimed he didn't have a copy of the handwritten codicil giving Cassidy custody of Alexis. He declared if the codicil couldn't be located, custody would go to the grandmother, or Brian and Susan, the next of kin.

Cassidy protested, "I know Kara posted you the codicil. She sent yours the same day she sent mine." After searching the files, neither he nor Sheila could find it.

Cassidy finally called Amy and had her run to Cassidy's home to find the copy Anna had promised was waiting. Amy faxed the copy to Mr. Morgan who gave in without further ado. Cassidy had legal custody of Alexis—along with five hundred thousand dollars—Kara and Jacob's life savings. Brian and Susan had been left a tidy sum of twenty-five thousand. And yet, Cassidy was worried.

Tears streaming down her cheeks, Susan's last words still rang in her ears. "You haven't heard the last of this. Alexis should be mine to raise. I want her. I love her. I don't know how you convinced Kara and Jacob to do this, but it's not over."

April 6

Thursday afternoon found Gabe staring out his kitchen window. His boat rocked gently against the side of the dock as the water rose and fell. The sun burned brightly. It would be a beautiful day for a ride on the lake. He wondered if Cassidy and Alexis would like to take a spin on it one day soon. Then he wanted to kick himself for thinking about her again. Why did his mind insist on replaying their days together?

He had blue skies, warm weather and three weeks of vacation left. He should be relaxing and enjoying life. Instead it just meant that he had way too much time to think.

He needed to keep his distance. Micah McKnight's memory kept popping up too much lately. Probably because of Cassidy. Once he started thinking about her, he started thinking about Micah. And when he thought about Micah, he thought about Cassidy. It was a vicious cycle he couldn't turn off. He knew he should stay away, but what if she was still in danger?

So far, Cassidy hadn't had any more problems since she'd arrived home, but that didn't mean it wouldn't happen. Unfortunately, Gabe knew he should continue to keep his distance from her as secrets had a way of coming out when you let your guard down. And when he was around Cassidy, she tended to sneak past his emotional armor.

But he owed her an apology.

Gabe reached around and pulled his cell phone from his pocket and punched in her cell number. He wondered if she'd answer.

"Hello?" She sounded distracted. Good.

"Hi, Cass."

Silence from her end didn't reassure him. He cleared his throat and tried again. "So, what are you doing?"

"Checking my e-mail. Obviously not checking my caller ID."

Gabe choked back a surprised laugh. "I, uh, called to apologize. I was a jerk." There. No dancing around the topic.

"Yes. You were." Apparently, she wasn't in the mood to dance, either.

"You're not going to make this easy for me, are you?"

Her sigh reached his ear. "I suppose I should. After all, you did save my life."

"Yeah, you would think that would count for something these days."

That earned him a weak chuckle. Progress.

He turned serious. "Listen, Cass, I'm really sorry. I thought about what you said, and you're right. I was judgmental. I was just…I can't really…" He sighed. "I'm sorry."

"Okay, Gabe, you're right, you were a jerk and I was mad, but I forgive you."

"Just like that?"

"Just like that."

Silence.

Gabe asked, "Does God forgive like that?"

"Of course. If He didn't, I sure wouldn't be able to."

He gulped. "Do you think you'll be able to forgive me about Micah?" Maybe they'd salvage a friendship.

More silence. Then she said softly, "I'm working on it, Gabe. Mentally, I understand how the military works. It's my heart that has a hard time accepting it. And his body was never found, which gives me this irrational hope…"

Gabe sighed again and decided to change the subject. He knew Micah was dead. His injuries were too severe. "Cassidy, we need to figure out who set you up to be snatched from that orphanage. And we need to figure it out fast before they strike again. You need to keep bodyguards close by."

"Gabe, I'm surrounded with security. This place is well protected, although I suppose when we leave, I'll have to consider the bodyguards. Especially in light of the will."

Gabe mentally smacked his head. He should have thought to ask about that. He'd come back to the security issue in a minute. "Yeah, I meant to ask. How did the reading go?" Silence from the other end. "Cass?"

A deep sigh whispered across the line. "It went. Let's put it that way."

Gabe wondered what she wasn't saying. "Tell me, Cass."

"Alexis inherited some money and her aunt and uncle were not happy about not getting custody. It's not over yet. They'll sue. To be honest, I think Susan really does want Alexis. But Kara was adamant that she didn't want Brian around the child. Kara loved her sister, but hated the way Brian came between them."

"Ah, man, I'm sorry. Not only could you have a fight on your hands to keep Alexis, you might still be fighting to stay out of a killer's way. We need to figure out how to keep you safe."

"Well, why don't you join me for dinner tonight and we'll see if we can do some brainstorming about who could possibly benefit with me out of the picture—and how to avoid that happening."

Gabe thought that an excellent idea. Before supper, he'd do a little research of his own. After they said their goodbyes, he ran up the stairs to turn on his computer. He still had friends in high places. One of them was Craig Monahan, a detective with the local police force who had a lot of pull with the higher-ups in law enforcement.

TWELVE

Cassidy hung up the phone feeling better than she had in weeks. Amy had been a good listener over the past couple of days, and Cassidy appreciated her friend's attentive ear, but settling things with Gabe definitely helped ease her mind.

Marguerite stepped into the room as Cassidy powered down her laptop. She said, "Your parents went out with Amy's parents, so I just cooked up a casserole. One of your favorites. Chicken potpie."

Cassidy smiled at the cook. "What a great idea. I invited Gabe to join us."

Marguerite laughed. "That's fine. There's always plenty."

"I know. Thanks, Marguerite."

Three hours later the doorbell rang and Cassidy two-stepped her way to the door and then paused to get her breath and calm her racing pulse. When she pulled the door open, Gabe stood on the front porch wearing jeans and a black T-shirt that did wonderful things for him. She drank in the sight then remembered her manners. "Come on in, we're in the kitchen going casual tonight."

"Hi, Cass, you look great."

Cassidy felt herself flush at the admiration in his eyes and smiled. "Thanks. Feeling safe agrees with me, I guess."

He frowned. "Don't remind me. We'll talk about that later."

Cassidy led the way into the kitchen. The enticing aroma made her stomach growl.

Alexis grinned when Cassidy stopped by the high chair to drop a kiss on the tot's head. "Hi, my Cass-ty."

"Hi, my Lexi." She turned to Gabe. "It's a game now."

Alexis banged her spoon on the high chair and said, "Hi, Gabe. Kiss!"

Cassidy snickered and Gabe walked over to bow in front of the little girl. "Your wish is my command, little princess." Then he leaned over and placed a kiss on her upturned nose. That sent her into peels of giggles and Gabe's face softened to mush. He smiled and buried his face against her neck and blew raspberries until Alexis was breathless from laughing. At that moment, Cassidy knew what a great dad he'd be one day.

Gabe smiled a sad smile and said, "She sure does look like Kara with those blond ringlets and blue eyes, doesn't she?"

Cassidy nodded. "Yeah, she does. She's going to be beautiful, just like her mama."

Alexis perked up. "Mama? Where? My mama?" She held up her little cracker-covered hands, palms up, as she asked the question.

Tears surfaced and Cassidy quickly blinked them back, but said softly, "She'll forget her soon."

Gabe lay a hand on her shoulder. "You'll remind her."

Cassidy nodded. "You bet. Okay, let's lighten things up a bit. Marguerite, that smells wonderful."

Cassidy noticed Marguerite take a sneaky swipe of her eyes with a paper towel before turning around. She'd known Kara as long as Cassidy had, but the cook put on a smile and said, "Thank you, darling. Here we go."

Finally, everyone was settled around the kitchen table that seated twelve comfortably. Marguerite joined them for supper and Cassidy enjoyed catching up with her. Gabe seemed to enjoy the atmosphere also. Conversation flowed from topic to topic then Gabe finally said, "I did some research before coming over. We need to talk when you have a chance."

Marguerite stood, her dinner finished. "All right, I can take a hint. I'll get the little one ready for bed while you two chat."

"Oh, but you don't have to do that," Cassidy protested.

Marguerite waved her off. "Please. I love doing it."

Cassidy acquiesced. "All right then, thanks. Gabe, you want to move into the den?"

"Sure." Gabe pushed his chair back and followed Cassidy into the plush, comfortable living area. Polished hardwood floor gleamed and the Oriental rug had Gabe wondering if he should take off his shoes. The plasma television that hung on the wall played the March Madness tournaments.

He gestured toward the screen as he took a seat on the couch. "You like basketball?"

Cassidy grinned. "Love it."

"No way!" He leaned back, relaxed. Cassidy dropped beside him on the couch. Amusement gleamed in his dark eyes. "The princess is into sports?"

"Ah, Gabe, there's a lot you don't know about me."

Sadness flickered briefly. "Yeah, I know. Maybe once we figure all this out, we can do something about that, huh?"

What did he mean by that? He was interested in possibly pursuing something between them? Romantically? Or just as friends? Fingers of hope danced along her nerves as butterflies took flight in her stomach. Somehow she managed to nod once and say, "Maybe."

Gabe shifted and opened the folder he had brought with him. "So, here we've got some information on Brian and Susan Cooper, Alexis's aunt and uncle."

Cassidy frowned at him. "What kind of information?"

"Financial stuff."

"Why would you need that?" Surely he didn't think Brian and Susan had anything to do with her being kidnapped.

"Cass, someone is out to get you. I simply tried to think about who would benefit the most with you out of the picture. I came up with two names. Brian and Susan Cooper. If they got custody, they not only get the kid, but the money that comes with her."

Cassidy sucked in a deep breath as she thought about that. "Yes, I suppose if something were to happen to me, a judge would most likely award custody to them. I don't think the will ever actually stated that they *weren't* to get custody. What else did you find out?"

"They're swimming in debt."

Cassidy felt her eyes go wide. "Really? Wow. How much? I know they just got twenty-five thousand. Surely that'll take care of most of it."

Gabe shook his head. "Not even close. We're talking well over a quarter of a million."

Cassidy felt as though someone had sucked all the air from the room. "But how?"

"Living way beyond their means...and gambling. Mostly gambling. And I bet Brian is in pretty deep with some not-so-nice characters. Which is probably why he needs the money that comes with Alexis."

"Oh, no. Gambling?"

Gabe pulled out more papers. "Craig was able to get a court order and got copies of everything, from phone records to airline info. Tickets to Reno, Las Vegas, etcetera. Receipts for drafts on credit cards. Loans from the bank. They're going to lose their home if something isn't done fast."

Cassidy felt sick to her stomach. It certainly sounded like a motive for a kidnapping to her. With Cassidy gone, the Coopers would no doubt gain custody of Alexis—along with her money.

"So, what do we do?" she asked.

"Keep digging. See if I can find some proof that the Coopers are behind your abduction. It's a good theory, but without proof that's all it is…a good theory. But—" he held up a finger and pointed to a stack of papers beside him "—Craig also got ahold of Brian's and Susan's cell-phone logs. Being a suspect in a kidnapping investigation opens all kinds of legal doors."

"What does that tell us?"

"Not much at the moment, but there were an awful lot of calls made to the lawyer from Brian's cell. Nothing much showed up on Susan's."

Cassidy shrugged. "So? He's their lawyer. There's nothing illegal about calling your lawyer a dozen times a day."

"True, but the calls started up in earnest about a week after Kara and Jacob were killed."

Cassidy rubbed her eyes. "So you think when Brian and Susan learned that Kara and Jacob were killed, they started making plans to get custody of Alexis—no matter the cost?"

Gabe nodded. "Yeah, I do, and I think they came to the conclusion that if you weren't a factor, they'd get Alexis. Plus, they knew you'd be in contact with Oliver Morgan about the will. So, my guess is, they were all working together. Maybe bribing Morgan to give them information on your travel agenda."

"And arranged to have me disappear into the jungle. But what's in it for Oliver Morgan?"

Gabe rubbed his thumb and fingers together for the universal sign for money. "I bet he got a nice little bonus added to his legal fees if all went well. Craig's still looking into his activities. But it looks like the two men have known each other for a long time."

"So that's why the lawyer tried to say he never received the codicil?"

"He probably figured it was worth a shot. If you didn't have a copy, there'd be nothing you could do. Of course, I'm sure they didn't plan on you coming back to provide the copy. But since you did, he didn't have a choice but to follow it. However, I bet they're still trying to hatch a plan to get custody—and the money. Craig's also going to request the guy's computer hard drive and do a little investigating on that."

Cassidy narrowed her eyes. "They can plan all they want, but Kara and Jacob entrusted Alexis to me. And nothing short of death will keep me from fulfilling my promise. Nothing."

THIRTEEN

April 7

The next morning, Cassidy decided that she would move home to her gated community. She and Alexis needed the time alone together, and she needed to be in her own space. The tension between her parents ran high and they didn't need her in the midst of it. She'd decided against bringing her bodyguard for now.

Within a few hours, she'd e-mailed Amy, fed herself and Alexis and had her car delivered. Anxious to get home, she moved quickly to pack the vehicle and say her goodbyes with promises to bring Alexis to visit often.

Cassidy breathed a sigh as the entrance to her subdivision came into sight. She was so fortunate to live in a beautiful neighborhood with manicured grounds, a clubhouse, pool and tennis courts. Her home was on the back side of the subdivision with a flat green yard that was the perfect host for the brand-new wooden play set complete with swings, a sliding board and sandbox.

Thank goodness Amy had been willing to come decorate the room for Alexis while Cassidy had been in Brazil.

Everything should be just perfect. She pulled up to the gate, rolled down the window and waved to the guard. Frederick had been working the gate for as long as Cassidy had been living here. He was in his late sixties, and with his bald head, gold-rimmed glasses and snow-white beard, he reminded her of Santa Claus. She had a feeling he did that on purpose. Frederick returned her wave and opened the bar to let her through. She wove through the streets until she came to her house.

When she pulled into the driveway, she paused. The attic window above her garage was slightly open. She'd have to tell Amy to be more careful next time. She had probably been looking for something during her decorating frenzy and opened it to let out the heat and then forgotten to close it before leaving.

Cassidy pressed the button on the garage opener and pulled into the space. She shut off the engine, pushed the button to close the garage door behind her. She turned to Alexis in the backseat and said, "We're home, kiddo."

Alexis looked puzzled. "Home?"

Poor kid, she probably was really confused being jerked from one unfamiliar place to another; being stuck with people she didn't know. Cassidy was immensely grateful that she'd taken the time to get to know Alexis in the child's environment before whisking her off to the United States.

Cassidy climbed out of the car and opened the back door to unbuckle the child's car seat.

"Phone." Alexis proudly waved the device at Cassidy.

"Yes, that's my phone. I'm glad it kept you occupied for a while. Just hold on to it while I get you out of this contraption."

A scraping sound directly above her raised the hair on

the back of her neck. Goose bumps pebbled her flesh. She pulled back and looked around the garage, up at the ceiling.

Nothing.

"Out?"

Cassidy focused back on the little girl, yet uneasiness quivered through her and made her pulse pick up a bit of speed. Was someone there? How could there be? She wanted to laugh and convince herself she was just being paranoid. Still…

She clicked the child's belt back into place so she couldn't get out. Alexis would be safer in a locked car… just until Cassidy made sure everything was okay.

God, please let me be just hearing things.

Another scrape.

Cassidy jumped, heart thumping. That was not her imagination. What was up there? Had a squirrel found entrance through the open window or was something more sinister afoot? She clicked the lock on the car door. She had to keep Alexis safe.

Another scrape and this time some of the popcorn coating fell from the ceiling of her garage.

Granted, Amy had been over several times to take care of plants and fix up the nursery, but a stray rodent could have made himself at home without too much trouble. She kept telling herself that.

But in the meantime, she needed to climb back in her car and get out of here. Call the cops just to be safe. No one would question her skittishness. Not after the way her life had been going lately.

The garage-door button was located beside the door. She reached for it then stopped, her finger hovering.

Shock skittered up her spine. The light was out.

Usually, it glowed a steady orange.

And it had been on when she'd pulled in because she'd noticed it.

She pressed it anyway.

Nothing.

Had someone been able to cut the wire since she'd pulled in and shut the door?

Blood thundered in her ears as realization crashed. She was stuck in her garage—with a baby to protect. And someone was in her attic—her unfinished attic with scattered pieces of plywood laid for walking and storing small items. The rest of the flooring was covered with insulation. The wires to her garage door ran up into that attic.

The attic where someone hovered.

The phone rang from inside the house.

Panic made her gasp as she tried to decide what to do. Did she jump back in the car and try to call the police on her cell? But she didn't get good cell reception in her garage. The call might not even go through. Did she take a chance and grab Alexis from the car and run inside to snatch the phone? Or back up and smash through the garage door? Or was she just being crazy as a result of her life lately? However…

If someone hadcut the wire that powered the door, then that meant someone had deliberately waited until she pulled into the garage…and that meant someone was still here…waiting.

That spot between his shoulders itched. Gabe reached back awkwardly to scratch it as best he could. Pacing wasn't helping. The basketball game on television couldn't hold his interest.

He couldn't help feeling that enough wasn't being done to protect Cassidy and Alexis.

Worry chewed in his gut. What in the world was wrong with him? They were fine. They were protected better than the gold in Fort Knox behind the walls of her parents' estate.

He tried to distract himself by considering taking the boat out for a spin. The water and the wind always had a calming effect on him. Or he could continue his research into the Coopers and see what he could find, but doing that stirred up thoughts of Cassidy, which, in turn, made that spot between his shoulders itch.

Exasperated with himself, he muted the game on TV and picked up the phone. He dialed her number and listened to it ring. He hung up before her voice mail picked up. Just as he was about to dial her mobile number, his cell phone rang. Relief made him sigh. Cassidy's cell.

"Hello?"

"Gabe! Gabe, are…there?" Her voice came out in a whisper. "It's me. I…paranoid, but I think…someone's in my house. I called 9-1-1…bad…signal."

"Get out of there, Cass." Gabe clenched his fist around the phone and grabbed his keys.

"Gabe? I can't…you. I'm waiting…police."

He bolted for his car, yelling into the phone, "Cassidy, don't hang up. Are you there?"

Dead silence answered him.

He hung up then punched in her cell number.

No answer.

Wait, she'd said "my house." She must have gone home. On the way out to his car, he called her parents' house, hoping to get someone to give him directions to Cassidy's place.

* * *

Cassidy heard her cell phone ring. She flipped it open and it promptly displayed Call Ended. Then switched to No Signal.

She ground her teeth in frustration and shoved the useless thing into her pocket.

Was someone waiting?

Shivers of fear chased each other up and down her spine.

Think, Cass, think.

Thud. Scrape.

The intruder had somehow managed to climb up into the area above her. The open window above the garage. But how? He'd have to be Spider-Man to scale the brick wall. And why hadn't her alarm gone off? Amy had forgotten to reset it, obviously.

Another sound; another scrape. Cassidy swallowed hard and shivered. He would have to be careful where he stepped or he'd fall right through the unfinished flimsy flooring.

That did it.

She had to get back into the car. Her gun rested in the storage compartment between the seats. Decision made, she reached for the car door.

The ceiling above her opened up in an ear-shattering crash. A figure dressed all in black with a black ski mask came through and landed like a cat on the top of her vehicle. White plaster and insulation fell like rain around him.

Not bothering to waste her breath screaming, she yanked the door open and vaulted into the seat. When she tried to slam the door after her, a black-gloved hand reached down to stop it.

"No!" she cried. She struggled for a brief second then

a desperate idea crossed her frantic brain. She gave in to the hand pushing the door open and went with it. As soon as the figure stopped pushing and moved his hand to the top of the opening, Cassidy slammed the door as hard as she could on the fingers still gripping the top.

The furious scream of pain sent a shaft of satisfaction through her that overrode her fear for a brief moment. As soon as the hand jerked back, she quickly pulled the door shut and slapped the automatic lock. She hoped every bone in his fingers was broken.

The black ski mask appeared in front of her face through the windshield. This time, she couldn't hold back the scream that ripped from her throat. Evil stared at her. She knew those eyes. Had nightmares about those eyes.

Rafael! From the jungle. How had he found her here?

Oh, Jesus, protect us.

Alexis started crying in the background, scared and confused about all the commotion. With shaking fingers, Cassidy shoved the keys into the ignition and turned the car on.

A black-gloved hand rose as if in slow motion and pointed a snub-nosed pistol against the glass. Cassidy slammed the car into Reverse and stepped on the gas but kept herself upright in case he pulled the trigger. Her body would have to be Alexis's shield. There was no time to grab the gun from the storage compartment.

Wheels screamed against the concrete, then caught traction, and the car shot from the garage, bringing the door…and Rafael…down with it. Cassidy didn't care about the door or the car. She just wanted to get herself and Alexis away alive.

* * *

Gabe sped to Cassidy's subdivision. He drove fast. Weaving in and out through traffic on Highway 9, he finally made two more turns and arrived at the gated community.

He pulled up and flashed his military badge to the security guard. He hoped the man wouldn't question him. "Let me through, will ya? Cassidy McKnight's in trouble. Police are on the way." Gabe stuffed down his impatience, tapped his right foot against the gas pedal, his left rode the brake. Nerves zinged along his spine.

The guard frowned at him. "She just came through here not ten minutes ago. She thinks someone's in her house?"

The bar raised as though in slow motion and Gabe didn't bother answering. He sped through the minute he could get under it and wove through the streets until he came to the number Marguerite had given him.

The garage door exploded.

"What the…?"

Slamming on the brakes, Gabe threw his car into Park and jumped out without bothering to shut the door. Cassidy's battered SUV came to a stop at the end of the driveway.

Dirt and debris littered the area.

He started toward her, when he noticed a figure dressed in black stumbling through the hole left in the garage door.

"Hey!" Gabe hollered.

The figure halted, swore and lifted his hand in Gabe's direction.

A gun.

Gabe dived for protection behind his car door and flinched when the bullet shattered the driver's-side window. Glass rained down on him, but he ignored it and scrambled for the glove compartment.

Another shot sounded.

He managed to get the .45-caliber weapon from its case. He rolled back out of the car and ignored the glass crunching under his shoes. Slowly, he peeked around the edge of the door—and blinked.

Cassidy crouched behind her open car door with the window rolled down. A gun rested on the top edge where the window disappeared into the door.

The man in black lay amidst the mess in the driveway, blood flowing from the wound in his right shoulder. His left hand covered it while he groaned and cursed.

Gabe wanted to go to Cassidy, but first quickly approached the wounded man to kick the gun out of his reach. No sense in tempting him to try target practice with his left hand.

"The police are on the way," Cassidy's shaky voice assured him.

Gabe held his gun on the man while he spoke through gritted teeth. "What just happened here?"

Trembling, Cassidy slid the safety on and lowered the gun to her side.

Sirens screamed in the distance as Cassidy answered Gabe. "I got home and pulled into the garage. Somehow he managed to cut a wire or something after I pulled in and shut the door. He had us trapped." Gabe heard the hysteria bubble close to the surface, but she managed to continue. "He was in the attic above the garage and then he just… burst through it onto the car…and somehow I managed to get back in the car…and…"

Three black-and-white cruisers pulled up; tires screeched on the asphalt. Six uniformed officers jumped out with guns pulled. Two covered the man on the ground. Another ordered, "Freeze! Hands in the air. Now!"

"Cassidy, raise your hands and keep your gun in plain sight," Gabe ordered.

She did as directed. Gabe did the same while explaining, "Officer, I have my ID in my back pocket. Is it all right if I get it?"

The man responded, "Put the gun on the ground and move slow." Again, Gabe did as ordered.

Another officer had already cuffed the masked intruder and yet another retrieved Cassidy's weapon. She dropped her arms and scrubbed her eyes, then told him, "I need to get my daughter from the car. She's probably scared to death. Is that all right?"

The officer's head whipped around toward her car. "Daughter? Come on."

Gabe watched the officer and Cassidy head for the SUV. She pulled a confused but quiet Alexis from the backseat. An ambulance screamed to the curb and paramedics jumped out.

Gabe fished his ID from his pocket and flipped it open to his SEAL military identification. Then he pulled out his weapons permit.

The officer visibly relaxed and handed everything back to Gabe, who said, "Cassidy lives here. This guy broke into her home and tried to kill her."

"Why?"

"Good question. Why don't we find out."

Approaching the silent, sullen handcuffed figure, Gabe ripped the mask from the man's head.

"Rafael." The whispered word brought Gabe's attention

to Cassidy who stood with Alexis on her hip. She stared at the man and asked, "Why? Who hired you to kill me?"

He answered her by spitting in her direction and looking away. Gabe grabbed the man by the collar and pulled him up. Rafael winced at the stress on his wound but didn't make a sound. "The lady asked you a question. Who are you working for?"

Hard black eyes stared back at Gabe and he knew the man wouldn't talk. Demands were useless. Gabe shoved him back down and resisted the urge to kick him.

"Get this scum out of here."

FOURTEEN

Rafael had been hauled away, and after Cassidy provided appropriate documentation, her gun had been returned. Charges against her assailant ran from breaking and entering to attempted murder. Cassidy's shot was definitely self-defense.

Foremost in her mind was the breaking-and-entering aspect. How had Rafael gotten inside her attic? Obviously, he'd climbed over the hedge and fence surrounding her community to gain access to her home, but how had he gotten past her security system? No wires had been cut other than the one that operated her garage door. Rafael had used her home code.

It took a while to give their statements to the police, but finally Cassidy was able to make the necessary arrangements to have her garage cleaned up and the door replaced first thing in the morning. And her alarm recoded.

At eight o'clock, the sun was just disappearing beyond the horizon and darkness slowly crept up on them. Coils of tension began to unwind themselves in her stomach. Gabe walked into the kitchen as she hung up. She felt like throwing her arms around his neck and having a good cry. Instead she reached up to rub the tense muscles in her neck.

Gabe walked over and pulled her against him. At first, she resisted, then gave in as he gently replaced her hand with his and took over the massage. She said, "That feels wonderful. Is Alexis okay?"

"She's fine. But you need to lie down, put your feet up and relax."

"I don't think I'll be able to close my eyes all night." She gave a shudder and Gabe squeezed tighter for a brief moment then let her go only to reach up to cup her face. She leaned into it, relishing the comfort he offered. He told her, "You need to go back to your parents' house. You need that security."

Cassidy protested, "I left there for a reason."

"Well, I would think almost getting killed would overrule that reason," he snapped, and stepped away from her.

Instead of snapping back, Cassidy sighed. "I do have more than myself to think of now, don't I?"

Gabe's expression eased and he nodded. "Yeah, that little girl in there," he said, indicating the living room. "Not to mention my peace of mind. Come on. Let's keep an eye on Alexis and talk about how Rafael got in here."

"I don't suppose he would have signed in at the gate." Weariness dripped from her words.

Gabe sat on the couch and smiled at her attempt at levity. Cassidy grimaced and pulled Alexis away from the fireplace tools. The DVD no longer held her interest. "You need to be in bed sleeping."

Alexis grinned up at her and shook her blond head. "No, no sleeping. Play."

Gabe stood back up and took her from Cassidy. "I'll put her to bed while you rest. After I get her to sleep, we'll talk."

Fatigue pulled at her. "I'll take you up on that. Her room is down the hall and to the left. You can't miss it."

"You want to call Amy and see if she can stay with you tonight?"

"Let me think about it." Cassidy closed her eyes and thought about the scene being played out down the hall. It felt like family. Very cozy. She liked it and wanted it on a daily basis. With Gabe. Guilt speared her. Could she let herself fall in love with the man who wouldn't tell her about Micah? She knew she needed to hold her emotions in check as long as Gabe wasn't right spiritually. But she thought he seemed to be coming to terms with whatever it was that had him so moody all the time. He smiled more. And she loved being with him. But he couldn't stay all night. That wouldn't look good for either of them.

He came back into the room and announced, "Got the munchkin settled. You call Amy yet?"

Cassidy opened her eyes. He looked tired. "No, I haven't felt like moving."

"I'll get the phone."

"Thanks." He could be so sweet sometimes for such a bossy person.

He returned in seconds and handed her the cordless. "Here. While you're talking to Amy, I'm calling in some reinforcements. Your dad can spare a couple of guys to stand watch over you."

Cassidy knew she could count on him to make the necessary arrangements. She took the phone from him and dialed Amy's number.

April 8
Saturday

Cassidy's scream woke her from the nightmare. Sweat beaded above her upper lip and her breath came in short gasps.

Amy rushed in. "Hey, you okay?"

Cassidy closed her eyes and leaned back against the pillow. She was still on the couch. "Yeah. Yeah, I'm okay. Just a nightmare about some guy jumping out of my ceiling."

A knock on the door startled both of them then Amy smiled. "That's probably the guard. I'll go let him know everything's okay. Then I'll check on Alexis."

Cassidy voiced her thanks and Amy opened the door to the guard.

She ignored the muffled voices and shuddered against the images that still flashed like a slide show. She pushed the dream firmly aside and prayed for peace. *Please, Jesus, continue Your supernatural protection.*

Amy finally came back with Alexis in her arms, and Cassidy, glad for the distraction, sat up and patted the cushion beside her. "Have a seat. Oh, I wanted to ask you. Did you leave the window above my garage open when you were fixing up Alexis's room? The one that leads to the attic?"

Amy frowned. "No, I didn't even go in your attic. Why?"

"Because we think that's how Rafael got into my house. But we can't figure out how he got in my window." Cassidy shrugged, then said, "I guess Gabe and Craig will have to figure it out. Tell me what happened after I crashed last night."

Alexis crawled over onto Cassidy's lap and Cassidy hugged her tight, inhaling her sweet little-girl scent. "Hey there, sweetie. You hungry?"

"Hungry," Alexis agreed.

Amy said, "I stuck a waffle in the toaster. It'll be ready in a minute."

Cassidy had never been so grateful to have Amy for her friend as she was at that moment. "Come on, munchkin, let's get you that waffle."

"Mmm. Waffle. Yummy in my tummy."

Cassidy grinned at the tot, happy to see that she was picking up more English sayings every day. She placed Alexis in the booster seat and while she filled a sippie cup with milk, Amy swiped the waffle from the toaster and placed it on a kidproof plastic plate. After cutting it up into smaller pieces, she squirted syrup over it and placed it in front of Alexis.

While Alexis entertained herself with the sticky treat, Cassidy waited for the coffee to finish brewing and once again pressed Amy for details from last night.

Her friend answered Cassidy's question. "Nothing exciting. You were asleep when I got here, Gabe left and I crashed in your guest room. Your mom called to check on you."

Cassidy smiled. "I'll call her later. She's such a great mom. I just wish…" She didn't finish the sentence, but Amy filled in the blanks.

"You wish she was a Christian and that she understood your faith."

"Guilty."

Amy nodded. "I know the feeling."

"How's it going with your mom?" Cassidy probed the sensitive subject gently.

Amy grimaced, but didn't dodge the question. "I don't know, Cass. I get around her and she just…it's all about money, appearances, climbing the social ladder. I'm not into that, so she doesn't understand me. I don't understand her. Nothing is easy with us. Did I tell you she crashed my laptop. I wish I had the patience to sit down and give her some computer lessons. I got it working again, but…"

"Ooh, not good," Cassidy sympathized. "How's your dad doing?"

"Okay, I guess. I think when he lost the ambassadorial appointment to your father, he just kind of rolled over. I also think he's just marking time until your dad retires or moves on so he can be up for consideration again. You know, it's funny, my mother is from Brazil but has absolutely no desire to ever return to that country. And yet, she wants my father to be the ambassador. True, the salary would be bigger, but my family has no need for more money. Like I said, I have no understanding of the woman. You just know it's all about the status." Amy rolled her eyes and Cassidy ached for her friend.

She wished she could do something, but Amy was the only one who had the power to do anything about her situation. Cassidy refused to feel guilty about her father's appointment to the ambassador job. The two families had discussed the situation when the two men had been in the running for the appointment and both families agreed they'd not let this ruin years of friendship. So far, it hadn't.

Amy jumped up and said, "All this bonding is wonderful, but frankly I've had enough, and right now, this munchkin needs a dunking in the tub."

Alexis gave a toothy grin through the syrup she'd managed to smear all over her face. She even had it in her hair. Dodging the sticky hands, Cassidy released the safety belt and pulled the child from the chair. "I'll do it."

"Are you in the mood to do some shopping?"

"Ha—" Cassidy laughed "—when am I not in the mood for shopping?"

"Well, Easter's coming up and we need to get Easter dresses."

Cassidy squealed. "Wonderful! Let me give mom a call, then we'll go."

Amy took Alexis from Cassidy and said, "You go call your mother. I'll try to find this baby's face somewhere under all that syrup." She carried Alexis into the bathroom and Cassidy grabbed the cordless phone from the base to dial her parents' number.

After a conversation with her mother, who asked Cassidy to find her something to wear for Easter Sunday, Cassidy hung up and turned to face her friend and child. "Ready?"

"Yep," Alexis said. "Go. Go now."

They went.

Amy insisted on stopping by her house to pick up her other credit card. While there, Cassidy kept Alexis on her hip and wandered into the den where she found Amy's mother, Cecelia Graham, reading the latest crime novel.

"Hello, Mrs. Graham." Cassidy wondered why she'd never felt comfortable calling the woman anything else. Amy called Cassidy's mother Aunt Chris. But, for Mrs. Graham, nicknames just never…fit, she supposed.

"Cassidy!" The woman pulled her glasses from her nose and rose to give Cassidy a loose hug. "What a pleasure to see you. How are you?"

Cecelia had her dark hair with blond highlights pulled up into a smart bun. The hunter-green designer jumpsuit complemented her dark complexion and dark eyes. Cassidy knew the sparkling diamond earrings and bracelets she wore were genuine.

Cassidy responded, "Just fine right now. I'm sure Amy's filled you in on all of my troubles lately."

"She's told me some of it. I do hope everything gets resolved soon." She looked at the child in Cassidy's arms. "Now, is this the delightful Alexis I've heard so much about?"

Cassidy laughed and introduced them.

Cecelia sighed and stated, "One day, I hope to have grandchildren." She smiled at Alexis and asked her, "Do you want to color?"

"Color, yes. Make a picture?" Alexis asked.

"Absolutely, let's move into the study where I've got some paper and colored pencils." Cecelia took Alexis from Cassidy and walked down the hall to the first door on the left. Cassidy followed them into a room that smelled of leather and expensive cigars.

Cecelia placed Alexis on the burgundy leather couch then set a wooden tray on the child's lap. "Ah, here we go. Paper and pencils." She pulled several sheets of plain white paper from the printer on the desk, then opened a drawer and pulled out a multicolored box. She shut the drawer and walked back around to place the items on the tray.

Alexis eagerly picked up a blue pencil and started scribbling on the paper in front of her. Cassidy smiled and glanced around the masculine office. As children, she, Amy and Kara had played hide-and-seek in here often enough. At least until the senator or Mrs. Graham—or most often Amy's nanny—chased them out.

"Here you are." Amy breezed into the room. "Mother, have you been using my computer again?"

Cecelia looked up from Alexis's drawing and frowned. "Yes, but only to check my e-mail. And to print off some articles about your father. You know how he likes to read what the press is saying about him."

Amy rolled her eyes. "Let Daddy print it off from his own computer, will you? Or, not to be rude, but get your own. Honestly, as much money as this family has, you'd think you would just go buy yourself a laptop."

Mrs. Graham gave a low laugh. "I guess it's about time, isn't it? But we really don't need another one. Between yours and your father's I get what I need."

Amy rolled her eyes, but dropped the subject. "Could I show you something real quick?"

"What is it, dear?" Now Amy's mother was beginning to sound exasperated. Cassidy gave a silent sigh. When these two got together, it was never peaceful.

Amy was saying, "I've decided that I don't want those paintings after all. I had them hung in my room and they just don't go at all."

"Amy," the woman said sharply, "you harassed me for weeks about those things. And now you don't want them? What do you propose I do with them now?"

Amy rolled her eyes and grumbled, "Take them back and use the money to buy your own laptop." Cassidy smothered a chuckle and watched Alexis color. Amy told her mother, "Come with me and let me show you." She turned to Cassidy. "You don't mind, do you?"

Cassidy shook her head. Amy had a nursing degree and could work in any medical facility with no problem; could afford to live anywhere she wanted, yet chose to stay in her childhood home with a mother that drove her crazy.

But that was Amy's choice and Amy's life. Cassidy would stay out of it—for the most part. Since Amy had become a Christian right before Cassidy left for Brazil, she did seem to be trying a little harder. It would just take some time—and prayers.

The two women left and Cassidy shrugged. She turned to Alexis and said, "How you doing, munchkin?"

Alexis laughed and held up her picture. "Pretty?"

"Gorgeous," Cassidy affirmed with a laugh.

Fifteen minutes later, Amy was back. "You ready? I think Mother and I got things straightened out. She's going to use the paintings somewhere else."

"Sure, I'm ready."

"Mother also said she would be glad to keep Alexis if you wanted her to."

Cassidy frowned. "That's sweet, but I couldn't ask her to do that."

Amy laughed. "You didn't ask. She did. You know the security around here is impregnable. She'll be safer here than out with us anyway. And besides, Mother would love nothing more than to have the opportunity to make another conquest. I think she's already fallen in love with the munchkin."

"It's not hard, is it?" Cassidy laughed and nodded. "Okay, that sounds great. I think Alexis would enjoy being the center of your mother's attention more than she would like being dragged from store to store."

Amy exclaimed, "Great! Let's get going."

Cassidy hurried after her energetic friend. In the foyer, she offered her thanks to Mrs. Graham for the impromptu babysitting service and then returned to the office to kiss Alexis goodbye. "I'll be back soon, sweetie."

Alexis didn't look worried at all about being left behind. With all the upheaval in her life, Cassidy knew she'd either be clingy or independent. Apparently, Alexis had chosen the independent route. "Bye, my Cass-ty."

Cassidy wiggled her fingers at the child. "Bye, my Lexi."

The two women made their way out the front door to Cassidy's waiting car. She did her best to ignore the body-guard, Joseph, following several cars behind.

Two hours later, Cassidy groaned and hung the dress back on the rack. While she'd found the perfect dress for her mother and one for Alexis, she'd had no luck finding anything for herself.

Cassidy followed her friend out onto the sidewalk to head to the next store and felt her phone vibrate in her purse. She reached in, pulled it out and flipped it open without checking the caller ID.

"Hello?"

"Cassidy. It's Gabe. How're you feeling this morning?"

Cassidy felt her stomach curl at the sound of his voice. His image swam to the front of her mind and she smiled. "I'm better. Thank you so much for everything you did yesterday."

"You're welcome. What are you doing for lunch?"

"I'm actually shopping with Amy right now. She felt like I needed something normal to do. And as long as I can ignore my shadow back there, I can almost believe the past several days were just a bad nightmare."

"Well, they weren't and you need to be careful."

The worry in his voice touched her and she promised, "I'll be careful, honest."

"So, a rain check on the lunch?"

"You bet."

"Good. Just to let you know, Craig's working on the break-in at your house. Rafael had a grappling hook on him."

"A what?"

"It's usually used by the military. But anyone can make one. It's a hook that's attached to a rope. The hook has a shaft with a hole at the base…think of a really big needle with an eye. At the other end of the shaft are three equally spaced hooks. Picture trying to catch three fish at the same time. So all he had to do was toss the hook up on your roof and walk up the side of your house, jimmy the lock on your window and haul himself in. He pulled the rope in with him. Easy enough."

Cassidy shuddered at the image Gabe presented to her. "But why didn't the alarm go off when he opened the window?"

"Craig checked with the alarm company. It did go off for about ten seconds, then the code was punched in. As long as the code is entered within thirty seconds of the alarm sounding, the company just considers it a false alarm—the owner accidentally tripping it. They don't respond to those."

Her stomach rolled. "How did he get my code, Gabe?"

"That, I don't have an answer for. But we're working on it. Also, I found out something interesting about your lawyer."

Cassidy gripped the phone and ignored the people shoving past her. She stepped over to an empty bench and sat down. Amy motioned she was going into the store behind her. Cassidy nodded and then asked Gabe, "What is it?"

"My detective friend decided to do a background check on everyone you've come in close contact with over the last few months. He got a court order and got Mr. Morgan's bank and phone records. The man's made quite a few large deposits to his checking account over the last several months—and some hefty withdrawals."

"Well, that could be from anything." Cassidy tried to rationalize the money. She didn't want to believe her friends had trusted a crooked attorney.

"You're right, it could be. I also found out Mr. Morgan is the attorney of record on all of Brian and Susan Cooper's real-estate holdings."

Cassidy frowned. "But that's crazy. He's not a real-estate attorney."

"Doesn't matter. He was also referred to Jacob and Kara by Susan. She gave Oliver their names and he contacted them. Susan and Kara didn't have much communication going on, did they?"

Cassidy snorted. "Try none. Although I know Kara tried. She sent letter after letter to Susan, who returned them unopened." Then she said, "Okay, so there's a connection. But if he was on Brian and Susan's payroll, why read the will and give me custody and the money when he could have forged a new one? And why would Kara and Jacob use Mr. Morgan when she didn't trust Brian? Although, I'm sure she would have had him checked out first. His background check must have been clean."

Amy stuck her head out the door of the shop, saw Cassidy was still on the phone and ducked back in. A twinge of guilt struck her and she feared that she was ruining Amy's shopping trip by staying on the phone.

But she had to get to the bottom of this.

Gabe was saying, "First of all, maybe Mr. Morgan's background turned up clean because he probably has other people do his dirty work. Second, too many people knew about the new will and Jacob and Kara's wishes for anyone to do any kind of tampering with it. My guess is that Brian and Susan are biding their time until you are out of the picture. Then Mr. Morgan will make sure that the Coopers get the custody—and the money. And then take his share, which is probably a lot more than just doing the legal part of his business."

Anger at Brian and Susan built slowly, like a tsunami getting ready to crash and destroy everything in its path. Cassidy tamped it down and focused on what she needed to do. She said, "Well, we have to make sure that doesn't happen. I will not lose that little girl and have her brought up in that kind of environment. I'd just give them money if they'd leave Alexis alone."

"I know you would, but that's not what Kara and Jacob wanted. And it wouldn't be fair to Alexis."

"I know. I just wish I knew what to do."

"We'll get there, Cass. Just hang in there."

Amy popped out of the store again and this time Cassidy didn't feel right staying on the phone. "Listen, Gabe, I've got to go. Could you come over tonight?"

"You move back in with your parents yet?"

"No. I'm staying where I am." Before he could protest, she continued, "I have two bodyguards on the house at night, the alarm system recoded and my garage all fixed. Alexis needs the stability—and so do I."

His sigh reached her ear, but then he said, "All right. Yeah. I don't like it, but I understand. I'll bring dinner, okay?"

"Make it Chinese and you're on."

FIFTEEN

Amy had stayed to chat for a while, but left about five minutes before Gabe knocked on the door. Cassidy opened it and drank in the sight of him. She'd missed him. He wore comfortable blue jeans and a sweatshirt. When he smiled, her insides quivered.

"Can I come in? I brought food."

A flush started up her neck when she realized she'd been standing there staring like a starstruck teenager. She'd have to process that stupefying realization later. She coughed and stepped back to let him through the door.

"You brought Chinese food. Of course you can come in."

"Gabe!" Alexis ran over and grabbed him around the knee. "Hi. Want up. Kiss."

Cassidy watched his expression melt the way it did every time he was around the little girl. He planted the requested kiss on the tiny upturned nose and Alexis giggled. Cassidy laughed at the pair and said, "Here, give me the food and you can bring her."

Cassidy carried the goodies into the kitchen and set them on the table. Gabe followed and sat Alexis in the high chair. He handed her an egg roll and the little girl batted her lashes and said, "Thanks, Gabe."

Cassidy giggled and Gabe laughed. "You women sure learn young, don't you?"

"Yep," Alexis agreed, and bit into her food. Cassidy put a cup of milk on her tray and then turned her attention to her garlic chicken and brown rice. She shared the noodles and some plain chicken with Alexis. Gabe had thought of everything.

They enjoyed a companionable supper avoiding any topics that would ruin the meal. While they ate, Cassidy watched the interaction between Gabe and Alexis and felt the pang of longing that had become a familiar ache lately.

"You want to put her to bed while I clean up?" Gabe asked.

Cassidy looked at the two paper bags that now held the remains of their dinner. All he had to do was walk them over to the garbage can and drop them in. She raised an eyebrow and said, "Don't strain yourself."

Gabe burst out laughing and Alexis laughed because Gabe did. Cassidy allowed a small smile to pull at her lips as she released Alexis from her high chair. "Knock yourself out. I'll put her pajamas on her and get her into bed. It may take me thirty minutes or so, but if you don't mind waiting, we can talk after she goes to sleep."

"I don't mind. You want some help? I was just kidding about the cleaning-up thing."

She shook her head. "But you can start a fire in the fireplace if you want. It's April and feels like February out there. The weather is crazy. Blazing hot one day and freezing the next."

Gabe agreed and Cassidy moved to the back of the house, Alexis in her arms.

Forty-five minutes later, she returned to the den to find

a roaring fire popping and snapping brightly behind the screen—and Gabe asleep on the couch.

She walked up and stood beside him to look down at him. Frown lines cut deep grooves in the sides of his mouth. His forehead was drawn tight and his brows pulled together. He twitched, stirred and mumbled something under his breath.

Cassidy moved closer. Should she wake him?

"Gabe?" she whispered, and touched his face.

His eyes flew open and his hand shot out to catch her wrist in a painful grip. "Gabe! Wake up!" Cassidy forced herself not to struggle against him. She desperately tried to ignore the flashes from her kidnapping, concentrating on the pain in her wrist and getting Gabe to full consciousness.

"Cassidy?" he whispered, still somewhere between his nightmare and reality.

"Gabe, you're hurting my wrist."

He immediately unclenched his fingers, regret clouding his tense features. She clutched her throbbing wrist to her chest, but didn't move away from him.

He sat up more fully and rubbed his face. "Cass, I'm sorry. Let me see it." He held his hand out. She shook her head. "It's fine. What were you dreaming about?"

"Nothing. Let me see your wrist." He reached out and very gently took her hand to pull it toward him.

Refusal would get her nowhere. She let him look, but insisted, "It's fine. It might bruise, but I wouldn't worry about it. I bruise if a fly lands on me." She tried to smile. The intense pain in his eyes stabbed her heart and she knew he would never have hurt her had he been aware of what was going on.

"Ah, Cass, I'm so sorry." He pulled her closer and

tugged her into a hug. His heart beat a wild rhythm under her right ear.

"I promise," she insisted. "It's okay. You were dreaming."

"I know, but I hurt you and I would never…" His voice trailed off.

She looked up into his dark eyes. Eyes that seemed haunted with something she couldn't figure out. "What is it that won't let you sleep without invading your dreams?"

He closed his eyes and tilted his forehead to rest against hers. The fire snapped in the background; Cassidy just noticed the classical music playing softly on the stereo.

When he opened his eyes again, a fierce determination played through them. He swallowed hard and said, "Cassidy, I don't want anything to happen to you. You've brought a light into my life I didn't know was missing. You even got me talking to God again. I'm just afraid…" He trailed off again.

Cassidy was thrilled to hear his words, but sensed there was something more, something he wanted to say; he just couldn't get the words out.

Gabe tried to think, but it was too hard to do that with her this close to him. He wanted to answer her questions in detail. He wanted to tell her everything he knew about Micah. Maybe then the dreams would stop. And the guilt would quit eating away at his insides. But he'd lose her for good.

So he changed the subject.

"How did you get involved in your dad's work?"

"In college, after I broke up with my fiancé, I started listening to my father's speeches. I realized that although he wasn't a Christian, he had some deep beliefs about what was right and what was wrong. And he wanted to make a difference in the world. One person at a time. I dug in to help and the rest is history."

"You're amazing."

Cassidy flushed and Gabe felt his heart sputter. How different they were. Instead of being brought closer to God through tragedy, he'd pushed God away. Gabe stared at her and thought he probably loved her. And yet if he told her the truth, she'd hate him—maybe. So he asked, "What made you change from the flighty party girl I used to read about in the paper?"

Cassidy laughed. "Ah. Now, that's a story."

"Yeah?" Gabe lifted an eyebrow.

Cassidy nodded. "As you know, Kara and I grew up together. When you call me 'princess' with such disdain, it makes me mad." Cassidy gave a short laugh. "But if I'm honest, I understand why you do it. It's an accurate description of my life up until about two years ago. Kara became a Christian a few years before I did. All of a sudden she was this person that I didn't understand anymore. I saw her change. I watched her become a selfless, giving person and it confused me—made me jealous."

"Jealous, how?"

Cassidy shrugged. "Overnight, she had other interests. No more parties, no more sleeping in on Sunday mornings, and she was hanging out with people I couldn't relate to. *Church people.* It really bugged me. I felt like I'd lost my best friend and someone had replaced her with this lookalike. Amy and I became closer during that time. She didn't understand what had happened to Kara, either. But Kara kept working on me. E-mails, letters, pictures. Stories of how wonderful her God was. I decided to try it. I've been hooked ever since." Cassidy smiled then waved a hand as though to dismiss her story. "But enough about me. Tell me about your dream," she prodded.

No way. "Can't get out of it, can I?"

Cassidy stared at him for a few moments then shrugged. "It's late. As much as I'd like you to stay, we both know that's not an option. You can save that story for next time on one condition."

He arched a brow. "What's that?"

"You have to come to church with me tomorrow and on Easter Sunday."

"Church?"

"Yep."

"Will Alexis be there?"

She frowned at him. "Of course she will."

"Okay, then I'll seriously consider it."

"Why, you rat!" She punched him in the ribs and Gabe rolled off the couch laughing. She leaned over the edge, trying to frown down at him but failing miserably. She finally gave in to the grin struggling to break free.

Tenderness filled him. He needed to go. He stood and pulled her up against him to hug her, inhaling her sweet fragrance. Maybe he'd dream about that instead of the fact that not only did her brother die in the jungle, it was because of Gabe that Micah was there on a mission he never should have been involved in.

SIXTEEN

April 9

Cassidy put the finishing touches on her makeup and threw Alexis's diaper bag together. She'd chosen a flower-print short-sleeved dress that swirled about her calves as she walked. The white low-heeled sandals were comfortable and cool.

Church started in twenty minutes and she really didn't want to be late. Gabe had decided not to go and Cassidy still felt the sting of disappointment. But she wouldn't let it ruin her day.

Finally, she had Alexis in her car seat with a cup of juice, her sweater on the seat beside her, in case she was cold in the sanctuary, and the diaper bag on the front floorboard.

Fifteen minutes later, she pulled into the church parking lot and hurried to gather Alexis and her accessories. She made it to the entrance to the Sunday-school classroom with a minute to spare. She walked in and immediately re-laxed as she saw people mingling and talking around the food table. She laughed to herself for worrying about being late. Several people approached her and welcomed her back. All exclaimed over the child who sat happily on Cassidy's hip.

Marcie, a physical therapist from the local hospital and Sunday-school coordinator, came up and gave her a side hug and said, "Cassidy, it's so good to have you back and with Alexis." Sadness flickered over her features. "I didn't know the Fosters personally, but I'd been keeping up with their mission updates they sent to the church and posted online. It's hard to understand why God lets good people like the Fosters die while doing His work, but it's good to know they planned ahead. You'll be a great mom for Alexis. Thanks for bringing her to introduce her."

Cassidy blinked back tears and said, "Thanks, Marcie. I appreciate that and it's my pleasure." She set the squirming child down for a minute and looked around the room. "We've got quite a few visitors here, don't we?"

Marcie laughed. "Actually, a lot of them are new members. You've been gone awhile. When I called your parents to see why you weren't answering your phone, they said you were on an extended vacation in Paris."

Guilt stung Cassidy, but she pushed it aside. She'd done what she'd had to do. "It's a really long story, Marcie. One day I'll share it with you."

Marcie smiled and wandered over to welcome a latecomer.

Alexis was exploring the room and soaking up the attention being lavished on her. Cassidy gave her an indulgent smile and walked over to pick her up. She tapped the child's nose and said, "You're an attention junkie." Alexis giggled.

Cassidy took a seat in one of the chairs that had been placed in a semicircle around the perimeter of the room. She shifted Alexis in her lap and turned when a woman beside her tapped her on the shoulder. "Hi, I don't remember meeting you. I'm Cindy Patterson." The woman had curly reddish-blond hair and green eyes. Dressed conservatively in a black pantsuit, she smiled sweetly as she spoke. "I just started coming a couple of weeks ago."

Cassidy shook her hand and introduced herself and Alexis. "I've been gone for a few weeks and I come back and we've got all these new faces. That's great. I'm so glad you decided to join us."

Cindy asked, "A few weeks? Do you travel on business?"

Cassidy decided not to go into detail. She just said, "I became guardian of a child from Brazil and went to pick her up. So, we've been adjusting to life since we got back."

"Oh," the woman crooned, "that's so sweet. She's adorable. What does your family think about it?"

Cassidy laughed. "They're adjusting, too."

Marcie stood to make the announcements, so Cassidy shifted her attention to the topic at hand. Alexis squirmed and Cassidy wondered if she'd make it through the entire class. It didn't really matter. She didn't want to put the child in the nursery yet, so if she had to get up and leave, she would. But it was good to be back into something resembling her normal Sunday routine. Cassidy handed Alexis a cracker and the little girl said, "Thanks."

Everyone laughed and Marcie said, "Cassidy, why don't you officially introduce her."

Cassidy laughed along with the others and said, "This is Alexis. Most of you knew Jacob and Kara Foster. Kara grew up in this church and was one of my best friends. She named me guardian of Alexis in her will, and when she and Jacob were killed—" she still had a hard time saying those words, but took a deep breath and finished "—I went to pick her up, and here we are."

Everyone wished Cassidy well, several offered new-mom advice and babysitting should she need it. When it came time for the lesson, Cassidy realized she'd forgotten her Bible. Cindy, recognizing Cassidy's predicament, scooted over to place hers so Cassidy could see.

Cassidy whispered, "Thanks."

Cindy leaned over and said softly, "True sign of a new mother. You remember everything pertaining to your child, but forget something obvious—like your Bible for church."

Cassidy giggled under her breath and followed the lesson as best she could while entertaining and keeping Alexis quiet.

April 10

Monday morning dawned sunny but rainy. Gabe shoved a hand into the pocket of his khaki pants and waited under the shelter of the porch that led into the lawyer's office. Craig Monahan had agreed to meet him here. Cassidy would arrive any minute. Stubborn woman insisted on being there. Said she had some papers to drop off anyway, so would join the men. Gabe told her she'd just be in the way, but she'd been unmovable.

While he waited, Gabe thought about Cassidy's invitation to join her yesterday at church. He almost went, but then called at the last minute and wimped out on her. She was sweet about it, but he'd heard the disappointment in her voice. Something just continued to hold him back.

Regrets. Guilt. The gun in his ear. He flashed.

Three, two, one. Bye-bye.

Gabe sat frozen. Fear, rage, sorrow and guilt—and uncertainty over his eternal resting place—boiled within him.

God, I want to come to heaven!

Click.

An empty chamber.

Gabe brought his elbow around with whiplash ferocity and crashed it into the man's chin. The gun fell and Gabe snatched it up. Still shaken, he held the weapon on the man who choked, sputtered…then lunged. Gabe felt the searing agony crash through him. A knife in his gut.

He'd been careless.

A gunshot blasted. Surprise flickered in the evil eyes before the man fell at Gabe's feet. Dead.

But who killed him?

Weakness hit him hard. He dropped to his knees. Clumsy fingers gripped the handle of the knife and yanked. "Ahhhhh!"

Nausea churned, blackness swirled; he fought it. He had to know.

"Who…" he gasped.

His radio crackled. "Chopper's on the way. ETA ten minutes."

"Gabe, you okay, man?" a voice said to his left.

Disbelief hit him. "Micah?"

"Did…I…get him?"

"Yeah, you did. Are you okay? I thought you died."

Gabe crawled to the jungle undergrowth where Micah had collapsed. Red and black burns covered his friend's face, agonizing and painful looking. Blood flowed from a deep gash on his head. But he still held his Ruger. Micah gasped, "Getting…ready…to. Can't…breathe…good."

Fierce anger at the injustice of it all hit Gabe hard. Good men dying, a child's life cut short. All for what? Drugs? Money?

Where are You, God?

His breathing labored; he desperately tried to ignore the fire in his belly as he inched toward Micah, dragging the medic bag behind him. Breaking open some thick, sterile gauze, he stuffed it into his knife wound, struggling against the darkness threatening to close in. He popped an antibiotic pill and pulled out supplies for Micah.

"Anyone else make it out? The men? The boy?" Gabe worked the oxygen mask over Micah's face.

Micah sucked in the life-giving air. "I had him, Gabe… right behind me…" He closed his eyes and Gabe saw a tear leak out. Even SEALs had emotions, regardless of what most people thought.

Gabe pulled out a shot of morphine and aimed it where it would do the most good, but Micah opened his eyes and managed to shove the syringe away. "No drugs."

"I don't even know how you're alive, but we've gotta get you out of here. Backup's coming."

"I'm not going to make it, Gabe." Micah coughed, spit out the blood and sucked in another gulp of oxygen. "We've got a traitor in the loop somewhere."

Hard news. "Who?"

Micah coughed again. Gabe would worry about who the traitor was when he had Micah stabilized. He grunted and reached for the morphine shot again. "Don't worry, buddy. I got you into this, I'll get you out."

Micah pushed the shot away again. "Take…care…of Cassidy."

"Micah…" Gabe gritted his teeth and thought about jabbing the syringe wherever he could reach.

Gabe felt like passing out. He was losing blood fast.

He moved as fast as he could and still felt like he was

trying to race his way through quicksand. Helicopter blades thumped the air somewhere to his right.

Hopefully that was the help he'd been told was on the way. He'd go out into the open to wait for them.

Micah had passed out...or died. But there was no way he was leaving him here.

Gabe used the last of his strength to move away from the bushes. He'd just wait...here...for...rescue. Then he'd tell...them about...Micah.

Darkness closed over him.

"Gabe?"

Motionless, Gabe fought the memories and struggled to focus on the man who had called his name.

Craig.

"Hey, man, you all right?" Craig asked, concern etched on his rugged face.

Gabe shuddered and forced a tight smile. "Just waiting on Cassidy to get here. Said she had some papers to drop off. I think she just wants to be in on every aspect of the investigation."

"Can't say I blame her," Craig said, but scrutinized Gabe's features. The man's gray eyes saw too much. His hair had turned silver by the time he was thirty, making him look a lot older than his actual thirty-six years. He had the build of a weight lifter and Gabe knew he ran seven miles a day.

Craig held out a hand and Gabe shook it, saying, "Thanks for making the time to be here."

"No problem. I've been looking over the stuff you gave me, and I think you're onto something."

"If this guy is the one threatening Cassidy, I want him put away for good."

"If he's the one, we'll arrange it," Craig promised.

"She's here."

Cassidy's Armada pulled into an empty spot. She hopped out of the vehicle and dashed through the drizzle. Just watching her sent his world into a tailspin again. It wasn't just the physical attraction, although there was definitely that, but the emotional pull she had on him that threatened to overpower him. Was this love? Maybe. He wanted to protect her, laugh with her, cry with her, raise children with her.

Lock her away and keep her safe until this madman was found. But Micah stood between them.

If he ever had clearance to tell her the truth, would she be able to forgive him? If she knew that it was at Gabe's insistence that Micah was even on the mission?

He sent up a silent prayer as Cassidy skipped up the steps to greet him. *God, I know I've been out of touch for a while and there are still a lot of things unresolved between us, but I'd appreciate it if You'd show me where to go with all this.*

"Hello, Gabe."

"Hey, Cass. This is Craig Monahan, a friend and detective with the police force."

Cassidy smiled at Craig and held out her hand, "Pleased to meet you, Craig."

"Likewise. Sorry to hear about all the trouble you're having."

"Thank you. Maybe today we'll get to the bottom of it." She shifted her small purse to her other shoulder.

Gabe asked, "Where's the munchkin?"

Cassidy's features softened into maternal love. "She's with my mother today. Mom's really getting into this grandparenting stuff."

Joseph followed discreetly behind Cassidy. He'd been doing security for her father for the last two years. Gabe knew Cassidy liked him and that she felt safer knowing he was around.

"I see your shadow is doing his job," Gabe observed.

Cassidy rolled her eyes. "Yes. He'll wait close by while we're inside. I have to say that I'm grateful for his presence, even though I resent the need for it."

He took her hand and led her through the door. "Let's get this show on the road."

The three of then entered the office. Leather and expensive cologne mixed together to give an enticing scent of wealth and power.

The receptionist looked up and smiled her cool professional smile. "Hello, Ms. McKnight. How can I help you today?"

Cassidy took over since she'd been the one addressed. "We're here to talk to Mr. Morgan, if he has a moment."

Gabe stepped up. "Actually, we're here to talk to him whether he has one or not."

The woman's lips tightened, but she didn't argue; she simply picked up the phone and dialed an extension. "Mr. Morgan, you have some visitors in the lobby. Would you mind stepping out here for a moment?"

After she set the phone on the hook, she turned her icy gaze back on the trio. "He'll join you in a moment. Please, have a seat."

Gabe flashed his toe-curling smile. "Thank you so much."

Cassidy picked up a magazine and flipped through it without really seeing it. Gabe settled into the chair beside her, and Craig took the one on the opposite side facing them.

Fifteen minutes later, the inner door finally opened behind the receptionist's desk and Mr. Morgan appeared. "Well, this is a surprise."

A vein throbbed in his forehead, and his smile was forced, telling Cassidy that he wasn't pleased by the unannounced visit. She smiled as charmingly as possible and said, "Thank you so much for seeing us."

Mr. Morgan adjusted his glasses and cleared his throat. But his smile relaxed and he gestured down the hall. "Right this way."

The three followed Mr. Morgan to the same conference room Cassidy had been in for the reading of the will. Once they were all settled around the table, Mr. Morgan got right to it. "What can I do for you?"

Craig took this moment to break his silence. "Mr. Morgan, someone broke in to Cassidy's home this past Friday and tried to kill her."

The man's jaw dropped and he stuttered, "Th-th-that's terrible. Who? Why?"

Craig and Gabe exchanged a look. "That's what we're hoping you could tell us. You see, we're investigating everyone who's had close contact with Cassidy over the last few months and who would have the most to gain should she disappear."

Confusion glittered in Mr. Morgan's eyes, "What exactly are you accusing me of?"

The detective spoke in a quiet voice. "We're not accusing you of anything—yet."

"You've had some rather large deposits made to your checking account lately—and some large withdrawals," Gabe said mildly. "Care to explain those?"

Mr. Morgan narrowed his beady eyes and said, "Look,

I'm telling you. I don't have a clue as to why someone would attack Ms. McKnight." He shrugged. "As for the money, I've sold a lot of stock lately. I made some good investments and cashed in on them." Then he sucked in a deep breath and admitted, "I also like the horses. I was at the track with those withdrawals. Feel free to check it out. I'll have Sheila give you my stockbroker's number. Now, you people are wasting your time—and mine. I'll see you out."

On the way out, they waited for Sheila to look up the number.

The three stepped onto the porch, grateful for the covering, as the rain still fell. Lightning split a jagged path in the sky to the west and thunder rumbled. Gabe and Craig dwarfed her small frame as they huddled together, but for once Cassidy didn't really mind.

"Anyone think to bring an umbrella?" Cassidy asked. Both men shook their heads. "And I left mine in the car. Brilliant, huh?"

Craig laughed. "Well, I've got to get back to the station. I'll be honest with you, though. I think the man's telling the truth. No doubt, I think he has the potential to be slimy, but I didn't get the impression he was lying about this." Craig shrugged. "I could be wrong, though."

Cassidy didn't think so. She had the same impression. Another crack of thunder made her jump. Movement to her left caught her eye and she turned to see her bodyguard step under the cover of the porch next door. He stumbled and grabbed the railing with his left hand. His right hand flew up to clutch his chest. He fell to his knees.

A heart attack?

"Joseph!" Cassidy called. She dashed through the downpour.

"Cassidy!" She heard Gabe follow.

It only took a few seconds to reach the man's side, but it seemed as if she moved in slow motion. She dropped beside him. "Joseph, what's wrong?"

Something sounded above her and splinters dropped from the ceiling. Gabe tackled her to the floor of the porch. "Get inside! He's been shot. Craig, call for backup!" Cassidy scrambled to open the door to the building.

Once inside, she turned to help Gabe pull the wounded man through the opening. Gabe slammed the door shut, locked it and pulled out his cell phone.

Drenched, shivers and adrenaline racked her as she leaned over Joseph to grasp his chilled hand. "Joseph, please open your eyes." Fingers felt for a pulse. It beat, but was faint and slow. "Please, please don't die." Her tears mingled with the rain on her face.

Through a foggy haze, she heard Gabe barking orders to the emergency medical team on the way, telling them about Joseph. She offered up a string of prayers, for Joseph, for their safety, for the shooter to be caught.

Finally, the sound of sirens screamed through the air.

"How is he?" Gabe demanded as he shook the rain from his head.

She looked up through the sheen of tears. "Not good. He needs an ambulance."

"Let me look at him."

With relief, Cassidy complied. Gabe was a doctor. He'd help him. Gabe stripped off his outer shirt and made a pad to press against the wound. "Here. Hold this. Lots of pressure."

Cassidy obeyed and pressed down on Joseph's chest while continuing her prayers. "Please, Joseph, look at me." His eyes flickered. Cassidy applied more pressure. "Joseph?" Water from her hair dripped down on his face. His eyes opened briefly then shut again.

"Keep fighting, Joseph," Gabe whispered as he held the man's wrist. "Come on, people, come on. Where are you?"

As if in answer to his question, Craig's voice called out, "Sinclair, you okay in there?"

"I've got a man who needs a hospital, now!" Gabe reached up to unlock the door. Cassidy continued the pressure until the emergency personnel rushed in and took over.

The room spun and she felt faint. She swallowed hard and concentrated on staying upright. As they loaded Joseph into the ambulance, she whispered a silent prayer. *Please, Lord, let the madness stop.*

"Why shoot Joseph?" Cassidy demanded as she paced the den area of her house later that evening. "I was standing right there. Why not me? And why didn't we hear the shots? Never mind, dumb question. We did hear them. I just thought it was thunder."

Anguish worked its way across her face and Gabe wanted to grab her in his arms and keep her there. Protect her. They'd just received word from the hospital that Joseph was out of surgery and doing well. His wife was with him.

The police were heavily involved now and after taking Gabe and Cassidy's statements, they'd released the two of them. Craig would take care of the final details. Cassidy had wanted to go to the hospital, but Gabe convinced her she couldn't do anything productive there and besides, she needed to pick up Alexis.

The ambassador had been notified. Extra security had

been ordered for him and his wife and now Cassidy would be covered even more heavily. The six o'clock news ran the story.

Cassidy stood in front of him. Gabe watched Alexis stack blocks while he thought. "It looks to me like the shooter's sending you a message."

Wrinkles creased her forehead as she offered Gabe a frown. "What do you mean? What kind of message?"

"If he can't get to you, he'll get to the ones you care about."

"But…but…no attempts have been made on my parents. No one's tried to hurt Alexis or you."

Gabe's heart stilled and he even wondered if she realized what she'd just admitted. She cared about him. He knew it, but it was nice to hear.

"So, what do we do? How do I keep him from getting close to those I love?" Cassidy sat on the floor next to Alexis and started stacking the blocks so the child could gleefully knock them down again.

Gabe watched them play and wasn't even shocked when the desire for this to be the real thing swept over him. He wanted Cassidy and Alexis. He wanted them to be a family; someone he could come home to every day. Going home to his empty lake house left him aching for something more. This.

"There's nothing else you can do. Everyone's got bodyguards. And you're doing everything right short of shutting yourself up inside and becoming a hermit."

"There's no way I can do that." She shuddered at the thought. "Besides, I have that speech to make on behalf of Dad at that dinner in two weeks. It's been on the calendar for six months."

"Well, you'll have to cancel it. It's too dangerous."

Cassidy frowned. "I can't cancel. It's too late. I'll just have to be extra careful."

"Cass…" Gabe warned.

"Seriously, I can't back out now. This event is too important. And besides, security is top-notch. The word needs to get out about this problem of human trafficking and the only way to do that is to have as much communication as possible with people who have the power and the money to do something about it. And that's where I come in. Passing bills to force harsher punishments and raising money to help the hurting families is my cause, my calling right now. There's no way I can miss this dinner."

Gabe noticed the fire in her eyes and heard the passion in her voice. She cared deeply for those less fortunate and had made it her goal in life to help change lives for the better. She had become such an incredible woman. Gabe didn't feel worthy to be in her presence knowing what he'd done.

Like getting Micah into the jungle and then leaving him to die.

He shook off the thought and said, "I understand. You've convinced me. I had no idea how involved you are in your father's politics. We'll just have to make sure that you're protected."

"Security will be extremely tight anyway simply because of the high-profile people who'll be in attendance."

Gabe stood. "Okay. I'm going to make some calls. Rafael's behind bars, which means whoever wants you out of the way has already hired someone else to do his dirty work. I think it's too big a coincidence that we confront Oliver Morgan with our questions, and then on the way out of the office Joseph gets shot. I'll call Craig to see if he's got any new information." Gabe needed to do something productive before he did something stupid like pull Cassidy into his arms, spill his guts and beg for forgiveness.

Cassidy was still thinking about the dinner long after Gabe left. Maybe she should back out. Get someone else to give the speech for her. Cassidy made a mental note to double-check with Craig about the safety of the other people that would be in attendance. There was no way making her speech was worth putting lives in danger.

As she was pondering what to do, she heard the security buzzer sound and stepped into the kitchen to press the button. "Yes?"

Frederick said, "Miss Cassidy, there's a lady here to see you. Says her name's Susan Cooper."

Cassidy flinched and looked over at Alexis. She sat in the middle of a pool of toys, playing contentedly. Should she let the woman in? Her last words had not been nice. And she had threatened to sue.

"Miss Cassidy?" Frederick asked.

Lord, what do I do?

And yet, the woman was the child's aunt. "All right, you can send her on."

"Will do."

Cassidy clicked the intercom off and stood by the window. Approximately two minutes later, Susan Cooper's silver Mercedes pulled into the driveway.

Taking a deep breath, Cassidy opened the door before the woman had a chance to ring the bell. "Hello, Susan."

Susan slipped the sunglasses from her eyes to the top of her head, pushing her blond hair back behind her ears. Cassidy noticed the dark circles underneath the flawlessly made-up eyes. She'd used makeup concealer, but that hadn't helped much. Clearly, the woman was under stress, suffering. Cassidy's heart softened.

"Come on in. Would you like to see Alexis?"

Susan bit her lip and nodded. "Thank you. I appreciate this."

Cassidy led the way into the den area where Alexis still played. The little girl looked up when the two women entered the room.

Susan sucked in an audible gasp and said, "She looks just like Kara at that age. I still look at pictures every once in a while…"

Cassidy nodded and said, "Alexis, this is your aunt Susan."

Alexis looked up and grinned. "Hi."

Cassidy heard Susan give a choked laugh and respond to the child, "Hi there. You're a very pretty little girl."

Alexis nodded and said, "Yep. Pretty." Then she held up a wooden puzzle piece and asked, "Play?"

Susan seemed to forget Cassidy was in the room as she dropped to her knees and helped the child put the puzzle together. Cassidy just watched, her heart going out to the woman who obviously loved her niece. If only Brian wasn't in the picture.

Cassidy beseeched, "Susan, please reconsider your idea of suing. I know we left things tense in the lawyer's office, but…somehow, surely we can work something out."

Susan looked up, anguish reflected in her tired eyes. "Will you reconsider and give her to me?"

Cassidy sighed. "I can't, Susan. Kara…"

"This child is my family, the only piece I have left. I can't have children…we've tried for so long, and now here is this precious…" Tears appeared and Susan blinked rapidly. "I'm sorry. Maybe this was a bad idea. But I can't give up. I won't give up."

Susan sounded almost sad as she said the last words. Cassidy shook her head and escorted the tortured woman out the door. She stood staring at the empty driveway long after Susan's car disappeared from view.

SEVENTEEN

April 13

With no further incidents, Cassidy and Alexis had settled into a routine of eat, play, sleep, then play some more. And while she'd been thinking about it, she'd written a six-digit check to the orphanage in Brazil to help cover the damages the rebels had inflicted.

Thirty minutes ago, Amy, along with two bodyguards, had stopped by to pick up Alexis to take her to the zoo. Cassidy was supposed to be putting the finishing touches on her speech. Instead, she needed a distraction.

Friday night was fast approaching and Cassidy had sucked in a deep breath, shoved aside anger, resentment and other emotions, to call her father and ask that a bodyguard be assigned to her temporarily—again. She hated this estrangement, the stiffness between them, but she couldn't just act like the past hadn't happened—or that things weren't vastly different now. She'd prayed and prayed and still couldn't figure out how to forgive—or even what she was supposed to feel and think. She'd keep working on it. In the meantime, she had a new bodyguard.

Anderson Wilmont was a large man from Jamaica who had a lilting accented voice and kind dark eyes which seemed at odds with his choice of profession, but her father assured her that the man knew how to do his job without being intrusive.

Cassidy's one requirement was that he wear a bullet-proof vest.

She powered down her laptop and jumped up from her chair. Concentrating on her e-mail helped keep her thoughts in order; however, that couldn't last forever. She needed to do something. The shooter had escaped and still roamed the streets; out there somewhere, waiting to make another move.

The phone rang.

Cassidy looked at the caller ID. Morgan, Cline and Edwards. Ugh. What now? "Hello?"

"Cassidy, this is Sheila Simons with Morgan, Cline and Edwards."

"Hello, Ms. Simons. What can I do for you?"

"Mr. Morgan asked me to call and inform you that Brian and Susan Cooper have filed a lawsuit, suing you for custody of Alexis."

Cassidy dropped into the chair next to the phone. Weakness shook her and stars danced in front of her eyes for a brief moment. Then anger kicked in.

"I figured this would happen." Almost to herself she said, "I suppose I should call my lawyer immediately."

"I'm sorry, Ms. McKnight. I wish I had better news for you."

"No, I kind of expected it. All right, I'll get right on it."

Cassidy hung up feeling as though she'd been side-swiped. Although Susan *had* warned her she would sue, Cassidy had high hopes after the woman's visit that maybe she would change her mind. She ran her fingers through her hair, glanced at her laptop and gave a tearful, humorless chuckle. Well, she'd gotten her distraction.

The Bible lay on the end table next to the recliner. It had been a while. Life had been so crazy lately that she'd neglected her daily quiet time. Not that God was keeping score. Still, she realized she missed God; missed her quiet moments in the morning gazing out her kitchen window while she listened to what He had to tell her.

Cassidy picked up the Bible and flopped into the recliner. She opened the book and searched for something that might help her understand why her life had gone crazy all of a sudden. Certainly, she'd had a rough few years as a rebellious teenager, but now that she was trying to do the right thing, everything was going wrong.

I don't understand, God. Show me. Keep my faith strong and my trust in You unfailing. I know Moses didn't have a clue of all the trouble he was going to face when You chose him, he just had to trust You. You've chosen me to go through this trial right now and I guess I'm just going to have to trust You. No matter what. God, I don't know what I'll do if I lose that little girl, but I have to give it to You. Keep Your hand on us; Your protective shield around us. I know You are the ultimate protector and I thank You for that.

Cassidy went on to pray for her family, Brian and Susan Cooper, Amy and her family and, of course, Gabe.

April 15
Saturday

Gabe's cell phone rang as he jogged up the steps to his front porch. He'd just finished a three-mile run, as being active seemed to clear his mind and allow him to think. Sitting around worrying about Cassidy just made him insane.

He let the phone ring one more time while he caught his breath, then he pulled the device from the clip on his shorts.

"Hello?"

"Hey, Gabe. Craig here. I called the hospital and they said you had the morning off."

"Craig, good to hear from you. How are you?"

"Doing all right. Staying busy, unfortunately. I have some bad news for you. You know your pal Rafael?"

Gabe's gut tightened. "Yeah? He wasn't released, was he? Or he didn't escape?"

"Nope. He's dead."

"Whoa! What happened?" Gabe sat on the top step, stunned.

"He committed suicide. Guess he wasn't going to talk no matter what."

Gabe blew out a breath. On the one hand he felt relieved that the man couldn't hurt Cassidy anymore. Yet on the other hand, he felt sorry for the waste of human life.

"So, guess there's not going to be a trial, huh?"

"No, guess not. You can pass the word on to your lady friend. Now we've just got to figure out who shot the bodyguard."

"You got any leads?"

"We think the shots came from the roof of the building across the street. We questioned a group of people there, but no one saw anything."

"What do the surveillance cameras say?"

"There are four cameras, so we've got our guys going through them now. So far, nothing's turned up. But, we did find one thing pretty interesting."

Gabe stretched his legs in front of him and flexed his legs to cool down the muscles. Then he stood to pace while he talked. "What's that?"

"A black outfit tossed in the Dumpster around back. The person wasn't too careful. Obviously in a hurry. They left gloves, hat, stretch pants and a pullover shirt."

"Any DNA?"

"Working on it. You know how long it takes the lab to do anything."

Gabe clenched his jaw. "Tell them to work faster. You've got lives at stake."

"I know. I already told them. We'll see if it makes a difference."

"Any idea where the clothes were purchased?"

"All the tags were cut out."

"Wonderful. All right, well, keep me posted." Gabe ran a hand through his sweaty hair. Time for a shower. "Let me know the minute you hear something on the DNA or anything else."

"You got it. You know, Gabe, I could use a man like you in my business. You want a job at the precinct?"

Gabe laughed. "No way. I'm not into stress. That's why I like the emergency room."

Craig barked a short laugh. "Oh, yeah, no stress there, right? Okay. I'll catch up with you later."

"Later, man." Gabe hung up the phone and walked into his house. After he showered, he'd call Cassidy and break the news to her. First, that Rafael was dead and second, that he, Gabriel Sinclair, was going to set foot in a church tomorrow morning for the first time in two years.

April 16
Easter Sunday morning

Bright morning sun streamed through Cassidy's bed-room window and she stretched under the covers.

Then she remembered and smiled.

Last night, Gabe had called to say he'd join her at church this morning. She'd already prepared herself for his negative response, so when he'd agreed to come, she'd been flabbergasted—and thrilled.

Yesterday, she'd delivered her mother's Easter dress and the woman had raved about it, declaring she was going to hire Cassidy to do all of her shopping from now on. Cassidy was glad her mother had liked it, but never would she tell her she'd found it on the fifty-percent-off rack. She giggled to herself. Excitement finally propelled her from the bed and she hurried to shower before Alexis awoke and demanded her undivided attention.

It was amazing that the little girl had adjusted so well considering the upheaval she'd been through. But other than an occasional waking during the night to call for her mama, Alexis seemed content.

Thank You for that, God.

Cassidy dressed and applied a light coat of makeup while listening for sounds of Alexis. Finally, she heard, "Me up. Come get me, my Cass-ty."

Cassidy felt her heart warm to the call and hurried to finish swiping the mascara on her lashes. "I'm coming, sweetie," she called. "Be there in a second."

Finally, she had herself dressed in a light blue sundress with a matching shawl. Alexis looked adorable in one of her new outfits; a pale pink dress with a matching hat.

Anderson, Cassidy's bodyguard, would accompany her, but she would be careful, not take any stupid chances or be careless in any way.

Today was going to be such a sweet day—in spite of the custody battle the Coopers had threatened. Tears prickled behind her eyes and she blinked. No time for that; time to go to church and meet Gabe. She smiled. Now, *that* was cause to feel better about everything.

She'd instructed him to sit near the back as she didn't feel comfortable leaving Alexis in the nursery yet. Not only for security reasons, but because she simply wanted to keep the little girl with her.

When she pulled into the parking lot of First Community Church, she glanced in her rearview mirror and saw Anderson pull in behind her. Satisfied, she got Alexis from her car seat in the back and walked up the steps to the sanctuary.

"Cass, hey," Gabe called to her.

He came. *Thank You, Jesus.* She smiled. "Good morning."

"Gabe! Kiss," Alexis squealed.

Cassidy laughed. "I think she likes you better than me."

Gabe took the little girl in his arms, hugged her and planted a smacking kiss on her nose. "Hi, munchkin. You look really pretty in pink. I've missed you."

"Missed you." Alexis nodded her agreement.

Gabe smiled at Cassidy and she noticed his eyes lingered on her face. She blushed. "Come on." She grasped his upper arm and pulled him in the direction of the sanctuary. "Let's get a seat in the back before the only ones left are in the front row. Mom and Dad will meet us inside."

"Where's your bodyguard?"

Cassidy shook her head and grinned as she stepped into the sanctuary. "He's around. I saw him pull into the parking lot behind me. Now, stop worrying."

"I wish I could," Cassidy heard him mutter.

Cassidy slid in the seat beside her mother. "Hi, Mom, Dad." She'd yet to deal with all her feelings about her father ever since her mother told her about his past, but she was praying about it and working on it. The shock was wearing off. And the evidence her father presented of being a changed man made it easier to believe everything might work out. "I'm so glad you guys came."

"Well, I couldn't very well say no after you found this beautiful dress for me, now, could I?"

Cassidy forced herself to shoot a grin at her father as she lightly asked her mother, "And Dad didn't have a thing to do with it, huh?"

"Not a thing." But her mom winked and Cassidy felt her heart lighten tremendously. Her father seemed to relax. He'd been nervous about seeing her. Cassidy's heart clenched. She wouldn't mention anything. This problem was between her parents and things certainly seemed to be better. They were trying. Both turned to Gabe and welcomed him with a few kind words.

"Gaga." Alexis reached from Gabe's arms to her mother and he released her to climb up in the woman's lap.

Movement caught the corner of her eye. She tilted her head and the day turned perfect. Amy walked up the outer aisle of the church and slid into the pew next to Cassidy's father. Amy wiggled her fingers in a small wave, and Cassidy didn't bother to hide the grin she felt spread over her face. Everyone she cared about was here now.

Then Cassidy felt a hand on her shoulder and turned to

see Cindy Patterson sitting in the pew behind her. She smiled and said, "Hi, Cindy, how are you doing?"

Cindy smiled back and said, "Things are a little crazy at work, but other than that, I'm fine."

Cassidy introduced her parents and Gabe.

The service began and Cassidy drank in the peaceful atmosphere. She'd ask Cindy what kind of work she did at a later time. Maybe they could have lunch together one day this week.

The pastor talked about Jesus's death and resurrection. The fact that He'd died for her. And the fact that He forgave her for all the bad things she'd ever done was enough to bring tears of gratitude to her eyes.

Yes, Christ loved her and He was allowing her to go through this time of craziness for a reason; she just prayed that she would remain faithful and not give in to despair before this mad person was caught.

Gabe found his jaw relaxing. This morning, he'd almost called Cassidy and reneged on his promise to come, but at the thought of the disappointment he was sure to hear in her voice, he just couldn't make the call.

So, here he sat. Listening to how much God loved him. Enough to die for him. Him. Gabriel Sinclair. The preacher went on to describe the Crucifixion in detail, telling about the suffering Jesus endured in order that people might be forgiven to live and see heaven one day. The crown of thorns. The mocking and humiliation. Cat-o'-nine-tails ripping the flesh from His body. The nail-pierced hands and feet. The sword in His side. Buried three days to rise again. Unconditional love even from the Cross for the men who'd crucified the one who only wanted to love them.

A punch in the gut wouldn't have been any more effective than this sudden realization. Oh, he'd been to church and prayed to God and had a lot of the head knowledge, but this overwhelming heart knowledge bowled him over. And then he flashed to that day when that madman, Cruz, pulled the trigger and the hammer fell on an empty chamber. Gabe remembered his prayer right before that.

God, I want to come to heaven!

All of a sudden he knew that his prayer had saved his life. God had spared him *that* day so that he could live to see *this* day. Like he told Cassidy in the jungle, he had believed there was a God all his life. He just hadn't believed Him. Believed Him when He said, "I am the way, the truth and the life. No one comes to the Father, but through me."

Gabe believed Him now.

He didn't need fanfare or a big production. He didn't need to go forward at the end of the service. There was no need to wait until then. He needed to get his heart right with God right now. *God, I know the prayer. But I don't think I've ever prayed it. In all these years I never asked You to forgive my sins. I never stopped to understand the extent of Your love. I'm sorry, God. I've done some really rotten things. You know I've killed. And You know I've only done that in order to defend myself, my country or my team. God, forgive me. I'm sorry. You've given me more than a second chance. This time let me make a difference. For you.*

Lightness filled him. He couldn't wait to tell Cassidy and he would, just as soon as they had some time alone. Then came the crashing thought.

What do I do about Micah?

Telling Cassidy was a must if he wanted their relationship to progress. He wasn't even shocked when he pictured himself standing at the front of this very church waiting for his bride to come down the aisle.

Gabe knew he didn't deserve Cassidy, but he wanted her beside him.

But Micah stood between them.

What do I do, God? We're in this together now. I need to lean on You and I'm not very good at leaning.

"Gabe?"

He jerked his head up at Cassidy's voice. "What?"

"The service is over. Are you okay?"

Gabe smiled as he thought about the peace he'd just experienced. "Better than okay."

Relief swept her pretty features and she nudged his shoulder. "Then could you let us out?"

Parishioners milled about, heading for the back of the church. Gabe gave her a sheepish grin and stood to slide out of the pew. Cassidy followed and she took Alexis from her mother. The child had been entertained with coloring books and paper throughout the service, but she was ready for some action now. Cassidy set her on the floor, but kept a tight grip on her hand.

People stood around to talk and make lunch plans. It had been a packed service, as it usually was on Easter. Gabe watched Anderson struggle to keep Cassidy within his line of sight. Gabe moved in closer to her and saw Alexis pulling on Cassidy's hand while Cassidy tried to talk.

A woman bumped into him and muttered an apology. Another person shook his hand and told him how glad he was that Gabe had come to visit. Gabe lost sight of Cassidy for a brief moment, but knew Anderson was close by, along with the ambassador and his bodyguards, so Gabe smiled through gritted teeth and begged God to get him out of here.

"Alexis?"

Cassidy's voice caught his attention.

"Alexis!" Sharper now, worry snagged the edge of her call. Gabe hurried through the mass of bodies, not caring if someone thought him rude.

Frantically, Cassidy locked her eyes on his. Gabe caught her by the arm. Christina McKnight stood next to Cassidy twisting her necklace as she turned in circles looking, searching. "What's wrong? Where's Alexis?"

"I don't know! She was just right here."

"Did you put her down?"

"She wanted to go to my mother, so I handed her over. Mom held her for a moment then put her down for just a second so she could adjust her purse. She bent down to pick Alexis back up and she wasn't there." Tears sparkled on her lashes.

Gabe decided not to waste any time. He stood on the nearest pew, stuck his fingers in his mouth and let out a piercing whistle. Silence claimed the church. Everyone stared at him.

"Sorry, folks. I need your attention. We seem to have a missing little girl. Could you look around you and see if you can spot Alexis Foster? She's wandered off some-where. She's wearing a pink dress with white tights and a pink hat with a yellow ribbon on it."

Immediately, everyone pitched in to search the area, under the pews, up in the balcony. Even in the baptismal. Anderson Wilmont moved to stand in the door, guarding it as he kept his eyes on Cassidy, who frantically moved from one pew to the next, calling the little girl's name.

Gabe was on his hands and knees looking for tiny feet when he felt a hand on his shoulder. Cassidy stood there, shoulders slumped. "She's not here, Gabe. She's gone. Oh God," she cried out her despair in a desperate prayer, "she's gone. Someone took her. How did Anderson let this happen? Why wasn't he watching?"

Amy rushed up to them slightly out of breath and grabbed Cassidy by the hand. "Cass, someone said they saw a lady carry a little girl out the side door of the church about ten minutes ago. The little girl had on a pink dress with a matching pink hat. She also described the woman who was carrying her—and it sounds like Kara's sister, Susan. And get this. She got into a silver Mercedes."

Susan Cooper drove a silver Mercedes.

Amy paced the sidewalk. Cassidy watched her and felt like throwing up. Her parents had finally left, but not without giving strict instructions to call as soon as they heard anything.

How had this happened? With all the bodyguards and all the careful attention, how had Alexis been snatched from right under their very noses? Cassidy looked up from her seat on the church steps. This was where Alexis had disappeared. How could she move?

She and Gabe talked to the police for over an hour. The questions swirled endlessly in their monotony. Who could have taken her? Do you have any enemies? Why would Susan Cooper kidnap the child when you were open to visitation rights?

She clutched her head and choked back her desperate scream.

Craig Monahan had arrived within minutes of Gabe's call and as soon as he realized that Susan Cooper was a possible suspect, he'd put in a call to the FBI, who'd gotten right to work.

Pastor Bridges had offered his condolences and told Cassidy to call him if she needed anything. He'd offered to stay, but Cassidy told him there was no need. The police were here and would handle it. He left reluctantly, and only because he had someone in the hospital having emergency surgery. He promised to be in touch as soon as he could.

Gabe and Craig came to stand beside her. Gabe looked so secure, a shelter from the storm. She wanted to climb into his arms and forget the world existed, if only for a few precious moments. A headache pounded behind her eyes and she rubbed them, wishing for some relief. Gabe sat beside her and put an arm around her shoulders. Grateful, she leaned into the comfort while Craig stood in front of them.

Cassidy sniffed back tears. "She was suing for custody."

"What?"

Cassidy looked into Gabe's shocked eyes. She nodded. "I haven't had a chance to tell you. They filed Friday."

Craig frowned. "But if they're suing, why would she kidnap the child? Filing suit Friday and then kidnapping the child on Sunday doesn't suggest this was a planned thing. If she's the one who took Alexis, then she must have just come upon an opportunity. I mean, all she had to do was bide her time and let the court decide. She could have won without worrying about anything."

"Unless she was afraid she wouldn't win." A tall man with thick black hair and reflective sunglasses came up to the three and said, "We're waiting on Brian Cooper to arrive. He agreed to meet us over here."

Cassidy looked up, hope written on her features. "Does he know where Susan and Alexis are?"

"Cass, we don't even know if it was really her or not."

"I wish there was some way—" She broke off and sat up straight. "Wait a minute. The security cameras."

"What?"

"Look." She got up and walked to one of the poles that marked a parking-lot row.

Gabe looked. A camera mounted at the top. Craig caught their excitement. He said, "Where's the control room?"

"Follow me." She ran into the media building. Not bothering to knock on doors, she called out, "Hello? Mr. Dewitt?"

Gabe and Craig thundered up after her.

"Hey, what's all the commotion?" Mr. Dewitt emerged from the men's bathroom to her left. Cassidy gasped, "We need to look at the security tapes from just after the service ended today. Can you help us?"

"This about that little girl that's missing?"

"Yes, please."

"Sure, come on." He walked down the hall at a quicker pace than normal. He was in his late fifties, with gray hair and a wide girth. He was one of the nicest men on the face of the earth and had been weekend security for the church as long as Cassidy had attended.

Craig said, "I'm going to get the FBI guys. They'll want to be in on this."

Gabe nodded. "I'll stay here with Cass."

Mr. Dewitt opened a room to reveal TVs set up, each depicting a different part of the church, and about three angles of the parking lot.

The men from the FBI arrived with Craig and the viewing began. It was so simple, it was silly. A flick of a switch. Rewind the tape to about twelve-fifteen and push play. The first tape showed the parking lot with cars lined up to exit the premises.

Nothing on that one.

Mr. Dewitt shoved in the second one.

A view of the second parking lot.

"Hey, what about that?" Cassidy pointed to a car parked along the curb just outside of the lot. Since the video was in black and white, she couldn't really tell what color the vehicle was, just that it was light with a Mercedes symbol on the trunk.

"Can you enhance that?" one of the FBI agents asked.

Mr. Dewitt responded, "Well, I don't have all that fancy equipment you fellows have, but I can do my best." He zoomed in on the light-colored car.

"Got the license plate. Let's see who it's registered to. I'll call it in." The dark-headed agent stepped into the hall to have a brief conversation with someone on the other end of his cell phone.

The tapes kept rolling.

Finally, the mass exodus from the church.

"Stop right there. We don't need the license-plate confirmation," Gabe said. "I've never met Susan, but I'd know Alexis anywhere. That's her."

"And that's Susan." Cassidy let out a pent-up breath as she watched the woman clutch the child as she hurried down the front steps of the church while glancing back over her shoulder.

Craig called it in. The FBI put out an APB on Susan Cooper and arranged for another agent to go to the home and question Brian Cooper since he hadn't bothered to show up at the church.

Cassidy slumped to the floor to have a good cry.

EIGHTEEN

April 17
Monday morning

Cassidy stared at the phone willing it to ring by sheer mental willpower; she held back the tears with the same thing. Her throat ached with the need to release the emotion.

It was raining again. The dreary day fit. Breakfast had been a handful of grapes and a cup of the strongest coffee she'd ever brewed. The FBI had questioned Brian yesterday afternoon and gotten nothing from him except that to his knowledge his wife was visiting an old college friend in North Carolina. He vehemently denied any knowledge of Susan even thinking about taking Alexis and stated there was no way she would have acted on it if she *had* thought about it.

Craig entered the living room of her house and shed his coat. The FBI were officially on the case. Craig was there as a friend. She looked up, trying to assess the expression on his face.

"Well?"

He shook his head. "Mrs. Cooper's not there. The friend that she was to visit said they had no plans to get together and she hadn't heard from Susan since Kara's and Jacob's funerals."

Cassidy wilted.

Amy's voice called from the foyer. "Cass?"

"In here, Amy."

Amy came over to sit beside Cassidy and grasp her hands. "Nothing, huh?"

"Craig just said Susan wasn't at the friend's house."

"Where's Gabe?"

"On his way. He's been at work at the hospital all night and now he's coming here." Cassidy frowned and shook her head. "He needs to go home and sleep."

Amy patted her shoulder. "He'll be where he wants to be. And besides, you didn't sleep last night, either."

That was true. She'd prayed and paced. "Any phone calls?"

Cassidy grimaced. "Just from Dad asking if we'd heard anything. I really expected Susan to call." She shrugged and sighed. "Although, I don't know why. She's not going to ask for ransom." Cassidy swallowed hard. "She wants Alexis, not the money."

"Brian wants it, though."

"Yeah, maybe."

Anderson entered the room and Cassidy looked up. After Alexis disappeared, Cassidy learned that Anderson had been in conversation with her father at the church. Distracted for half a minute. Which is all it had taken.

Gabe followed him into the room and Cassidy felt her heart trip then skip into a faster rhythm. He'd come. But of course he would. Gratitude swam through her and she wanted to run to him and bury her face in his chest. She realized she often wanted to do that. He offered a weary smile although his eyes sparked when he saw her.

Two FBI agents stepped in behind him. Cassidy had learned their names were Adam Greene and Mac Smith. Adam stood about three inches over six feet and had piercing green eyes. She had a feeling he didn't miss much. He would also win any bodybuilding contest he entered. Mac was about an inch shorter and had close-cropped red hair and freckles. He looked to be an easy-going fellow with a sense of humor. When he wasn't involved in a kidnapping.

She stood and walked toward Gabe. Before she reached him, he was stepping around Anderson to pull her into his arms.

She didn't resist; she relished the feel of him, the comfort his touch held. Finally, she pulled back and asked, "Gabe? What is it?"

He let her go and scrubbed a hand over tired eyes. "Nothing. I just needed a hug."

"And a nap."

"Yeah, that, too, but first things first."

"What?"

"Come here." He spotted Amy on the couch and said, "Hey, Amy, glad you're here." Amy scooted over to make room for Gabe and Cassidy. Anderson stood by the fireplace and the agents settled onto the love seat that faced the couch.

Gabe pulled papers from his pocket and showed them to his audience. "Craig did some background investigating of the Coopers. I know he already gave you everything he found, but I dug a little deeper. On a whim, I did a search on Brian's parents and their real-estate holdings. I hit the jackpot. A house in the mountains of Asheville, North Carolina. According to Brian's father, Susan uses it more than anyone else in the family. I'm guessing this is where she's run to."

Mac leaned forward and took the papers from Gabe. He asked, "You got an address?"

"Right there on the back."

"I'll get on it." Mac left the room to use his cell phone.

Adam scooted to the edge of the couch. "And her bank records show she withdrew five thousand dollars on Friday afternoon."

Cassidy gasped. "So she was planning this!"

Adam nodded. "Maybe. Probably. I don't think she meant to snatch the kid this soon but was just watching you. Going places she knew you would go. And, like we said earlier, when she saw a golden opportunity Sunday morning, she couldn't let it pass by. I don't think she knew about the cameras or she would have been a lot more careful. This is the act of a desperate woman."

Cassidy felt the tears clog her throat again and forced them back.

Mac came back in and announced, "We've got a team headed up the mountains to this address to check it out. They'll get back to me when they know something. Should be within the next couple of hours."

Gabe cut loose with a jaw-popping yawn.

Cassidy ordered, "Go lie down in the guest room, Gabe. You're exhausted."

He gave a quick laugh and said, "And you're not?"

"Yes," she agreed, "but I didn't work all night. I just sat up praying."

Gabe's expression softened and he pulled her into another hug. "That's probably the best thing you could have done for Alexis."

Amy stood. "Cass, I'm going to head on home, but call me as soon as you know anything. Oh, and Mother said to let her know if she could do anything."

"Your mother is too busy running the Senate," Cassidy tried to joke. The attempt at humor fell flat, but Amy gave a courtesy laugh. Cassidy grimaced. "Sorry. Tell her I said thank-you."

Amy smiled her understanding and leaned over for a hug. "Bye."

She left, and Cassidy wanted to curl back into Gabe's arms. Instead, she stood and tugged on his hand. "Come on. These guys aren't going anywhere soon, so you might as well catch some sleep while you can."

"Should we drive up to the house ourselves?" Gabe asked.

Mac spoke up. "I wouldn't suggest it, sir. We don't even know that's where she is yet."

Cassidy gave him a nudge. "I'll wake you when we know something."

Gabe smothered another yawn. "That should be my line."

Cassidy didn't bother offering any more orders, she just pointed to the room down the hall.

"Right. Got it. Just for a few minutes, though, okay?"

"Sure." She walked with him down the hall. He stopped in the doorway and looked at her. He needed a shave and still he was incredibly attractive. He pulled her close and kissed her…like a husband kisses his wife after coming home from a hard day at work. It was a kiss that said, I care about you, thanks for being here and I'm here for you if you need me.

Cassidy leaned into it and felt cherished; protected. Loved. Everything all rolled into one. She immediately missed him when he stepped back. He placed one last kiss on her forehead, quirked a tired smile and shut the door.

Two and a half hours later, Cassidy occupied herself with washing the dishes by hand. She could have used the dishwasher, but then she would have had to find something else to do while she waited. In short order, her house sparkled. She'd even scrubbed the floor on her hands and knees.

Knuckles rapped against wood. Mac stood in the doorway, a smile on his face. Her heart leaped with hope. "You heard something?" she asked, drying her hands on the towel.

"Gabe called it. They're there. North Carolina police just confirmed it. A woman matching Susan's description and a small girl matching Alexis's are in the house. Plus, there's a silver Mercedes parked in the garage."

Cassidy wilted with relief. "Did they say how Alexis looked? Was she okay? Crying?"

"They said she looked fine. She was eating a bowl of cereal when one of the policemen snuck up and looked through the kitchen window."

Tears threatened to overwhelm her for the millionth time that day. "Thank You, God," she whispered.

She went to wake Gabe.

Gabe drove with focused concentration. Cassidy sat next to him twisting the antenna of her cell phone as she stared out the window. Unscrewed it, screwed it back on. Off, on.

He reached out with his right hand and gently removed it from her grasp and set it in the cup holder.

She gave a tremulous smile. "Sorry."

"We've got about fifteen more minutes."

"I can't wait to hold her. My arms feel empty." Cassidy worried her bottom lip with her teeth. Gabe's heart twisted at the pain on her face.

"We'll get her back, Cass."

Cassidy shook. "You don't think she'd do anything to hurt Alexis, do you?"

Gabe reached over again, but this time it was to grasp her hand in his and hold on tight. "I don't know, Cass. I won't lie to you. Desperate people do desperate things, but God's got it under control."

I won't lie to you. Gabe's own words echoed in his ears. *But you are lying, aren't you? I can't tell her about Micah,* Gabe reminded himself fiercely. *But,* he argued with himself, *you could tell her it was your fault he was even there.* That was worse. *He could lose Cassidy forever.*

Help me, Lord.

Then he was out of time. He saw the exit just ahead. Ten minutes later, he was parked on top of the mountain facing a beautiful log home. Police surrounded the area. A SWAT team stood on alert. No doubt a sniper had a bead on one of the windows in the house.

Curious neighbors stood behind the yellow police tape. Gabe stepped out of the car, and Cassidy came around to walk with him to find the officer in charge. He was tall with a commanding presence; an aura of authority clung to him. He introduced himself as Jackson Devereaux. He reminded her of the head army ranger from the television show, *The Unit.*

She shook his hand and said, "I'm Cassidy, Alexis's guardian. How is she?"

"Ma'am, our hostage negotiator's working on getting Ms. Cooper to talk, but she's not having much to do with him. The child seems to be unharmed."

Gabe spotted Brian sitting in a police car. "What's going on with him?"

The man raised a black eyebrow and said, "He wanted to bust in there to get to the woman. He was fired up mad, screaming at her. We had to restrain him. I really don't think he knew anything about her plans to kidnap the little girl. But he sure had a lot of other stuff to talk about."

Cassidy marched over to the car where Brian sat, eyes closed, with his head resting against the back of the seat. The window was down. "Brian! Did you know about this?" she demanded.

"That stupid woman ruined everything," Brian spat. "It was all supposed to be so simple. Finally, things seemed to be going our way. Kara and Jacob dead through some freak raid on their village, the grandmother incapacitated, and the one remaining sister, Susan, is available to collect the kid and the money that came with her. And then Oliver tells her there's no way a judge is going to grant custody, so she pulls this stupid stunt. Unbelievable."

"I promised her visitation rights!" Cassidy was so furious, she could hardly think straight.

"Visitation. Ha. She'd never settle for that. Susan can't have children. She's been begging me to adopt a kid for years." He gave a short laugh. "Alexis would have kept her busy and out of my hair. And all that money would have been enough to—" Brian clamped his mouth shut.

"Pay off most of your gambling debts," Cassidy finished for him.

Brian looked shocked, then groaned, "I owe some pretty nasty people some big-time money. If I don't get my hands on some cash soon, I'm dead." He looked ill at the thought, then looked up at Gabe and asked, "But how…"

Gabe answered the man's unspoken question. "We had you checked out when someone kept threatening Cassidy. We suspected you all along. So was it you? You and Oliver schemed it together after you got word that the Fosters had been killed, right? You hired Rafael to get rid of Cassidy and all your problems would be solved, true? You'd get Alexis and all the money, too."

Now Brian looked confused. "Get rid of Cassidy? What are you talking about?"

"But how did you know the contents of the will?" Cassidy asked, ignoring his question. "I know Kara and Jacob wouldn't have shared that with either you or Susan."

"No, Oliver did. After he got word that Kara and Jacob were dead, he called us up and told us about the will. He decided to see if he could get his hands on some of the money. He said that Cassidy would get custody, but if he lost the codicil then he might be able to work around that. We promised him if he'd get us custody, we'd cut him a nice deal financially. Then after Cassidy showed up with the original codicil, Oliver said that the will was pretty cut-and-dried and the only way we'd get custody is if something happened to Cassidy before she had a chance to write a new will."

"So you hired Rafael to kidnap me," Cassidy stated. "If the codicil and I disappeared, there was nothing standing in your way, right?"

Brian shook his head. "What are you talking about? What kidnapping? No! We hadn't even had time to come up with another plan before Susan pulled this harebrained stunt."

Cassidy didn't know if she believed Brian or not. He had to be lying. Didn't he? But if he wasn't… She mentally groaned. It was all just too confusing.

"Sir? Ma'am? I'm Steven McEntire, the hostage negotiator. I've been trying to talk to Mrs. Cooper and she listened for a while. Unfortunately, instead of de-escalating, she's going in the opposite direction. She's becoming more agitated and keeps telling us to leave her alone then hangs up on me. Would one of you be willing to try?" Steven stood a couple of inches over six feet tall and had on the protective body gear that all the SWAT team wore.

Cassidy forgot about Brian. She'd have time to deal with him later. "I'll talk to her." Agent McEntire pressed a button and handed Cassidy the phone. "Keep your cool. It's ringing."

"Hello?" Susan sounded scared…and determined. Cassidy cleared her throat. "Hello, Susan. It's Cassidy McKnight."

"No! You can't have her!"

"Wait, Susan! Don't hang up, please. I just want to talk. Please."

"Don't you see? My life is ruined. Brian—" She broke off to sob.

Cassidy felt her anger slip a notch. *Lord, help me know what to say to her.* "Susan, I understand you're hurt. Your sister gave your niece to me. It wasn't because of you. It was because of Brian." Cassidy tried to keep her voice even, soothing, when she wanted to scream at the woman to stop this craziness. *God, I need You.*

Deep breath. Relax.

Susan was crying so hard Cassidy had to strain to make out the words. "She told me not to marry him. She warned me he only wanted my money. That she didn't trust him and he would cause me only grief and heartache. But he loved me. He said he didn't care about my money and would even sign a prenup." Another hiccuping sob. Cassidy just let her talk. "But he spent it all. Every last dime."

Yeah, Brian had offered to sign a prenuptial agreement because he knew his starry-eyed fiancée would never let him. Jerk.

Steven gave Cassidy a thumbs-up for approval. Men in black gear moved slowly toward the back of the house. Cassidy said, "Kara told me she hurt for you and wanted to be there for you, but you wouldn't let her. All of her letters were returned unopened."

The sobs stopped. Another hiccup, then all was still. Silence on the line.

"Susan?" Cassidy glanced at Steven who motioned for her to keep going. The woman was still there. "Talk to me."

"Her letters?" Susan finally asked. "That's because I didn't want to read about how stupid she thought I was. About how I'd made the wrong choices. About how Brian was no good for me…and how unworthy I was to be related to her."

Cassidy's stomach dropped. *Oh, please, God, don't let me say the wrong thing.*

"But she never said that. She just wanted you to know how much she loved you and how much God loved you. She sent you pictures of Alexis and their village where they had made a life in Brazil. When you never responded, she was too scared to call. She said your refusal to read the letters hurt, but she couldn't take you hanging up on her."

"But I never… I thought she just wanted to harp on my bad choice of a husband." Susan's voice changed. Cassidy heard the rage as Susan hissed, "Brian did this, too. He convinced me to return them unopened. You know, before Kara left for Brazil, she came to see me. She said she loved me and just wanted what was best for me, but I didn't believe her because Brian said it was all for show. That, as a missionary, it wouldn't look good for Kara to tell me how stupid I was in front of the family and that…and that—" Her voice broke and she cleared her throat to finish. "He brainwashed me, didn't he? Convinced me that Kara rejected me and that she was still angry with me for marrying him. That her letters weren't worth opening. I can't believe I've been so stupid!"

"Oh, Susan, I'm so sorry." Cassidy felt her heart soften. She pleaded, "Come out so we can help you."

Cassidy realized she held no anger toward this poor woman who had felt unworthy of her sister's love for so long, only to find out Kara had relentlessly pursued a relationship with her that was too late to accept. Kara had loved her and Susan had missed out on a loving relationship because she'd believed the lies of her husband. How sad.

"Please bring Alexis out so no one gets hurt. I know you only took her because you were hurting so bad. I'll make sure you get to see her, I promise."

Susan sniffed and sighed. "Oliver told us there wasn't much chance to overturn the will. He said the codicil was too strong and that that woman, Anna, from the orphanage, would come testify if called, so he said it was hopeless and I should just give up." Her voice squeaked on the last word. "And I just can't. I'm sorry."

Cassidy cajoled, "We'll work something out, I promise. I don't think Kara meant for you to never see Alexis. I just know she didn't want her around Brian. I'll let you see her anytime you want."

"Promise?" Another quiet sniff.

Steven motioned for his men to stand down. Cassidy was talking the woman out. The sniper on the roof of the house across the street lowered his rifle.

"Absolutely."

"I wouldn't have hurt her, Cassidy."

"I understand. Just come out. Bring her out and we'll do whatever it takes to get you help, okay?"

"O-o-okay. Don't let them shoot me."

"Nobody is shooting anyone." Cassidy looked over at Steven and he gave the thumbs-up sign again.

"I'm scared," Susan sniffled.

Cassidy reassured her. "You'll be fine. Do you want me to meet you halfway?"

Out of the corner of her eye, Cassidy saw Steven frown and Gabe adamantly shook his head. She ignored them. Whatever it took to get Alexis. "Okay, I'm heading your way." Cassidy carried the cell phone and walked slowly toward the front entrance of the house.

Susan's shaky voice said, "I'm coming out. Alexis is in front of me."

The door cracked open. Steven took the phone from Cassidy and spoke into it.

"Ma'am, send the little girl out, then you come out and lie facedown on the ground, you understand?" He listened for a moment then nodded to Cassidy. She walked closer.

Nerves shot, Cassidy almost expected to feel a bullet from somewhere slam into her body, but she kept walking. *Cover me, Lord.* Alexis peered around the door and her eyes grew large. She screeched, "My Cass-ty!"

"Hi, my Lexi." Somehow she choked the words out. When Alexis fairly flew from the house, Cassidy half expected Susan to jerk her back, but the little girl made it safely into Cassidy's arms. The minute she had Alexis in her grip, hands were pulling them to safety and Susan was stretched out on the ground, cuffed.

Gabe surrounded Cassidy and Alexis with a bear hug.

"Hi, Gabe!" Alexis squealed, then demanded, "Kiss."

"Hi, munchkin." He leaned over to plop a kiss on her upturned nose.

"Cassidy!"

Cassidy turned at the desperate cry.

"You promised." Susan's tear-stained face and defeated posture pulled on Cassidy's pity strings.

She nodded, "I promise, when you get out of jail, we'll work something out."

Susan smiled a tremulous smile and the officer led her away. Cassidy looked across the driveway and Anderson saluted her as Gabe pulled her toward the car. She nodded a silent thanks for his dedication and attentiveness.

Cassidy followed Gabe to the car and when he opened the door to put Alexis in the car seat, Cassidy swore she saw tears in his eyes before he could blink them away.

NINETEEN

April 18
Tuesday morning

Gabe stared at his ceiling. Life had a funny way of coming full circle. In the jungle, he'd failed. He'd let Micah die. When he'd finally regained consciousness, he'd been three thousand feet in the air with an oxygen mask on his face, a medic stitching up his stab wound and yelling in his ear.

"Stay with us, Gabe. You're gonna be fine. Just hang on."

"Micah," he whispered.

Of course, no one heard him above the thumping of the helicopter blades. He lifted a shaky hand and pulled the oxygen mask off and tried again. "Micah."

This time someone noticed. "Hey, leave that alone. What'd you say, buddy?"

Were they deaf?

"Micah!" He swore he yelled the name, but the medic leaned closer trying to hear.

"Micah? Who's Micah?"

"Micah McKnight. Back there." He forced the words out on a gasp.

"Man, you were it. No one else back there. Sorry."

"No, go back." Gabe struggled to rise, but strong hands held him down; he felt the prick of a needle and all went black again.

Shadows shifted on the ceiling.

They hadn't believed him. Because Micah wasn't supposed to have been on that mission. But Gabe insisted that he was there. And because he wouldn't give up, they told him to shut up.

Which meant that if Gabe kept up the questioning, other SEALs could be in danger because Micah never got to finish his original mission. And a traitor was still out there.

And so Gabe kept his mouth shut. There was nothing he could do for Micah at that point. Unfortunately, revealing what little he did know would only cause grief to those who loved Micah and the families of the other SEALs from that mission. And Gabe certainly didn't want to be responsible for anyone else's death.

His head ached.

Be anxious for nothing.

The words sounded in his head.

That's You, isn't it, God? I am anxious. I'm sorry, I'm a little new at this. I know I'm supposed to give this to You, but I hate that this family is suffering and I could end it. But if I do, I might put others at risk, other men who have families waiting for them to come home. How can I chance it? Cassidy wouldn't understand. The ambassador would, but Cassidy would demand an all-out search for the body of her brother and wouldn't believe him to be dead until she saw it with her own eyes. Give me peace in this matter,

please. I need it. I would also appreciate a few hours with-
out an emergency at the hospital. Thanks. I mean, amen.
You know what I mean, God.

April 19
Wednesday morning

Cassidy rolled over in her childhood bed. She and Alexis
had spent the last two nights with her parents. Gabe had
badgered her until she gave in. She'd tried to convince him
that everything was fine now that Brian was in custody and
Susan was getting the help she needed, but Gabe said
something about that spot between his shoulders itching
and demanded that she and Alexis stay behind the secure
walls of her parents' estate.

Feeling sorry for the man, Cassidy gave in without too
much argument. He'd also told her about his experience in
church. His eyes held a new light that made Cassidy's
heart swell with joy for him…and the knowledge that now
there was nothing holding them apart—except Micah.

She couldn't wait to see him again, but since he'd had
to work the past three days, she decided to figure out what
was going on with her parents. Like if they were making
any more progress toward working things out. She gave
Anderson the week off—with the exception of working
during her speech Friday night. He'd agreed.

Her cell phone chirped.

Cassidy rolled out of bed and snatched it from the
dresser. Caller ID indicated Mr. Morgan's office. Cassidy
frowned. What now? No charges had been made against the
lawyer as no one could prove he lost the codicil on purpose
or done anything illegal. It was Brian's word against his.

Sheila Simons called to formally tell Cassidy that the custody suit had been dropped. As soon as she hung up with Sheila, the phone rang again.

"Hello?"

"Hello, Cassidy, this is Cindy Patterson from Sunday school."

Cassidy smiled into the receiver. "Hello, Cindy, how are you?"

"I'm fine, thanks. I got the prayer-chain call that Alexis had been found. I'm so relieved for you."

Cassidy shuddered at the memory of the horrific experience, but said, "Thank you. I can't tell you how much it means to know that everyone was praying."

"I also had an ulterior motive for calling."

"Oh?"

"Nothing terrible. I read in the paper about your upcoming speech regarding the evils of human trafficking. I know the event is a benefit to raise money for those directly affected. I…well, I'm interested in attending. Would that be possible?"

"Sure! That would be great." Cassidy wondered if the woman was aware the plates were a thousand dollars each. But that information was in the paper, so…

"Who do I make the check out to?"

Okay, apparently money wasn't an issue. "Make it out to the Stop the Traffic Foundation."

"No problem. I'll get this in the mail to you this afternoon."

"And I'll have your ticket at the hostess podium where you enter the ballroom."

"I look forward to being there." A slight pause and Cassidy thought the conversation was finished. "You're a really good person, aren't you?"

The question took Cassidy by surprise. "What?"

"You do good things. You like to help people. I just think that's—admirable. I hope we can be friends."

Cassidy smiled into the phone. "Thank you, Cindy. Why don't we get together and have lunch one day."

"I'd like that."

"Great. We'll talk Friday night and set something up."

"Sounds good," Cindy said.

They hung up just as Alexis, book in hand, wandered into the bedroom and demanded total attention. Cassidy laughed and picked the little girl up to smother her with hugs and kisses. The high-pitched giggles did wonders for Cassidy's morning.

April 20
Thursday morning

Gabe's first thought when he awoke was that he'd missed something. Then he realized he had no idea what day it was. Oh, yeah. He'd had some brutal hours at the hospital starting with Monday evening around midnight and ending this morning around 3:00 a.m.

Cassidy. They'd played phone tag updating each other with what was going on, but he'd yet to have a real conversation with her since Monday night when he'd dropped her and Alexis off at her parents' estate.

He missed her. Like crazy.

Thank You, God, for keeping them safe. Thank You for letting me be a part of getting them home safe. You healed something in me by allowing that. It still hurts to think about that little boy and the men who were killed in that explosion, but hopefully, You can use it somehow. Anyway, thanks.

Gabe liked this new feeling of talking to a best friend.

He didn't have to be formal, he just talked to God like he did to a good friend—or his dad.

Cassidy's cell phone sounded loud in the quiet room. She jumped and closed her Bible. She and Alexis were in her father's office, just off the foyer on the main floor. Alexis played with books and blocks, and Cassidy had decided to have her quiet time.

She also planned to read over the guest list for tomorrow night.

And if she was honest with herself, the activity allowed her to shove thoughts of her parents to the back of her mind. They looked as if they were making progress since seeing a Christian marriage counselor, but one never knew. The phone rang again and she picked it up. "Hello?"

"Cassidy, this is Detective Craig Monahan. How are you doing?"

"Hello, Detective. I'm doing all right. Just trying to focus on tomorrow. It's such a relief not to have to worry about Susan or the custody anymore. But I'm still a little concerned about Brian. You really feel like he was the one that set everything up?"

"Yeah. We can't decide if he's telling the truth or not. He swears he had nothing to do with your kidnapping. Unfortunately, we don't have any proof that he did, nor do we have any other suspects."

Cassidy sighed. "So, what do we do, Detective? Assume he's lying? I don't know what to believe. I can't think of anyone else that would be out to get me, but all of this has made me just a little jumpy…and paranoid." She gave a weak laugh, but couldn't manage to inject any humor in it.

"Completely understandable. Also, security for tomorrow night is all set up. There shouldn't be any problems."

"Thank you so much, Craig. At first, I was adamant about not canceling, but after I thought about it, I can't risk anyone getting hurt. Tell me now what I need to do."

"I really think it'll be all right. Let me worry about security, okay? That's my job."

Cassidy sighed and agreed. "All right, but if you see *anything* that could be a problem, you let me know, please. I'll talk to you later."

Cassidy hung up the phone and stared at it as though it would give her the answers she sought.

"My Cass-ty. Play blocks. I share."

Alexis stood in front of her and held out a colorful block. Her blue eyes twinkled with life and mischief. Love rushed through her. Oh, Kara, she's beautiful. *God, please tell Kara thank-you for giving me this precious gift.*

Alexis lifted a finger and brushed a tear from Cassidy's cheek. She tilted her head inquisitively. "Owie? Me kiss?"

"Mmm. Yes, kiss it and make it better."

"I'd be happy to," a deep voice said.

Cassidy jumped and swung around to face the door. "Gabe!"

"Gabe!" Alexis echoed.

He stood in the door grinning at the two females. Alexis ran as fast as she could on her short, chubby legs and flung her arms around his knees.

Gabe laughed as he bent down and picked her up.

Cassidy felt her heart melt at the sight and wanted to do exactly as Alexis had and run to him to fling herself in his arms. Instead, she walked sedately across the floor and stood beside him.

"Okay, I'm ready," she told him.

Gabe's brows drew together in a frown. "Ready for what?"

"You to kiss it and make it all better."

Gabe froze and stared at her for two seconds before he snaked his hand around her neck and pulled her closer. The longing in his gaze made her catch her breath. He leaned over and settled his lips against hers for a brief second before pulling back and smiling down at her. "Your wish is my command."

Alexis's giggles brought Cassidy's attention back around to the real world—and their little two-and-a-half-year-old chaperone. Cassidy knew the red in her face could rival the red color of her father's restored antique convertible Mustang. She pulled back, but had to smile as Alexis planted her hands on Gabe's clean-shaven cheeks and demanded, "Gabe, kiss."

Gabe grinned at Alexis. He leaned in closer to her to blow a raspberry on her cheek. She threw her blond head back and howled with laughter. Cassidy felt a surge of emotion so strong it nearly choked her. She wanted this to last forever. *Please, God.*

April 21
Friday-night dinner

Cassidy shuffled her index cards one more time then set them down on the table in front of her. She didn't need them. Everything she needed to say was ingrained deep inside her brain, her heart, her very soul.

Sequined gowns sparkled under the lights of the chandeliers hanging in the ballroom. Black-tailed tuxedos competed with the white ones. Money, power and high-profile celebrities graced the tables piled high with plates from the

buffet. And while all of these highly influential people visited and sparkled on the surface, Cassidy knew that underneath the glitter their hearts were genuine. Amy and her
parents had arrived early to visit. Cassidy had appreciated
the support and encouragement. They would be down with
her parents shortly.

Black curtains lined the walls and swayed gently in the
path of the air conditioner. Nine crystal chandeliers hung
from the vaulted ceiling and gave a warm ambience that
promoted good feelings and hopefully, generosity. Fund-
raisers weren't exactly the reason her parents had built the
ballroom, but as far as Cassidy was concerned, it was as
good a reason as any.

Craig Monahan gave her a slight nod as her gaze passed
over him. She responded in kind, grateful for his presence.
Security was tight; there was only one way in and one way
out. Anderson stood guard at the door, subtly checking
and double-checking each person's invitation. Cassidy saw
the Grahams enter, followed by Amy.

Christina McKnight entered on the arm of her husband
and her posture would make her finishing-school madam
proud. Cassidy waved to her parents. They waved and
smiled, but Cassidy noticed her father appeared to have
aged a few years over the past couple of weeks. Cassidy
avoided thinking about the cause. Senators, congressmen
and women handed over their tickets and joined the crowd
at the buffet to chat and socialize.

Cindy Patterson, dressed in a simple black dress and
matching black purse, entered alone. Cassidy waved and
smiled. Cindy bit her lip, but offered a small smile in return. She seemed nervous and out of place and Cassidy

hoped she'd find someone to talk to. In fact, Cassidy decided, she'd just go welcome the woman personally.

She felt a hand on her arm and turned to speak to Congresswoman Shelton. By the time she spoke and turned back, Cindy had disappeared. She'd have to catch her later.

A band played off to the right and a few couples swayed on the dance floor. The buffet held roast beef, ham, turkey, caviar, an assortment of vegetables and a tower of fruit. The dessert table tempted even the strongest-willed dieter. The staff had done an excellent job.

Then Gabe entered the room and Cassidy felt her heart quiver. Oh, my. *Lord, is he the one You want for me? Because I'm with You a hundred percent.*

Amy came up beside her and said, "He cleans up real good, doesn't he?"

"I'm speechless," Cassidy admitted.

"That's a first." Amy's laughter drew the eyes of a few, and Cassidy smiled in spite of herself. Secretly she agreed with Amy's assessment. The man looked good. She watched him scan the room until his gaze came to rest on her.

Wow, he mouthed.

Cassidy grinned. *Ditto,* she mouthed back.

Gabe began moving toward her. He'd offered to pick her up in the foyer and escort her down to the ballroom, but she'd insisted that she needed to be there early and didn't want him to have to wait around on her.

"You look stunning," Gabe murmured as he leaned over to place what was probably supposed to be a chaste kiss on her cheek. However, the combination of the kiss and his spicy cologne caused her senses to spin.

She focused on his words. Stunning, huh? Cassidy *felt* stunning in her strapless green straight gown. Modest and

classy, she knew she looked her best. Her curls had coop-
erated and had allowed her to tame them into an elegant
pile on top of her head with a large pearl clasp. Several
loose ringlets curled around her ears. Matching pearl earrings and bracelet completed her ensemble of jewelry. She
almost felt ashamed to wear such nice things knowing the
reason for the gathering, but appearances often did matter
and the end result would be worth it.

Cassidy shoved aside the butterflies doing laps around
her stomach and looped her arm through his. She smiled
up at him. "Thank you. You clean up pretty well yourself."

Amy spoke up. "Since I'm obviously not needed
here—or noticed, for that matter—I'll just meander over
to the buffet."

Cassidy flushed. "Amy…"

Amy grinned and slipped away before Cassidy could
finish her warning.

"Cassidy, darling, what a lovely party."

Cassidy turned to find Cecelia Graham beside her.

"Senator Graham, Mrs. Graham. Thank you so much for
coming. I'm so glad you popped in early. It was nice
visiting with you." Cassidy grinned at Amy's mother and
leaned over to give the woman a gentle hug.

"And you, dear," Mrs. Graham answered. "That Alexis
is so precious. It was good to see her, too. We had such fun
that day I kept her."

Cassidy gestured toward Gabe and said, "You remember
Gabriel Sinclair, I'm sure."

"It's a pleasure to see you again."

Gabe took the woman's proffered hand and gave a slight
bow over it, charming her into an almost girlish giggle.
"My goodness, you are a smooth one, aren't you?"

Gabe quirked a smile. "I try, ma'am, I try."

Cecelia winked at Cassidy and said, "You'd better keep this one."

Cassidy mentally rolled her eyes. What was it with the Graham family and Gabe? Then he gave her a wicked cute smile and she decided that was about the dumbest question she'd ever asked herself. She grinned back and said, "I'm working on it."

Cassidy noticed one of the supporters trying to get her attention. She acknowledged the man with a smile and said, "Excuse me, please. I need to get this thing going here." She stepped away and up to the podium. Leaning into the microphone, she said, "Good evening, ladies and gentlemen."

Gradually the room quieted and focused on Cassidy. She continued, "Good evening. I hope you all have enjoyed the scrumptious feast provided by our local caterers, Food To Die For." A round of applause greeted this statement. Cassidy grinned. She'd loved the name and wanted to help the friend who was in her Bible-study group get her new business off the ground. Cassidy decided it was definitely airborne.

When the cheering stopped, she said, "And now, I'd like to thank each and every one of you for coming. I feel so blessed to be able to stand before you today and ask for your help in a project that has become near and dear to my heart. The Stop the Traffic Foundation has raised millions of dollars to help those victimized by human trafficking in Brazil. I know other countries are also affected by this evil. However, as they say, Rome wasn't built in a day. And the atrocities committed through modern-day slavery won't be eliminated in a day. But we can strive to make a difference—one day at a time."

Cassidy took a deep breath and continued. As she spoke, she scanned the crowd before her. All lightheartedness had long since faded from their faces. Serious expressions replaced the previous gaiety.

She went on, "As you know, my father, Ambassador McKnight, is a huge voice in the fight against human trafficking in Brazil. Each year, close to one million people are trafficked against their will. And close to twenty thousand of those victims end up right here in the United States of America—the land of the free."

Cassidy watched several shake their heads and frown at one another. Good, they were listening, absorbing it, processing it, ugliness and all. Cassidy spoke for several more minutes and then said, "There's so much information, it's impossible to give it all to you tonight. So, in closing, I just want to say. This is the twenty-first century. We cannot let this go on. Please, give from your heart to the Stop the Traffic Foundation that is dedicated to helping victims of human trafficking. We can change lives—one day at a time. Thank you."

Thunderous applause greeted Cassidy as she smiled out at the audience. A sudden movement to her left captured her attention. What? Was that a…

"Gun!" someone yelled.

"Cassidy, duck!" Cassidy heard Gabe's yell but felt frozen to her spot on the stage.

The ski-masked figure holding the weapon stepped from behind the curtain and approached Cassidy, swinging the gun back and forth. "Stay back," the attacker ordered. A woman. Small, petite.

Security had guns drawn but stayed back as ordered. Cassidy stood on the stage, the perfect target. "Why?" Her voice shook. "What have I done to you?"

The gun shook; the trigger finger jerked spasmodically. Cassidy flinched, expecting to feel the impact of a bullet any moment now.

Cassidy sucked in air. "Who are you?"

The figure steadied the gun with one hand and reached for the mask with the other. A slight tug pulled it off and Cassidy gasped. Reddish blond hair spilled out onto black-clad shoulders. Green eyes glared up at Cassidy.

"Cindy Patterson?" Cassidy stared in disbelief. "What…how…why?"

"Because he's my father. Mine. But he didn't want me. He left me and my mother to struggle on our own. He never called, never cared. Just sent the money that was never enough."

And Cassidy knew. Her father's child from his affair. Her half sister.

Cindy was on a roll now. "And then…that person called. Told me about all of you. Told me how to get revenge. And I agreed."

People gasped and stared. Her father groaned and closed his eyes. Cassidy focused on the woman in front of her. "Oh, Cindy. So, you set up my kidnapping?" She took a few steps in her direction.

"Cassidy, stop," her mother pleaded.

Cassidy ignored her but glanced again at her father's white face and strained features. His eyes, open now, begged her forgiveness, his sorrow over the situation clearly displayed by his slumped shoulders and clenched fists.

Cindy laughed, a bitter sound. "No, that wasn't me. I don't know who it was. But I'm going to finish it."

"Cindy, give me the gun. We can work this out. We can." Cassidy approached, but Cindy raised the weapon.

"No, we can't. I shot a man." Tears leaked down her ashen cheeks.

"Joseph. Outside the law office. Those clothes belonged to you," Cassidy whispered.

Cindy nodded and shrugged. "He saw me on the roof. He would have warned you. I didn't really want to shoot him, but I couldn't let him catch me." Tears watered her eyes, her attention focused on Cassidy, not the detective moving in behind her. Craig gave her a warning shake of his head not to let on that she saw him. Cassidy didn't even blink.

"Cindy, put the gun down. You don't want to kill me."

Craig chose that moment to rush Cindy. The gunshot sounded loud in the silenced room. Cassidy flinched and felt the hand on her wrist a second before her world tilted upside down. Then she was on the floor and under the table. Her elbow banged the leg of a chair and pain shot up her arm. Gabe pulled her close and covered her with his body.

Cassidy heard a grunt and the sounds of a struggle, then Cindy crying and saying she didn't mean it. Cassidy's heart ached for the woman, but right now she had to concentrate on sucking air into her squashed lungs. She pushed against Gabe.

"Move, Gabe, I can't breathe."

Through a fog of fear and fury, Gabe heard Cassidy's voice telling him to move. Reluctantly, he complied and pulled away. Cassidy scrambled up from the safety of his sheltering body. He wanted to pull her back.

Cassidy was brushing herself off and Gabe was just starting to breathe a little easier when he noticed a small stain spreading across Cassidy's shoulder. Before he could figure out what it was, Cassidy looked up with a startled expression, closed her eyes and dropped to the floor, the small stain becoming larger by the second. Gabe felt his world screech to a halt.

"Cassidy!" he whispered.

Chaos reigned for the next sixty seconds as security finally broke from their shocked stupor and sprang into action. Gabe dropped to Cassidy's side and pressed his hand against the wound. Cassidy's parents rushed forward, still surrounded by security, and Cassidy's mother dropped beside him. "Cassidy, darling, don't move."

Desperately, he struggled to shift into doctor mode, but it was a difficult thing to do when the woman he loved lay bleeding all over his hands. Cassidy's mother pushed the red curls back from Cassidy's forehead and Gabe saw her hand tremble.

Amy rushed up to him. "I called 9-1-1. Please tell me she's going to be okay." Tears dripped down her pale cheeks. "Tell me what to do to help."

Gabe shifted. "Grab that cloth napkin. Fold it into fourths and press it where my hand is. Keep the pressure on it." Joseph's shooting just a few days ago kept flashing through his mind. Grimly he thought to himself, it seemed his specialty was turning into gunshot wounds.

Amy obeyed. Gabe looked up at the ambassador and motioned for him to get his wife out of the way. The man nodded and reached down to pull Christina to her feet. She protested, but the man said, "Christina, they can't do anything for her if you're in the way. Gabe's a doctor. Let him work."

Reluctantly, she acquiesced.

Cassidy's eyes fluttered closed and Gabe leaned over her. "Cassidy, stay with me, honey." He pressed his now-bloody fingers against Cassidy's neck and felt relief sweep through him. Her pulse felt slow and faint, but at least it was there. She'd just passed out.

Sirens sounded in the distance and Gabe sent a thank-you heavenward. When the paramedics shot through the door, Gabe reeled off all the information he had and moved out of the way. Amy, too, let go and moved.

Finally, Cassidy was loaded into the ambulance and on her way to the hospital with her mother in attendance. Gabe would follow in his own car—and do some heavy praying on the way.

TWENTY

Gabe paced the hospital waiting room. Cassidy had been in surgery for three hours. He'd been in close contact with Craig, who told him that Cindy wasn't talking. He felt helpless, unused to being on this side of the situation. He'd have a lot more empathy for future patients. He rubbed his eyes, wishing for news. As though from his lips to God's ear, the doctor pushed through the double swinging O.R. doors and headed his way. He recognized him and called, "Max?"

"Gabe."

Cassidy's mother asked, "Well?"

Gabe tensed, trying to read Max's face. Sympathy oozed from him and Gabe thought his heart would give out. He croaked, "She's not…"

Max startled. "No, Gabe, no. It was a bit of touch-and-go there for a while. We almost lost her once, but she made it."

They'd almost lost her. He felt like he'd been punched in the kidney, the pain so intense it nearly knocked him out.

Max was saying, "Right now she's hanging in there. She's not out of the woods yet, but I've done all I can do. I'll be back with more information shortly."

Cassidy's mother pressed the young doctor's hand and said, "Thank you so much."

Max left and Jonathan paced from one end of the room to the other, his lips moving silently, praying. Amy sat as still as stone, her gaze fixed on the plastic green plant someone had tried to use to liven up the waiting room. Cecelia went to visit the son of a good friend who'd had hernia surgery. Amy's father vowed to make sure law enforcement caught the person responsible.

No one brought up the scene with Cindy.

Frustration clawed through him. He plopped into the nearest chair and dropped his head in his hands. How had the woman gotten a gun in?

What else, God? I need Your reassurance here. I need Your help. What do I do? I can't live without this woman and I need Your guidance about how to tell her about Micah even if it means losing her. Plus, how do we find this person that wants Cassidy dead so bad? And why? Why is this killer so determined to get rid of Cassidy? What has she done to make this person so mad at her? And, most of all, how did top-notch security fail?

Gabe's prayers ran nonstop. He knew God was listening, he wouldn't doubt that again. Unfortunately, Gabe couldn't seem to shut up long enough to listen. He needed a Bible.

Be anxious for nothing.

Trust in the Lord with all your heart.

Be still, and know that I am God.

Gabe froze. Then relaxed. He had the Word. All he had to do was listen to it. All those years of church and his parents' teachings came into focus. Gabe suddenly realized how fortunate he'd been…and still was. *Thank You, God, for my parents. It's been a long time since I've thanked You for them.*

He felt someone drop into the chair beside him and looked up. "Jonathan."

"This is my fault, all my fault. It's taken twenty-plus years, but it's finally caught up with me."

"You're a new man, Jonathan," Gabe reminded his friend.

"But sin is sin. Consequences can't be avoided forever."

"God's forgiven you. Now you have to forgive yourself." *Just like I have to about the situation with Micah.* But he couldn't add that last part.

"Cassidy's been…distant. I don't know if she'll ever forgive me. Christina's getting there, I think."

"Cassidy'll come around."

"If she lives." The man's voice cracked on the last word and Gabe felt his throat go tight.

"She'll live," he insisted.

Please, God, she has to. Although knowing Cassidy, if her death would be a way to serve You, she'd say fine. But I'm not there yet. And I think Jonathan needs to hear Cassidy say she still loves him and forgives him. Give us that, God, please.

An hour later, the doors opened again and Max reappeared. He smiled and said, "She's in recovery and doing much better. Thankfully, she's strong. I got the bone fragment out and while her blood pressure was scary low there for a while, once I found and repaired a small hidden bleeder, her pressure came back up. She's on some powerful antibiotics and some pretty strong painkillers, so she might not make much sense when she first wakes up. She'll be in ICU for a while, but if everything looks good, we'll transfer her to a private room."

"Thanks, Max."

"No problem. Glad I was here. Of course you can wait here or go on back, Gabe."

Gabe looked at the ambassador for a clue as to what the man felt he should do. Jonathan nodded and said, "Go on, Gabe, she'd want you with her."

"I'll let you know as soon as she wakes up."

What was that smell? Cassidy wrinkled her nose and grimaced. That was some strange cleaning solution. And why did her mouth taste like week-old rotten fish? And why did her shoulder feel like it was on fire?

She turned her head and nausea rolled with the effort. Ugh. A bad case of the flu, definitely.

"Hey," a voice said softly. Gabe. "How are you feeling?"

Cassidy ran her tongue across dry lips. "Thirsty."

She struggled to keep her eyes open, but they drifted shut. So sleepy. Sounds faded. But she felt something cool touch her lips. Ice. "Thanks."

"You're welcome. Can you look at me?"

Huh-uh. Going back to sleep. Darkness came, then receded several more times before she woke and was aware of someone standing over her, stroking her hair. Then warm lips pressed against her forehead.

"Gabe?"

"Hey. You with me this time?"

Cassidy tried to shift on the bed and winced at the pain in her shoulder and side. They ached. "Yeah. What happened?" Then the memory hit her. "I was shot. Cindy?"

Gabe's hand stilled for a brief moment then continued its soothing motion. "Yeah."

"Why?" Cassidy felt tears well up and tried to force them back. "What'd I do? I don't understand."

She felt Gabe wipe away the tear that trickled down past her temple.

"Ah, Cass, don't cry, love. She was just jealous of your relationship with the father she never got to know."

She sniffed and changed the subject. "Where's Alexis? Is she okay?"

"Marguerite has her. She's fine. Your parents are here and are very worried about you. Let me just go tell them you're awake and okay."

"All right."

The door opened and the nurse stepped in. "Ms. McKnight. So glad to see you're awake. Are you ready to move to your own room now?"

Cassidy blinked sleepily. "Sure."

Gabe got the room number then bent down and pressed another kiss against Cassidy's forehead. He headed for the door. "I'll let them know where to find you."

"Thanks," she mumbled. Sleep began to overtake her once again and she closed her eyes as the hospital orderly transported her from the recovery area to a private room on the third floor.

April 22
Saturday morning

She must have dozed off again because when she opened her eyes she could see sun peeking up over the horizon— and smell flowers. Lots of flowers. She shifted to get a better look and pain lanced through her whole left side.

She froze and eased back against the pillow, waiting for the throbbing to subside. The door opened and Amy stepped in. "Hey there." Without waiting for Cassidy to answer, she looked behind her and announced, "She's awake."

Apparently that was the cue. Amy stepped in first, followed by Cassidy's parents. Gabe popped his head in and said, "I've got a phone call, but I'll be back." He winked and Cassidy smiled at the warmth that flooded her. He loved her, he just didn't know it yet. Or maybe he did.

"Finally," her mother exclaimed, "she's awake."

"Hi, Mom." Cassidy lifted her cheek for her mother to kiss.

"Don't you 'Hi, Mom' me, young lady. I can't believe you're in the hospital because you were shot."

Cassidy didn't know whether to grimace or laugh. Surely laughing would hurt more. "That makes two of us, Mom."

"Hey, darling." Her father shifted, awkward and unsure in Cassidy's presence.

She struggled with the desire to hold a grudge and the desire to forgive. She'd almost died. What would her father have done if she'd died without making things right between them? He would have lived the rest of his life feeling regret and sorrow. Did she want to take a chance on that happening?

She settled for a slight smile. "Hi, Dad."

Relief relaxed his tight features and Cassidy realized she'd have to forgive the man. She loved him too much not to. Just like Jesus had loved her enough to die for her. She wouldn't forget, obviously, but she could start with the choice to forgive. "I love you, Dad."

Tears flooded the man's eyes.

"Are you and Mom…?" She trailed off, the question hard to ask.

He smiled down at her and gave a small nod. "We're going to be okay."

The door swung open again and Senator and Cecelia Graham entered. The senator stood awkwardly inside the door while Cecelia came over to Cassidy's side and took her hand. "Cassidy, darling, you gave us quite a fright."

"Mother, what are *you* doing here?"

The ire in Amy's voice surprised Cassidy. She knew Amy and her mother didn't get along, but she'd never seen Amy so openly hostile toward the woman. Especially since she'd become a Christian. Cecelia frowned at Amy but spoke to Cassidy. "The doctor said it was a close call. You're fortunate."

"Fortune didn't have anything to do with it, but thank you."

"Now that I know you're all right, I'm going to visit my friend's son again, but if there's anything I can do, anything at all, you just let me know, okay?"

Cassidy's mother stepped forward and gave Cecelia a hug. "Thank you so much, Cecelia."

Amy spoke up. "Yes, it's so wonderful how our families have just been such great friends all these years, isn't it?"

Cecelia frowned at her daughter and everyone else looked a little taken aback at Amy's tone. Cassidy decided something else was going on between mother and daughter but didn't have the energy to try to figure it out now. She'd ask Amy about it when they were alone.

After Cecelia left, Amy grimaced. "Sorry. You didn't need that."

"You still mad at your mother?"

Amy's lips tightened. "She just makes me crazy. I'll check in on Alexis and be back to see you before too long. Take care."

Then her parents were bidding her goodbye and she gave her father an extra-long—extremely gentle—hug. He had tears in his eyes when he pulled back. "I'm glad God wasn't finished with you yet, honey."

She studied his eyes. Total sincerity. He'd made mistakes in the past, but he was a forgiven child of God now. Cassidy felt her throat close up with emotion and had to clear it to speak. "Me, too, Dad. God's not finished with you, either."

He nodded.

Christina took his hand. "Come on, Jonathan. Obviously, everyone is giving credit to God for Cassidy's survival, so I guess I need to reconsider Him. After all, when Cassidy was lying on the floor bleeding to death, I did something I hadn't done in a really long time. I prayed. Maybe He was listening."

Jonathan's eyes shot wide-open and a grin split his lips. Cassidy's heart went wild with joy. Her parents left and she lay there feeling happy and dizzy. She didn't think it was all due to the drugs flooding her system. She slid into a light doze thanking God for His goodness—and the invention of painkillers.

Twelve hours later, Gabe sat in the hospital cafeteria contemplating the events of the last two days. Craig called and wanted to meet with him, so Gabe told him to come to the cafeteria. He'd traded shifts with another doctor so that he could be here with Cassidy. Right now her parents were visiting so she had company to keep her occupied until he could get back up there to check on her. Gabe swallowed the last of his coffee and tried to decide if he wanted another cup or not.

"Hey there, buddy. How's it going?" Craig dropped into the chair opposite Gabe and slapped a file folder on the table between them.

"Okay, I guess. What you got?"

"Well, DNA proves one part of Cindy Patterson's story."

"The black clothes."

Craig pushed the folder over to Gabe. "These are e-mails we pulled from her laptop. She was staying in a hotel on the west side of town. We ran her phone records, too, made and received calls from the hotel phone. No evidence of a cell phone." He pointed to several numbers that had been highlighted in yellow. "See these numbers here? It took us all night, but we've figured out that they're all from clone phones and only short quick calls to keep the legitimate subscriber from realizing someone has hacked into his cell. We checked all of them. Somebody was real smart. And I'd stake my pension on that somebody being Cindy's contact."

Gabe sighed, "Yeah, but who? This somebody would have to know how to hack into a cell-phone company's records." Frustration was giving him a headache. "Brian is the logical one, but there's no connection between him and Cindy. Her job was to simply get rid of Cassidy and report in to the number and e-mail address provided by her contact. No trails anywhere."

"Well, one trail." Craig flipped to the back of the folder and pulled out four sheets of paper. "Letters from a post-office box."

"Who's it registered to?"

"I'm waiting on that phone call. I've also got our department professionals working overtime to see where these e-mails came from. They're tracking the IP addresses. Unfortunately, they're well covered up and routed through several different computers. It's a waiting game right now."

Gabe sighed. "So our best hope is the e-mails or the letters."

"That would be it."

Gabe curled one hand into a fist and resisted pounding it on the table. He leaned forward, tension radiating from him. "Craig, we've got to find this person fast. Something just doesn't add up. Cassidy's got personal bodyguards, a state-of-the-art home alarm system that someone bypassed. She had extremely tight security last night at the benefit and Cindy was able to sneak a gun in and shoot her. How? What happened to the metal detectors? How did they fail? Unless…" Gabe trailed off, not liking where his thoughts were taking him.

"She didn't sneak it in," Craig finished the sentence for him.

Gabe went still then breathed, "It was planted."

"An inside job," Craig said.

"Yeah." Gabe blew out a breath. "But who would benefit from it? At first I thought it was the whole custody thing with Alexis. But that's been resolved. We've got Cindy, and while I'm not sure I buy the fact that she doesn't know who hired her, she's not talking."

Craig nodded his agreement. "So who else would benefit from Cassidy's death?" His cell phone rang and he pulled it off the clip to bark into it, "Monahan." He listened for a few moments. "Okay, thanks."

Craig snapped the phone shut. He looked at Gabe and said, "The post-office box is registered to a woman by the name of Juanita Morales."

Recognition zinged through him. "Juanita Morales. Why does that name sound familiar?" Gabe thought; realization dawned. He snapped his fingers. "Rafael's *sister?* Why would a woman who's been missing for over thirty years have a post-office box here in town and be sending letters to the woman who tried to shoot Cassidy? How would she even *know* about Cassidy and why would this woman want Cassidy dead?"

Craig shook his head. "I'm confused, man." His phone chirped again. Once again, he listened; this time his eyebrows shot up into his hairline. He hung up and looked at Gabe, consternation written on his handsome features. "You're not going to believe this."

"What now?"

"Those e-mails came from a computer in Senator Graham's house."

Gabe blew out a shocked breath. Craig was right. He didn't believe it. "Amy? It's a setup. It has to be."

"Think about it, Gabe. Amy is Cassidy's best friend. You just said it had to be an inside job. Who else would have access to all of Cassidy's information…and her home-alarm code? And she's good on a computer."

Gabe just had another thought. "Oh, man. And Amy was there fixing up Alexis's room while Cassidy was in Brazil, remember? She could have been the one to leave the attic window open for Rafael." Gabe shuddered. "And she was visiting Cassidy before the dinner. She could have easily snuck the gun in, then told Cindy where to find it." This would shatter Cassidy. Gabe questioned, "But why? What's her motive?"

"Jealousy?" Craig asked.

"Of what? She has everything Cassidy has."

"Except Cassidy's father beat out Amy's father in the bid for the ambassadorial position. If he were gone or incapacitated with grief, the senator just might move up without a problem."

Gabe let out a tense breath. "Well, whatever the motive, we've got to find Amy. Now."

TWENTY-ONE

Cassidy dozed in and out, thanks to the pain medicine. So when she heard the squeak of the door, she didn't bother to open her eyes. Her head felt heavy and her mouth dry. She wanted water but felt too fuzzy to try to reach for the cup on the tray beside the bed. Maybe her visitor would get it for her. It was probably Gabe.

She rolled her head toward the door and opened her eyes. Nope, not Gabe. She hid her disappointment, smiled and said, "Hi."

"Hello, Cassidy."

"Did you forget something?"

"No, I just had some unfinished business to take care of. I told you I'd be back."

Confusion made her frown. "Sorry, I'm a little fuzzy right now. What kind of business?" She gave a weak laugh.

The person moved closer and around the side of the bed to the IV pole. A syringe appeared in the well-manicured hand.

Cassidy struggled to think. "What are you doing?"

"Something that has to be done, unfortunately. I'm being kind, though." The hand waved the syringe of fluid. "You won't feel a thing. Potassium is a quick-acting little thing."

The syringe moved toward the part of the IV where medication was injected. A lovely little invention that saved the patient from having to be stuck with a needle every time medication was needed. However, it made it awfully easy to inject a fatal amount of potassium that would go straight to the heart.

Awareness exploded in Cassidy's brain, but she felt so sluggish she knew it would be impossible to fight. The needle entered the IV. She croaked, "Tell me why. You owe me that at least." The figure paused and glanced down at Cassidy.

"Yes, Mother, you owe her that." Amy stood in the doorway, tears trembling on her long lashes. Two spots of color stood out on her otherwise ashen cheeks. Gabe and Craig pushed in after her. Gabe started toward Cassidy, fear written all over his pale face.

Cecelia Graham didn't bother to lower the syringe, but a flicker of fear crossed her face before hardening back into a stony mask of determination. "I thought you would be busy a little longer."

Gabe's eyes flitted between the syringe and Cassidy.

Cassidy felt almost numb. Between the drugs and her disbelief that a woman she loved, trusted and respected was trying to kill her, she was reeling.

Dizziness threatened, but she pushed it back and moved her left hand over her right to find what she needed. Never taking her eyes from Cecelia and her needle, Cassidy slipped her fingernail under the tape. She had a large-bore catheter due to the blood loss she'd endured. If Cecelia pushed that potassium in, Cassidy knew she'd be dead before she could blink.

Cecelia's scornful voice twisted Cassidy's heart into a

painful thing. Amy was devastated. Her mother was a murderer. Cassidy whispered again, "Why?"

"I think I know," Amy rasped. "I've done a little research over the last several days."

"Research?" Wariness crossed Cecelia's features.

Amy hissed, "Oh, yes, Mother. You see, I got so frustrated with you messing with my computer that I went to lock it with a password. Then just out of curiosity I started researching what you'd been doing on it."

Cassidy felt it hard to stay alert but she had to. She pulled some more of the tape, hoping she wasn't making any noise. Fortunately, Amy had her mother's full attention. Gabe shifted closer.

Amy went on, "You'd been accessing my e-mail. That's how you found Cassidy's home-alarm code to pass on to Rafael."

"Amy, you need to shut up now."

Gabe took over. "You knew Cassidy was going to Brazil to get Alexis. You knew which lawyer's office was handling the case, and you also knew Cassidy's father had something going on because he was paying out a large sum of money each month for years. We found the letters you, as Juanita Morales, wrote to Cindy."

Cecelia turned white at this announcement.

Amy sobbed a ragged breath and said, "I found out who you really are."

"What?" Cassidy whispered. "What are you saying?"

Amy choked back a sob.

Gabe said, "Amy found us in the cafeteria and shared a lot of information with us on the way up here. What she's saying is that she's a pretty good computer hacker. She found all kinds of interesting stuff on her computer, Mrs.

Graham. And your husband's. Everything Jonathan has done in the last six years since his appointment as ambassador to Brazil. Apparently, you're more skilled with computers than you wanted anyone to know."

Cassidy couldn't take it all in. "But why? Just tell me, why?"

Cecelia hissed between clenched teeth, "Because he stole that appointment from my husband. Jonathan had no right to take that job. When he did, it messed up everything. Everything that I've worked for years to achieve."

Cassidy shook her head and tried to clear it. She still didn't understand. Amy advanced toward the bed. She'd dammed up the tears, determined to finish presenting the evidence she'd gathered. "Don't you see, Cass? When your father took that position as ambassador, my mother knew his main focus would be human trafficking. And while she had absolutely no intention of ever setting foot in Brazil again, she had to have my father in that position."

"Why should she care?"

At this, Amy let the tears fall.

Gabe shifted closer to the bed and spoke again. "Because that's where the money comes from. And has for years. There is no old family money in a trust fund. When Amy's grandfather died, he was broke. This sent Cecelia into a panic. She had to find a way to keep the cash flow steady. So she contacted the one person she hadn't talked to in years. Rafael Juan Morales. Her brother."

"That's enough. You don't know what you're saying. You…" Stunned disbelief crowded Cecelia's features.

"No, let's finish it." Gabe kept his eyes on the syringe and knew whatever was in it couldn't be good. If he kept her talking, maybe he could figure out a way to get it out of her hand. He said, "Once you knew Jonathan was going to become ambassador, you had to find a way to get rid of him. Only it would be too obvious, not to mention difficult, if something were to happen to him personally."

Amy took over. "You were so involved in Dad's bid for that appointment, you had to make sure it couldn't come back to haunt you if something happened to Jonathan. So you set up Micah. Jonathan's pride and joy are his children and you used that."

"Micah?" Cassidy asked, confused.

Gabe sucked the air from the room. Amy hadn't mentioned Micah when she'd brought them the evidence against her mother. Amy continued, "Since my father is on the United States Senate Select Committee on Intelligence, he works with the Special Forces and all their missions. Micah let my father know that he was changing missions briefly. Mother had my father's password that enabled her to access top-secret information. She found out about this mission Micah would be going on and alerted the drug lord." Amy glared at her mother through her tears.

"I can't believe you'd betray me like this," Cecelia spat.

"You had twelve men killed, Mother. A little boy died because of your interference in that operation. An operation you weren't even supposed to be aware of. The only one to survive was Gabe. All because Micah found out about your past. Yeah, I found that e-mail, too. After I found that, it all clicked into place."

Cassidy turned to Amy. "What did Micah find out?"

Cecelia's thin lips twisted into a disgusted curl. "Micah was working on something in Brazil and saw my missing person's picture posted on a wall in a police department.

It nagged at him until he realized who it reminded him of. He sent an e-mail with the wanted poster attached to our home, asking if it was me. Fortunately, I came across it first. If my husband…" She gave a shudder then said mockingly, "Poor little Juanita Morales, born to Brazilian trash. After years on the street selling myself, compliments of my brother, I got out. Snuck into the United States, changed my name, worked my fingers to the bone for an education, watched how the rich lived, talked, walked. And married a senator. If my past ever got out, I was finished. My husband would be dead in the political waters. So I set everything up to get rid of my problem. Micah died on the mission. Unfortunately that didn't distract Jonathan. After Rafael failed in Brazil," she sneered, "I needed something on the man. He was costing me money every day. Finally, my search paid off. An illegitimate child. Unfortunately, just revealing that he had a child from an affair wouldn't faze anyone these days. I had to go a step further. Once I found the money trail, contacting Cindy was simple. Finding out she was a bitter young lady who wanted revenge on the father that dumped her mother and never claimed her as his daughter was just pure luck."

"You're evil," Amy whispered with disbelief.

Craig stepped up and said, "You need to move away from Cassidy, Mrs. Graham." His gaze went to the needle in the IV.

Cecelia shrieked, "Get out! All of you, or I push this potassium in."

For the first time in his life, Gabe thought he would faint. *Sweet Jesus, please…*

Craig wheedled, "Mrs. Graham, you know we can't leave. There's no reason to kill Cassidy now. You're going to be arrested no matter what at this point, so why not give it up peacefully and we'll talk with your lawyer."

Cassidy pulled her hand out from under the covers. The end of the IV dangled from her fingers, but the hole in her arm bled in a thick steady stream.

"Could someone get me a Band-Aid, please?" she asked.

Cecelia screeched and lunged toward Cassidy, the syringe held to stab her. Cassidy ducked, Gabe swiped his foot across the woman's path. Cecelia let out another yell as she went down to the floor, spread-eagle. Craig stepped on the hand that still clutched the poison.

"Ow! You're hurting my hand." Cecelia wept uncontrollably, her sophisticated veneer stripped clean. Amy leaned against the wall, silent tears streaming down her cheeks.

As Craig led the deranged woman from the hospital room, Amy followed with a tearful glance over her shoulder at Cassidy. Gabe clamped a hand over the hole in the crook of her elbow and reached for the tissue box beside the bed.

It would do until he could get a sterile bandage. He wadded it up and placed it over the wound to put pressure on the wound. He looked down at the woman he loved and demanded, "Will you marry me, please? I think it's the only way I'm going to be able to keep you out of trouble."

Cassidy blinked and Gabe could see the yes dancing on her lips.

"I...I—" She stopped.

Gabe frowned. "I know, I know. I'm sorry. You deserve flowers, a seven-course meal, the works, but I almost lost you, Cass. I don't want to spend another minute away from you."

Cassidy gulped and blurted out, "I want to know what you know about Micah—and I want to know now."

Gabe froze. "What do you mean?"

Cassidy narrowed her eyes at him. "Micah was on your last mission. And there was a lot more involved than what's been told. I want to know. I have to know. And his body's never been found. Is he still alive?"

Gabe felt his entire soul go cold.

"Cassidy, the details are classified information. You know he's dead. Here, bend your arm to hold the tissues in place." She obeyed absently, her attention focused on him. Gabe got up to wash his hands while he racked his brains as to what to say to her. He watched the liquid swirl in the sink then go down the drain. He thought it ironically symbolized his relationship with Cassidy. If he told her, he broke a confidence he swore to uphold; if he didn't tell her… How much could he reveal without compromising his promise?

"You heard Amy. Tell me the rest of it, please."

Gabe sat on the edge of the bed and took her hand. "Cassidy, I love you, I just can't break an oath. If I tell you about Micah, I'll be betraying my country, the men still out there."

She pulled her hand away and crossed her arms. "No, Gabe, if you don't tell me, you'll be betraying the woman you love."

He felt her emotional withdrawal as keenly as her physical. "Cass, I can't."

She searched his face for a few tense seconds. "Then I need you to leave."

No, not this. His worst fear materializing. "Cass, come on. You know how things work in Special Forces. You know I have things that I can't talk about. That's one of them."

Tears dripped onto her cheeks. "Then I guess we have nothing more to say to each other. Because as long as you know something about Micah and won't tell me—" she gave a sad shrug "—then I can't be with you. I'd always wonder, it would always be there between us, and as much as I love you, I can't live like that."

Gabe honestly thought he could hear his heart split down the middle. She'd just admitted she loved him—and kicked him out of her life all in the same paragraph.

"If I could tell you, I would. But I made a promise and I have to keep it—just like you had to keep your promise to Kara." Doubt flickered in her eyes at that statement. He had her there.

Resolution swept the doubt away. "This is different, Gabe. This is between you and me." Tears shimmered in her green eyes, but she held them back. "I just want to know what happened to my brother."

"Do you really want to know that for sure?"

She nodded.

Gabe sighed and dropped his head. "All I can tell you is that it's my fault that he was on that mission. I pushed him into it. He didn't want to be there. Said that if he was on that mission, it could jeopardize whatever else he was working on. That's all I can tell you." He looked back down, held that position for about a minute then looked back up. "I have to get permission to talk to you about this. I can't just…Cass, I can't."

Admiration for his integrity warred with frustration at his refusal to talk. She finally said, "What do you mean, you pushed him into it? Gabe? You? It's your fault he died?" Tears dripped down her chin. Emotions swirled. She didn't know anything and needed some space, time to think. "Fine. You go get permission from whomever you have to, but don't come back until you do."

Gabe wanted to scream. *God, she's supposed to understand this. Please, make her understand.* Being a part of a SEAL team had been his job, his life. There was no way he would jeopardize anyone by saying something he'd been sworn to keep quiet about. And he still wouldn't. Not even if it meant losing the woman he loved.

TWENTY-TWO

May 20

Cassidy hadn't heard from Gabe in over four weeks. The last time she'd seen him had been the day after she'd been shot. Today was May twentieth and as she walked through the mansion's gardens before heading for her car, she gave thanks for her parents' reconciliation and the fact that there hadn't been much political fallout from Cindy's announcement regarding her parentage.

Her father had gone on with business as usual, apologized publicly for embarrassing himself and his family, but most of all for the pain Cindy had grown up with.

Cindy.

A complex young woman who truly regretted she'd allowed herself to be taken over with anger and bitterness. She'd been charged with two counts of attempted murder.

Cindy was in deep trouble, but Cassidy had forgiven her and visited her in jail. Maybe soon she'd be ready to hear about a heavenly father who forgave and loved unconditionally.

A glance at her watch told her that her weekly Bible-study group would be arriving in a couple of hours. She had come to her parents' house to drop off Alexis. Now she would go home, put together a snack for the ladies and do her best to put Gabriel Sinclair out of her mind.

Gabe. Was he as miserable as she? Probably. One thing she didn't doubt was that he really cared for her. But Micah would always be between them. Eventually, she'd come to resent him. And she wasn't doing that to either of them.

The pain that accompanied thoughts of Gabe zinged its way through her heart. By the time she reached her house, she didn't remember the drive home. She needed to snap out of it. Her wound only twinged as she pulled into the garage. It was healing nicely.

She climbed out of her car and opened the door that led to the kitchen. Then she pushed the button to lower the garage door. Maybe one day she'd be able to shut it before she got out of her vehicle.

Twenty minutes later she was ready for her guests. Cassidy had volunteered her living room this week. It seemed to be a good way to start getting things back to normal.

Someone knocked on her front door, then called, "Cass, you here?"

"Amy!" Cassidy hurried to greet her friend with a bear hug. This was the first time she'd seen her friend since the episode in the hospital. "You came." Cassidy frowned. "You've lost weight."

"Food isn't high on my list of priorities these days." Tears, never far from the surface for Amy, rose fast, but she managed to blink them back before they fell.

Cassidy gave her another squeeze, then ordered, "You get the ice cream. I'll pull out all the goodies to go with it. The bananas are there on the counter ready to be sliced."

Amy focused on slicing the banana. Cassidy asked her, "So, how's it going?"

"My mother's in jail. It's not going too well."

Cassidy didn't take offense. Her friend was hurting—bad.

Amy slapped the knife down on the counter. "This was a bad idea. I'm sorry. Maybe I'd just better go."

"No! Please, Amy, just give it a try. You're my best friend in the whole world. You helped save my life."

Amy picked the knife up again. This time she managed to slice the whole banana and put it into a bowl. "Well, I suppose it was the least I could do at the time considering it was my mother who…"

Cassidy sighed and placed her hands on her friend's shoulders, forcing her to turn and face her. "Amy, look. You are not responsible for your mother's actions any more than I'm responsible for my father's."

"Your father didn't kill anyone."

"No, but he still could have destroyed his family. Your mother made her choices, Amy. Horrible ones. But you're a different person. You can make right choices that are honorable and decent. Pity parties aren't fun. I know. I used to have them all the time. I'm not saying you shouldn't grieve over the loss of your mother and your family as you know it, I'm just saying don't let it destroy you and all the good you have in you—and all the good you can do for other people."

Tears slid down Amy's cheeks and Cassidy tore off a paper towel to mop them up for her. Amy sucked in a deep breath and grabbed the chocolate syrup. "So," she began as she twisted the top off the jar, "have you heard from Gabe?"

Cassidy winced. But if this topic would take Amy's mind off her mother… "No."

"And you haven't called him?"

"Uh-uh."

"Well, don't overwhelm me with details," Amy said dryly.

Deciding this called for the straight stuff, Cassidy squeezed the bottle to drizzle the chocolate into the spoon. She stuck it in her mouth, swallowed and sighed. "I'm sorry. It just hurts. He knew all along what happened to Micah but didn't breathe a word. He was the one who pushed Micah into that mission. That—" she jabbed the spoon under the water faucet to rinse it off and then let it clunk into the sink "—makes me mad. Really, really mad."

"Yes, I guess that would do it."

"So—" Cassidy decided to change the subject "—you ready for our Bible study? I heard someone pull up outside."

The doorbell rang.

Cassidy left the kitchen to go answer the door. "Hey, guys, come in. Go on into the kitchen and make yourselves a sundae, then come into the living area." Four young women single filed through the door and on into Cassidy's kitchen. Cassidy went into the den where Amy sat working on her sundae.

Everyone giggled and talked while they scarfed down the sundaes, then after opening with prayer, Marcie pulled out a small book with her notes in it. "Okay, since Cassidy was so gracious to let us use her place, I planned the devotional. I was reading in Solomon about how we deserve the best God has to offer—especially when it comes to relationships. In Solomon, the bridegroom went after his lady, probably a poor peasant girl. When Solomon approached her as her king, she was intimidated and ran from him. Unwilling to give up, Solomon disguised himself as a shepherd. Once she fell in love with him, he revealed himself to her and loved her with a love that said he would be right beside her and they would survive the toughest times. And rejoice together in the happy times. He showered her with gifts and compliments. He pursued her with a love that every woman deserves."

Cassidy nodded even though her heart pinched with fear that she and Gabe would never be able to work things out. She swallowed hard, but broke in to say, "I see just what you're getting at, Marcie. God loves us like that. He pursues us relentlessly. He carries us through the tough times. He showers us with blessings and gifts in our lives. He tells us how wonderful we are and how He knew us and had a plan for us when we were knit together in our mother's womb. And He meets us on our own turf where we are."

Amy blinked back tears and Cassidy reached out to wrap her hand around Amy's and squeeze it.

Marcie nodded and said, "That sounds like a first-rate love if you ask me. He chases us down to get our attention, our focus on Him."

Cassidy thought about something. "His love letter," she burst out. She gripped her Bible and held it up. "It's in here. All we have to do is read it to see how much He loves us."

Cassidy thought about Kara, who'd relentlessly, over the years, sought a relationship with her sister, Susan. And Susan, who'd refused to read her sister's letters. They were right there all the time, expressing love and acceptance. All she'd had to do was pick them up, open them and read them. Just like God's Word; His love letter to his people.

Two women, Amy and Susan. Both had had the opportunity to reach out and grab love with both hands. Susan had rejected it, choosing to wallow in her resentment and anger. Amy, however, had cried out to God to rescue her. And He did.

So where did that leave her and Gabe? He certainly wasn't pursuing her. She hadn't even heard from him in four weeks! *I need to forgive him, don't I, Lord?* But was there really anything to forgive? Had Gabe actually done anything wrong? Cassidy flinched at the thought. Gabe knew she needed to know about her brother and yet he hadn't told her.

But he'd taken an oath to protect his country and keep confidential what was confidential. Cassidy grudgingly admitted she had to respect that even though she couldn't live with it on a day-to-day basis.

He'd also professed to love her and yet had willingly walked away without a fight.

Solomon had been willing to do whatever it took to win his lady's hand. Would Gabe be willing to do the same?

May 22
First thing Monday morning

Gabe stepped out of his ex-boss's office and squinted against the bright summer sunlight. His heart felt lighter than it had in four weeks. Since Cassidy told him to get out of her life. Ever since then, Gabe had been fighting confidentiality, orders to stay quiet and the desire to bash several high-ranking heads together.

Instead, he'd kept his cool and persevered. And finally got the answer he wanted. Basically, he'd procured permission to tell Cassidy the bare essentials about the mission and her brother's involvement.

But she had to promise to keep it confidential and if she said anything, she could be arrested for treason. As long as

Gabe could get her to agree to this, he could tell her. This was highly unusual and Gabe had pulled more strings and called in more favors than he ever had in his life. But he'd done it.

Not only was he sticking his neck out by sharing classified information with her, his ex-boss's neck was also on the line. But Gabe knew if Cassidy made this promise, nothing would drag the words from her lips. She would carry them to her grave.

And he could ask her to marry him. Again.

Plus, he missed the munchkin, Alexis. But he'd honored Cassidy's request to stay away from her. Now he could find the stubborn woman, tell her about her brother and ask her to marry him.

But first, he had one stop to make.

Cassidy decided she had just lived through the longest weekend of her life. She'd prayed and paced, paced and prayed. Poor Alexis just watched her with a bemused expression then went back to her toys. If it hadn't been for the presence of the child these past few weeks, but more specifically, these past two days, she would have given up and gone certifiable.

Cassidy had come to the conclusion that quite possibly Gabe had done nothing wrong—other than not call her over the last four weeks. Of course, she had told him to get out of her life. He was an honorable man and he'd honored her request.

He'd also honored his vow to keep confidential what he'd been ordered to keep confidential.

So, how could she hold that against him?

She couldn't.

Call Gabe.

"Okay, Lord, I want to. But how can I? Can I love him like he deserves without coming to resent him for his silence?"

All things work together for the good of those who love Him.

"What good is going to come out of this? I mean, I believe You, I just don't see it… Don't get me wrong, I know You see the big picture, but…"

Forgive him.

"Forgive him? I've already done that."

Forgive him.

Cassidy sat for a brief moment as she considered this. She'd forgiven Gabe, hadn't she? Well, of course she had. Yes, she'd come to terms with the fact that he couldn't tell her about her brother. But then again, would she still be so turned inside out about his refusal to discuss a highly confidential case if she'd forgiven him and accepted the situation?

Probably not.

The doorbell rang and Cassidy jumped. Grumbling, she wondered who'd made it through front-gate security. Mentally, she ran down the names on her list that didn't require a call to let her know they were coming.

She peeked out the peephole.

And nearly passed out.

She opened the door and blurted, "What are you doing here?" Ouch, that came out wrong.

Before she could apologize, Gabe pulled his hands from behind his back and thrust a single rose under her nose. He said, "I've missed you, Cass."

"Well, you have a funny way of showing it." No, no, this was not going right at all. "I'm sorry. Let me start over." Deep breath. She took the rose, and its sweet fragrance gave her heart a lift. "It's beautiful, thank you. I'll just put this in water."

Gabe followed her into the kitchen. His intense dark gaze scrutinized her every movement, making her nerves jump up and down under her skin. She fumbled with the flower and finally got it into a vase and set it in the windowsill. Absently, she stroked a finger down a petal.

Cassidy took a fortifying breath and turned to face Gabe only to find her nose buried in his chest. Blood hummed through her veins. Goose bumps danced along her arms, the little hairs on her skin standing straight up. Gabe reached up and traced a finger down her cheek. "It can't compare to you."

She let out a shaky laugh. "Okay, Gabe. What's going on?"

"Like I said. I've missed you." He stepped back and Cassidy took advantage of the moment to scoot around him.

"Come on into the den."

Gabe's smile let her know he knew exactly how he was affecting her, but he willingly followed her into the den area and plopped down on the couch.

Little feet pattered down the hall.

"Alexis is awake." Cassidy smiled. "I can call Amy to keep her if you want me to."

"No, let me see her."

Alexis toddled into the den and spotted Gabe. She screeched to a halt and her jaw dropped. Her blue eyes lightened and she clasped her pudgy hands in front of her chest.

"Gabe!" she shrieked. Sheer joy propelled her little body torpedo style into Gabe's lap. Little arms wrapped themselves around his neck and squeezed.

Cassidy spotted the tears swimming in his eyes right before Gabe buried his face in the child's sleep-mussed curls. "Hey, munchkin. I've missed you."

"Yep." She nodded. "Missed you. Now, kiss!"

Laughter shook his shoulders as he bent down to plant a smacking kiss on her rosy cheek.

Cassidy choked back her own tears. Even if things didn't work out between Gabe and her, there was no way she could keep Alexis from him if he wanted to see her. They had developed a special bond.

Gabe lifted his eyes and the love she saw there threatened to undo her. He'd torn down all the walls and exposed his soul for her to see. She swallowed hard. *Help me, Lord.*

Gabe set Alexis on the floor after giving her another kiss on the top of her head. "Go play, okay?"

"You play with me?" She batted her baby blues and he couldn't stop the love that surged.

"Sure, I'll play with you after I talk to Cassidy, okay?"

"Nope. Now."

Cassidy gave a choking sound and Gabe grinned. "Gee, you're already taking after your new mama, aren't you?"

"Yep."

"Okay, munchkin, go get a toy and we'll play."

"Yippee!" She scooted down the hall and Gabe turned to Cassidy. His heart constricted at the look on her face. A mixture of fear, hurt, anticipation and resignation.

"Cass, come here."

Cassidy shook her head. "I can't, Gabe."

"We don't have a lot of time. Alexis'll be back in a second and I need to tell you some things."

"Micah," she breathed.

Gabe ran a hand over the back of his neck and nodded. "Yeah, he's one of them."

Confusion and hope ran across her features. "But I thought… No. I mean, you can't." This time she scooted closer to Gabe and placed her hand over his. "And I think I understand. I mean, I don't like it, that's for sure. But I've come to understand why you can't say anything."

"Cass…" he started to say. When she placed warm fingers over his lips and shushed him, he gulped. "Gabe, I've grown up a lot in the last several years, God has been so faithful and taught me some incredible things." She grimaced. "And not all of those things have been fun to learn. But one thing about God is that if you listen with an open heart, even to the things that you might not want to hear, then you'll come to realize that God's way is best after all. I can choose to accept that—or not."

Her slender fingers squeezed around his. "I guess what I'm trying to say is that it's okay. It's all right that you can't tell me about Micah. I understand that you took an oath, you made a promise that you would keep certain information confidential." She closed her eyes and leaned her head against his forehead. "And I have to respect that. I can't ask you to compromise your integrity."

"Ah, Cass." He sighed. "You take my breath away, you know that?"

"Well—" she brushed a tear off her cheek "—that's what I wanted to say. I guess it's your turn."

Gabe stood, paced. He shoved his hands in his pockets and said, "I can tell you the rest of the story about Micah now."

Cassidy blinked. "How?" she breathed.

"During those four weeks that you didn't hear from me, I was busy. I knew I couldn't approach you again until I could tell you everything. It wasn't easy, but I got clearance from the powers that be."

Hope and fear flickered through her eyes. She jumped up. "I've got to check on Alexis."

"Cass…" he called, but she kept going toward the back of the house.

Cassidy moved to the back room, where she found Alexis playing in her closet. Apparently the child had gotten distracted when she came to pick out a toy. Now the toys surrounded her and she made barking noises as she ran the stuffed animals around in circles.

Alexis was fine. And content. For the moment. Cassidy had no excuse to avoid Gabe; she had to go back out there and listen to him tell his story. The one that she'd wanted to know for the last two years but now wasn't sure she could handle hearing about. The one he'd gotten clearance from his superiors to tell her.

He'd actually done it. All this time she'd fretted because he hadn't called, he'd been clearing the way to tell her about Micah. *Oh, God, please give me strength.*

Cassidy put a Christian DVD in the TV/DVD combo on the dresser and pressed play. Squaring her shoulders, she took a deep breath and walked back down the hall to find Gabe building a fire.

"Uh, Gabe, it's eighty degrees outside."

Startled, he jumped and turned to offer her a sheepish grin. "I know. I'll help you pay your next power bill. I turned the air-conditioning down a few notches."

Cassidy laughed. "I'm not worried about the power bill, but Alexis will freeze. This is a familiar scenario. You like fires, don't you?"

Cassidy walked over and sat back down on the couch. Gabe placed the poker back in the stand and joined her. She said, "Okay, I'm ready to hear it. Or at least I think I am." She looked over at him. "Am I?"

A slight smile curved his lips but quickly faded. "Probably about as ready as I am to tell it."

Cassidy watched him shift into a more comfortable position then pat the cushion next to him. She scooted over and he curled his arm around her shoulders. After a brief hesitation, she folded into his side and waited.

"Micah was a great guy, Cass. The best. When we both joined the SEALs, we ended up on different teams. So, I hadn't seen him in forever then ran into him about five years ago during a practice mission. He told me he was working on something major but couldn't tell me what. He was worried though, I could see it."

Cassidy silently prayed while Gabe told the story.

"A lot of things happened during that year. Sometimes a mission is quick and dirty. Other times it takes a long time to go down. Micah was working on a lengthy undercover project." Cassidy heard Alexis laughing. The video had caught her attention.

"Anyway," Gabe went on, "we had this one mission two years ago. It had to do with a drug lord. We were supposed to do our job, get the kid out and be on our way."

She shivered. She remembered Amy's comment from the hospital. "That's the child Amy mentioned. The one who died."

"Yeah." He cleared his throat. "I…pulled Micah away from the job he was on by threatening to pull rank."

"What? Why?"

"I needed him. He was the best, and that little boy there

needed the best. I had to—" he broke off, his Adam's apple bobbing convulsively.

"Oh, Gabe…"

"So we got there, our plan established. Twelve men. I'm number thirteen. The man in charge of the mission and the team. The plan was clicking along, things going exactly as they were supposed to, then all of a sudden I hear Micah in my earpiece telling me something felt wrong. I trusted his intuition and ordered the men out immediately."

Cassidy squeezed his hand harder. She wanted to tell him to stop, she couldn't bear it, but she couldn't force the words past the lump in her throat.

"Then the explosion happened. The place just…" He coughed, emotion choking him up. "Sorry, this is…I've only told this story once. Right after it happened."

"It's okay, Gabe. You don't—" She stopped. Could she tell him he didn't have to go on?

"Shh." He stilled the words on her lips. "Let me finish it. After the explosion, they were gone. Good men. Family men who wanted to serve their country the best way they could. Gone."

Cassidy couldn't help the sob that escaped. "I'm sorry." She used the edge of the blanket to mop up the tears and struggled to get herself under control. "I knew he was on the mission with you and that he was killed in that explosion. But why all the secrecy?"

"Cass."

She settled back. "I'm sorry. It's just so unfair."

"That's not the end of it, Cass."

She stilled.

"What I'm about to tell you can go no further. I have permission to tell you the next part, but with orders to inform you that if you repeat it, which I know you won't, but if you do, you could put other SEALs in danger. You see, the mission's still not over. And if you say anything or do anything with this information, you and I, both of us, will be arrested for treason. I know you won't say a word," he reemphasized his trust in her, "but I have to be able to say that I informed you of this."

Cassidy gasped. "Then don't tell me."

He pulled her in front of him and looked her straight in the eye. "Can you live with not knowing? Can you look at me every day of our lives and not long to ask me?"

She held herself rigid then slumped and whispered, "Probably not."

He squeezed her fingers gently. "I couldn't live with you without you knowing the whole truth. It would eat me alive, day after day."

"Okay," she whispered, "go ahead."

"When I couldn't raise anyone on the radio, I started to move down the hill to go after the men. But before I could turn to grab my pack, a gun barrel jabbed me in the ear."

Cassidy gasped.

Gabe shuddered. "I knew I was a dead man. But before he was going to shoot me, he was going to get as much information as he could from me. When I wouldn't talk, he counted down from three. When he got to one, he pulled the trigger."

Cassidy couldn't breathe. "But…you…you're…"

"I had just finished a plea to God when that man pulled the trigger. It clicked on an empty chamber. We fought and unfortunately I got careless and he managed to stab me. Then a bullet came out of nowhere and killed him."

"God spared your life," she whispered in awe. In the

background she could still hear Alexis's TV and the little girl singing along with one of the silly songs. But Cassidy's attention was focused solely on the man beside her.

"Yes, He did. And He used Micah to do it."

She bolted upright. "Micah didn't die in that explosion?"

"No, he died after saving my hide. Some of his last words were orders for me to take care of you."

"But, how? What…"

"And he gave me orders that no one was to know that he was there. There was a traitor, who we now know to be Cecelia Graham, in our midst, and for some reason if anyone knew he was there, it would endanger other SEALs even though they weren't on that particular mission."

Gabe pinched the bridge of his nose. The memories still hurt, but for Cassidy he would face them. "After I gave him an oxygen mask and a whopping dose of antibiotics, I went to wait for rescue. But I passed out from my injuries and the next time I opened my eyes I was in the chopper. I tried to tell them Micah was still down there. But no one believed me. They thought I was delirious. By the time I could get anyone to listen to me, I'd already been in and out of surgery. And I was told the mission never happened. Micah McKnight was dead along with the others and I was never to speak of it again. And I haven't. Until now."

Cassidy sobbed, the pain of losing her brother fresh all over again. "Oh, Gabe."

"I pushed him to be there. He was the best for that kind of situation and I pulled rank to get him there. Then I let him die. I feel like I failed him, Cass. He saved my life and I just left him there to die." Gabe choked back tears of his own. "I was so afraid if you found out about this, you'd hate me forever, despise me for being the one to put Micah on the mission that got him killed."

Cassidy just cried harder.

Gabe hugged her, rocked her and let her cry. Did she hate him? Were his worst fears about to materialize?

She couldn't quit crying. But she had to. Finally, she was able to speak. "It wasn't your fault." Cassidy found she really did believe the words. It wasn't fair that her brother had died, but it wasn't Gabe's fault. He'd been wounded himself and by the time anyone would have listened to him, most likely Micah would have already been dead.

"Ah, Cass, thanks for saying that, but I'll always feel like I should have done more."

Cassidy said thoughtfully, "So you don't think Micah could possibly be alive?"

Gabe sighed and shut his eyes. "I just don't know. I don't see how and yet after an intense search, his body was never found. I just don't know."

Tears welled up in her eyes and she nodded, finally able to say goodbye to the brother she'd loved so much. "Okay, Gabe, okay."

"So, now you know."

Cassidy raised a hand and cupped his cheek. "Yes, now I know. And I don't hate you. I don't understand God all the time. If I did, I wouldn't need faith. So, I'm going to exercise my faith and trust that God had something good come from all of the horror. I may never know what it is, but I'm trusting He'll let me in on it one day in heaven. Of course, you and I wouldn't be together if you hadn't had to rescue me from the jungle, so…I guess I can actually see something good, right? I mean, I don't know why He

couldn't have just had you call me up and ask me out, but…
like I said, God works in ways we find strange but make
complete sense to him. I guess I won't complain, since he
sent you back into my life."

"You're amazing."

"And I'm in love with you. With the kind of love you
deserve. Not a silly schoolgirl crush," Cassidy said with
conviction.

Tears dripped from his eyes and mingled with hers and
he joined their lips together to seal the promise of the
future. A future based on their love for each other, and their
love for a powerful God who makes all things work together for the good of those who love Him. "I love you,
too," he whispered. "This is one mission I wouldn't have
missed for the world."

As Gabe's lips again moved sweetly over hers, she felt
a little warm body crawl in between them. She laughed
against his lips and he joined her in a chuckle as they
looked down to see Alexis, snuggling, right at home next
to the two of them.

Alexis saw them watching and grinned. "Brrr. Cold."

Gabe and Cassidy wrapped their arms around their
charge and squeezed. Alexis giggled and the game was on.
Gabe blew raspberries on the little tummy until they were
both breathless. Cassidy's cheeks hurt from the laughter.

Alexis's giggles died down and she reached up to grasp
Gabe's face in her small hands. She smacked a kiss on his
nose and said, "I love you, Gabe Daddy."

Cassidy gasped and teared up again. Gabe blinked
rapidly and pulled Alexis to his chest for a gentle hug. He
whispered, "I love you, too, little munchkin."

Alexis finally grew bored with the big people and wandered over to play with the blocks stacked on the other side of Cassidy. Gabe watched for a few minutes then looked up at Cassidy, unashamed of the tears on his rugged features. He smiled tenderly and Cassidy swiped at her own wet face. He crooked his finger, ran it down her cheek and said, "I could get used to this. I want to spend the rest of my life loving you. I thank God for bringing us together again. Will you marry me, Cassidy?"

Cassidy nodded and reached out to wrap her hand around his neck so she could pull his face closer. "You bet I'll marry you," she whispered. "Now, kiss."

He eagerly complied.

* * * * *

Dear Reader,

Time is such a precious commodity in this day and age. And out of all the books on the shelf, you chose to spend your time reading this one. I'd like to offer a deep-felt thank-you.

I've often been asked, "How do you come up with your ideas?" I came by the idea for this book while waiting in the Department of Motor Vehicles. I kept thinking, "What a jungle. I'm trapped in a maze—I'll never get out of here!" And so the character Cassidy McKnight came alive in my mind as a way to pass the time. I wrote the first chapter before my number was called. And, yes, I did eventually find my way out of the DMV, although I did worry about Cassidy a few times in the writing of her story.

My sincere desire as a writer is to let God's love shine from the pages of each and every story that I write. Getting kidnapped in the jungle is quite an adventure that probably won't happen to you in your everyday life. (Thank goodness!) That's not to say, however, that we don't sometimes find ourselves trapped in certain circumstances of our lives, desperately looking for a way out. I pray that you will lean on God and trust Him to be faithful to deliver you.

I would also love to hear your feedback on the story. You can e-mail me at lynetteeason@lynetteeason.com. Feel free to visit me online at www.lynetteeason.com. I love to discuss every aspect of writing with anyone who'll listen.

Again thanks so much!

Blessings,

Lynette Eason

QUESTIONS FOR DISCUSSION

1. Cassidy learns that her missionary friends have been murdered, and she's devastated. But instead of turning her back on God, she makes the choice to trust Him even though she doesn't understand. Describe a time in your life in which you trusted Him to see you through a bad time.

2. How can Cassidy's motives for going all the way to Brazil to get Alexis be compared to Christ's chasing after His children who need Him?

3. When the rebels arrive at the orphanage to kidnap Cassidy, she is required to push Alexis away to protect her. While God never pushes us away, sometimes He allows things to happen in our lives that we don't understand because He knows what's best for us. Describe something that's happened in your life that you didn't understand at the time, yet now you can look back and see God's hand protecting you.

4. When Gabe is asked to return to the jungle to rescue Cassidy, he must face his nightmares head on. Going back into the jungle forces Gabe to think about the God he's turned his back on. Do you think God arranges this situation to get Gabe's attention? What do you think about the idea that God will do whatever it takes to get your attention focused back on Him?

5. In the cabin Gabe assumes the worst about Cassidy, that she has questionable virtue because, as he under-

stands it, she's had a baby out of wedlock. He judges her unfairly and without all the facts. How does Cassidy respond? How would you respond if you were in Cassidy's shoes?

6. Jorge and Selena prepare for the worst and pray for the best. Do you think their digging the tunnel shows a lack of faith that God will protect them? Or are they just plain smart, perhaps employing God's command in Ephesians 6, "Therefore, put on the full armor of God…that ye may stand strong in the day of evil."

7. Gabe realizes his refusal to tell Cassidy everything he knows about the mission her brother died on is eating her up inside. And yet Gabe *can't* tell her without compromising his integrity. Have you ever been in a situation in which you were tempted to give up your integrity for something you really wanted, but didn't? Or did you fail and come up short? How did you feel in either situation?

8. The Coopers are willing to go to any length to get what they want. Susan out of love for her niece and Brian out of desperation for money. As a result, they both cross the line. What could they have done differently to get what they wanted and not have broken the law?

9. Amy is Cassidy's best friend. In the end, she puts it all on the line for Cassidy in spite of the pain that it causes her. She sacrifices her life as she knows it for Cassidy. What would you have done had you been in Amy's situation? Why?

10. Cassidy manages to forgive quite a few people in this story, including her half sister, Cindy, for trying to kill her. Think of a time when someone has wronged you. Have you forgiven that person? If not, would you start to pray for that person? If you have forgiven someone, how did that make you feel?

INTRODUCING

Love Inspired.

HISTORICAL

A NEW TWO-BOOK SERIES.

Every month, acclaimed
inspirational authors
will bring you engaging stories
rich with romance, adventure
and faith set in a variety
of vivid historical times.

History begins on **February 12**
wherever you buy books.

Steeple
Hill®

www.SteepleHill.com

REQUEST YOUR FREE BOOKS!

2 FREE RIVETING INSPIRATIONAL NOVELS PLUS 2 FREE MYSTERY GIFTS

Love Inspired®
SUSPENSE

YES! Please send me 2 FREE Love Inspired® Suspense novels and my 2 FREE mystery gifts. After receiving them, if I don't wish to receive any more books, I can return the shipping statement marked "cancel." If I don't cancel, I will receive 4 brand-new novels every month and be billed just $3.99 per book in the U.S. or $4.74 per book in Canada, plus 25¢ shipping and handling per book and applicable taxes, if any*. That's a savings of 20% off the cover price! I understand that accepting the 2 free books and gifts places me under no obligation to buy anything. I can always return a shipment and cancel at any time. Even if I never buy another book from Steeple Hill, the two free books and gifts are mine to keep forever.

123 IDN EL5H   323 IDN ELQH

Name _____ (PLEASE PRINT) _____

Address _____ Apt. # _____

City _____ State/Prov. _____ Zip/Postal Code _____

Signature (if under 18, a parent or guardian must sign)

Order online at www.LoveInspiredSuspense.com

Or mail to Steeple Hill Reader Service™:

IN U.S.A.: P.O. Box 1867, Buffalo, NY 14240-1867
IN CANADA: P.O. Box 609, Fort Erie, Ontario L2A 5X3

Not valid to current Love Inspired Suspense subscribers.

Want to try two free books from another series?
Call 1-800-873-8635 or visit www.morefreebooks.com

* Terms and prices subject to change without notice. NY residents add applicable sales tax. Canadian residents will be charged applicable provincial taxes and GST. This offer is limited to one order per household. All orders subject to approval. Credit or debit balances in a customer's account(s) may be offset by any other outstanding balance owed by or to the customer. Please allow 4 to 6 weeks for delivery.

Your Privacy: Steeple Hill is committed to protecting your privacy. Our Privacy Policy is available online at www.eHarlequin.com or upon request from the Reader Service. From time to time we make our lists of customers available to reputable firms who may have a product or service of interest to you. If you would prefer we not share your name and address, please check here. ☐

LISUS07

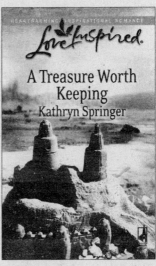

Love Inspired SUSPENSE

TITLES AVAILABLE NEXT MONTH

Don't miss these four stories in March

WILDFIRE by Roxanne Rustand
Snow Canyon Ranch
Years ago, Josh Bryant broke Tessa McAllister's heart. When he showed up again in *her* town, Tessa counted the days until he'd leave. She had enough to handle with drought, wildfire and underhanded rivals—she couldn't bear to risk her heart again.

DON'T LOOK BACK by Margaret Daley
Reunion Revelations
Cassie Winters was overjoyed when her brother got a job as a journalist...until his latest story resulted in a fatal end. Determined to find the truth, Cassie sought help from her former professor—and not-so-former crush—Jameson King.

BROKEN LULLABY by Pamela Tracy
Growing up in the Mob had left Mary Graham with emotional scars. Still, after years in hiding, Mary had nowhere to go but home. Home offered little safety, though, and fear soon drove Mary to turn to the last man *anyone* in her family could trust—policeman Mitch Williams.

MIA: MISSING IN ATLANTA by Debby Giusti
Finally home, returning war hero Jude Walker was ready to reunite with the woman he'd met on his last leave. Her last known address, though, was a homeless shelter. Shelter director Sarah Montgomery wanted to help, but she feared it would all end in heartache...for *both* of them.

LISCNM0208